FAMILY SKELETONS

FAMILY SKELETONS

BOBBIE O'KEEFE

FIVE STAR
A part of Gale, Cengage Learning

Detroit • New York • San Francisco • New Haven, Conn • Waterville, Maine • London

ROM
O'Keefe

Copyright © 2011 by Bobbie O'Keefe.
Five Star Publishing, a part of Gale, Cengage Learning.

Set in 11 pt. Plantin.

LIBRARY OF CONGRESS CATALOGING-IN-PUBLICATION DATA

O'Keefe, Bobbie.
    Family skeletons / Bobbie O'Keefe. — 1st ed.
      p. cm.
    ISBN-13: 978-1-4328-2499-0 (hardcover)
    ISBN-10: 1-4328-2499-6 (hardcover)
    1. Family secrets—Fiction. 2. Skeletons—Fiction. 3. Cousins—Fiction. 4. Missing persons—Fiction. 5. California, Northern—Fiction. I. Title.
    PS3615.K43F36 2011
    813'.6—dc22   2011007372

First Edition. First Printing: June 2011.
Published in 2011 in conjunction with Tekno Books and Ed Gorman.

Printed in the United States of America
1 2 3 4 5 6 7 15 14 13 12 11

For families, immediate and extended.
For all the joys and triumphs, losses and pain, and the love therein.

CHAPTER ONE

Headlights appeared without warning on the dirt road—on her right where they didn't belong. Sunny Corday jerked the wheel left and the other vehicle crashed into her right front fender.

"What the—!"

Smashing the brake to the floor had stalled the car, but out of habit she switched the ignition off. She couldn't tell what the headlights belonged to, but it was bigger than her compact, and its driver's door was opening. She threw open her own door but the seat belt wouldn't let her out. Impatiently, she fumbled the buckle open, narrowly missed falling into a ditch as she exited the car, and then she splashed through puddles on her way around the back of the vehicle.

The afternoon rain had been heavy, but she'd barely noticed it then. She'd been distracted by a packet of snapshots she'd found in a junk drawer in her father's kitchen, featuring her parents and herself as an infant. Typical of him that he'd put them there. She'd let the discovery hold her up and had gotten a late start out of there.

The driver exited the other vehicle, tall enough to be male, and he looked all in one piece. She shielded her eyes against the glare of headlights.

"Are you all right?" Yes, it was a male voice, and he stopped at his front fender, giving space to them both. Too bad he hadn't thought about space before he'd crowded her off the road.

"Yes." She clipped the word off, still shaky from the close

call. Didn't he know what side of the roadway he was supposed to drive on? "Can you kill the lights? You're blinding me."

"Is that why you ran into me? My lights startled you?"

Huh? "Hey, wait a minute. I ran into you? In case you didn't notice, I was on the road, and you're—you were—well, where the hell were you?"

"I was just pulling off the shoulder when you came out of nowhere."

"*I* came of nowhere?" She covered her eyes with both hands. She'd already asked him once, quite nicely, considering the circumstances, yet the lights still glared at her. "Will you please turn those damned lights off?"

He walked back to the driver's door, reached inside, and the lights mercifully blacked out. "You've got quite a mouth on you." Though he had his head inside the truck, he'd spoken loud enough she'd caught both the words and disapproving tone, just as she was sure he'd wanted her to.

Well, he had a lot of gall to be so unconcerned about the fright he'd given her. And even more nerve to blame her for his mistake. In the wake of the glare, exploding pinpoints of color now attacked her eyes.

"I hate to break it to you, Mr. Civility, but my mouth isn't my only problem." She massaged her eyes with the fingers of both hands. "Thanks to you, I'm now also blind."

She heard his heavy exhale. The man must be feeling really put upon.

"My apologies," he said stiffly. "Once you've sufficiently recovered, perhaps we could exchange insurance information and be done with this unfortunate encounter?"

"That's what you call it? I thought it was a fender bender." Vision was slowly returning. Water was seeping into her shoe, so she stepped out of that puddle and into another one. The cold water made her think that if she toned herself down, the situation might cool off as well.

"You scared the hell out of me, mister," she said apologetically, hoping to explain away her confrontational attitude. And then, too late, she realized she'd stuck another bad word in there.

"And sent you straight into attack mode?"

Well, yeah, but . . . "Me? Somehow I'm in the wrong here?" So much for toning herself down.

"Actually, you were traveling a little fast for this road."

"I know the road and how to drive it. I also know enough not to pull into traffic without first checking for traffic."

"If there is any, which—"

"You still check. You do not blithely assume—"

"Blithely? Is there really an educated vocabulary lurking in there somewhere?"

Well, he sounded a little teed off, too. About time a crack appeared in his composure.

Then, as if he'd also noticed his control slipping, he waggled his hand and drew in another heavy breath. "Excuse me. I admit I erred—"

"Erred?" This guy's sphincter muscles must be extremely tight. Though that observation might be considered another example of an educated vocabulary, she decided not to share it with him.

"And of course I'll make restitution." Pausing, he withdrew his wallet from his back pocket. "Here's my card, and if you'll give me a moment . . . ." He went back and ducked inside the truck, one of those oversized sport utility vehicles that were so popular, and leaned across the seat.

She walked forward, hoping to find a dry spot on his side of the road. Which had been hers until the gas-guzzler had bullied her out of it. In the overhead dome light, she noted the meticulous look of the man's creased slacks and the caked mud on the sides and soles of his shiny black shoes.

He snapped the glove compartment closed, eased out and stepped down, walked to her and extended the card. "I wrote down the name of my insurance company and the number of my policy on it. Contact them. I won't contest anything."

Since he was accepting responsibility, she kept her mouth shut lest another bad word accidentally escape.

He returned to the truck then paused and looked back. "I'm sorry about this. It really wasn't your fault, and I don't want you getting into trouble over it." He hesitated with his hand on the vehicle's doorframe. "I can follow you home and explain to your parents."

"You think?" He wasn't the first person to make that mistake. She was a quarter inch under five-two and not quite a hundred and five pounds. In jeans and a sweatshirt and her short blond hair probably messy and windblown, she doubted that she was a picture of maturity. She turned her back and splashed through the same puddles on her way around the compact's trunk, then addressed him over the top of the car. "Thanks anyway, but I'm closer to thirty than fifteen. And if you follow me anywhere, I'll lead you to the nearest police station."

She settled in the driver's seat. The engine caught on the third try, giving her plenty of time to worry that it might not catch at all.

He stood watching her. Unfortunately, he wasn't in position for her lights to also blind him. When he jerked up his hand, she pressed the button to lower the passenger's window to half-mast.

"You forgot to give me your insurance information," he called out.

She glanced at her purse on the passenger's seat. It'd spilled over, dumping half its contents onto the floorboard, and some of it was peeking at her from beneath the seat. She tried to think of where in that mess her proof of insurance might be. And this wasn't her car, and she didn't even know if she had a copy of the owner's insurance, or even where the registration was. *Oh, crap.*

"I'll mail it to you," she called back. He'd given her some kind of business card, so some kind of address had to be on it. And he'd hit her anyway; he was the one who'd erred.

She pressed the window up, reversed, then shifted into drive and maneuvered the compact around the truck without landing it in the ditch, and then resumed the long drive home—two hours south to San Francisco on crowded Highway One-Oh-One. And wasn't she lucky; rain started to spatter the windshield.

The next morning, in the parking basement below the condo she shared with him, Sunny stood next to Ryan. They'd been friends since high school and housemates since she'd been released from the hospital four years ago and had started divorce proceedings against the guy who'd put her there.

"Whoa, baby!" His hands measured the newest dent in the compact's exterior. The car was the most economical model Reviler Automakers produced, and there were some who claimed that it was made out of plastic and that was why it was so cheap. The ugly implosion was about eight inches in diameter and looked worse in daylight, especially with its owner examining it.

Sunny winced. "I really am sorry."

He straightened and pulled her to his side with one arm. "Sunny, sweetheart, lose the frown. If it'll make you feel better, I'll go out today and get a matching one on the other side." He stretched to look around her. "If there isn't one there already."

"Wish I could say the other one looks worse, but it was too dark to tell. His card's in the glove compartment. When you get the estimates, take the most expensive one. Please."

"Nah, not worth it."

"What do you mean? It—"

He dropped his arm to point at the car. "Look at it, Sunny. It's a clunker. Before they finally took Gran's license away, she'd aimed it at everything and anything that caught her eye."

"But . . ."

"You want to get even with the guy and his tank, you'll have to find another way to do it." He gave her a curious look. "Who was he, anyway? He live around there?"

"I don't know. I didn't look at his card." With a shrug, she changed the subject. "Will you give me a ride to the dealership to pick up my car? It should be ready."

"Nope. Call came in when you were in the shower. A different part was delivered than what was ordered so it'll be another week."

"*Week?*"

He took a quick step back, putting his hands up in a defensive posture. "Hey, don't kill the messenger."

"But the only reason I came home was to pick up the car."

"I know. Call 'em up and give 'em hell."

She waited a beat. "No. Not worth it."

He gave her a slow smile. "Is that a touch of maturity I hear?"

"Whatever you want to call it." She headed for the stairs leading out of the condo's parking area, and he fell in step. A gray and white cat was waiting on the other side of the door when she opened it. Sunny blocked its exit with her foot, then scooped it up.

"Where do you think you're going?" She ruffled its fur as she carried it to the door marked *Manager*. A young girl about ten answered her knock. Sunny smiled and handed the cat over.

"Hi, Anna. Jojo got out again." She was careful to keep censure out of her voice. "He almost got into the garage."

Anna thanked her and was scolding Jojo as she closed the door. Her voice held no censure either.

Sunny turned and caught Ryan's grin. Giving in, she returned it. "I know, I know. Rough and tough exterior, marshmallow interior."

His grin grew. "A true sign of maturity is knowing oneself."

"Oh, shut up."

Arriving at their apartment, he unlocked the door.

"Guess I still need the clunker, then," she said without enthusiasm.

"Sure, no problem."

She led the way inside the standard San Francisco condo, nothing special and not cheap either, but she only had to pay half the rent. Ryan was gay and the best friend she'd ever had. She was straight, but romantically gun-shy, and their housing arrangement had worked well for the last four years.

He pocketed his keys and sent her a sidelong look. "How's it going up there, cleaning out that old house? Difficult dealing with the memories?"

She lifted her shoulders. "What memories come up, I just ignore." At his silence, she frowned and shook her head. "And don't look at me like that. I don't wish to be psychoanalyzed right now, thank you."

"Phone hooked up yet?" he asked, proving that a shrewd psychologist knew when not to push.

"They promised it for today. I wrote down the number for you. Hopefully I'll find a dial tone when I get back up there."

"When do I get to see this place?"

"When you get the time. You tell me." Entering her room, she paused and turned back with a defiant air. "You know what? I'm not rushing back up there. The place can do without me for one day. I'm gonna sack out, just read, maybe cook something special for dinner. What would you like?"

shower, only a claw-footed bathtub she'd scoured until she felt okay putting herself into it.

She mounted the stairs, deposited her suitcase on her bed, and then stopped, dead-still, eyes and ears alert. Something was wrong. Stepping back to the doorway, she stood sideways in it, turning her back on nothing. The skin at the back of her neck prickled as she surveyed the bedroom, then the hall leading to the other two rooms, the door opening into the bathroom—

That was it!

Her gaze shot back to the open door leading into the right front bedroom. It was supposed to be closed like the other one. The house was chilly, and she kept the unused rooms closed off to save the meager heat from the floor heater in the hallway below.

She didn't own a gun, but she kept a baseball bat under the bed. She got it and crept down the hall toward the door that most probably hadn't opened itself. A prowler must have broken in one of the back doors and was long gone—she hoped—but her heart was beating double time and a chill had settled over every part of her.

The room emitted a snore.

CHAPTER TWO

Sunny froze.

No phone. No damned phone.

Forget the phone and the baseball bat. Get the hell out of here.

Another snore caught itself in the middle. She heard a huge intake of breath, a pause, and a loud exhalation. Sheets and blankets rustled, bedsprings creaked, and feet hit the floor.

Keys! Where are the car keys!

Not in your pocket . . . purse still on the passenger's seat . . . the trunk. The keys are sticking out of the trunk's lock.

Brilliant, Sunny. Brilliant.

She backed up a slow step at a time, gaze glued to the open doorway. The baseball bat was poised over her right shoulder, her fingers rigid around it.

Cell phone! It's in your purse.

The floor creaked as someone walked across it, and he appeared in the doorway before she made it back to the top of the stairs. When his gaze lit upon her, he uttered an inarticulate sound and jerked to a stop.

Run. Attack before he gets his wits together. Do something, Sunny!

"Who are you? What are you—" He squinted. "You're the girl from the other night, with the foul mouth. So you're the one who's been living here."

She swallowed.

"Relax, whatever your name is. You don't need that bat."

He moved slightly, probably just settling where he was, but

she stiffened her stance.

He grew still. "But if you feel better holding on to it, then by all means keep it."

Slowly, as if he didn't want to startle her into attack, he held up one hand, then looked down at his t-shirt and boxer shorts. "Let me back up and put some clothes on, okay?"

"No."

"No?"

"Who are you? What are you doing here?"

"I asked you first. But we'll play it your way. I own this place. I—"

"Corday? You're Jonathan Corday?"

Smart, Sunny, you fed it to him.

Calmly, he nodded. "Yes, I am. Now it's your turn."

"I'll need to see identification."

"I gave you my card the other night. Remember?"

"Oh. Yeah, but I didn't look at it. I still need to see identification."

He appeared annoyed, but when she didn't relax her stance, he nodded toward the room's interior. "It's in there. May I?"

She considered, gaze not wavering, then gave him one curt nod of her head. He stepped back into the room and she followed as far as the doorway, afraid to let him out of her sight. He got a wallet from the dresser, withdrew a driver's license and extended it toward her.

She indicated the end of the bed with a flick of her eyes. He flipped it there and backed up to the far wall. She grabbed the license and got the basics with a quick glance.

Jonathan Louis Corday. Five-eleven. One sixty. Hair brown. Eyes green.

She checked the picture, him, then the picture again.

"Okay." She lowered the bat and felt her energy level lower along with it.

"May I get dressed now?"

"Of course. I'm sorry, I—"

"It's okay. We can talk over coffee. I think I mastered that old percolator in the kitchen."

"Never mind. I brought a new coffeemaker with me. It's still in the trunk. I'll go get it."

She barely caught the curious look he gave her as she left.

Outside, when she caught her frowning reflection in the car window, she forced her expression to clear. No sense wondering what he was doing here. Just ask him.

While she was filling the glass coffeepot in the kitchen, the upstairs toilet flushed and the flow of water reduced to a dribble. Talk about poor water pressure. She turned the spigot off, waited a beat, then turned it back on and filled the pot.

Corday still hadn't shown when she poured the fresh brew into a cup. He was either deliberately giving her time or he was the slowest creature on two legs she'd ever met.

Then he showed, dressed in tan slacks with a sharp crease and a button-down, pinstriped shirt. And clean-shaven. No wonder he'd taken so long. She pointed to the mug she'd placed next to the coffeemaker. He filled it and sat at the table across from her. They stared at each other.

"Well." He cleared his throat. "How did you get the electricity on?"

She squinted. "Huh?" There had to be more important considerations to discuss than that one.

"Evidently you've moved beyond trespassing. I suppose the correct term for you would be squatter."

Her spine straightened. "I'm not a squatter."

"When I saw signs of someone living here I immediately thought of you, and I surmised you'd been scared off when you met me." His tone was calm, matter-of-fact; not accusatory. "This is the only place I could've been going to."

"I am *not* a squatter!"

He was remarkably unruffled. Being met at his bedroom door in his underwear by a strange woman armed with a baseball bat had thrown him for only a quick second.

"And I need to see identification before I'm going to believe you're closer to thirty than fifteen," he went on. "Even in this light, it looks like I might have a runaway teen on my hands, and that puts me in deep trouble."

"You're in deep trouble, all right. You're pissing me off, buddy."

His facial muscles tightened.

"You want proof?" She raised her chin in challenge. "In case you didn't catch it, I knew your name before you told me. Thanks to good old Franklin Corday, a long lost uncle you probably didn't even know you had, you now share ownership of Corday Cove with his equally notorious daughter, Laurel. Your cousin, twelve or twenty times removed. Now how is a . . . *squatter* . . . going to know that?"

She took a deep breath and blew it out in a noisy rush. "You want some history to go along with that? After their divorce, Franklin's wife won a judgment on their daughter's behalf, stipulating that at his death Corday Cove would go to, and I quote, 'surviving blood kin, including offspring, Laurel Frances Corday.' It was that poorly written, and it gave him an out. He searched until he found another heir—you—just so he could stiff his daughter and her mother one last time." She paused, then added, her voice dripping scorn, "You really lucked out, buddy."

"My name is Jonathan, not buddy." Temper was beginning to show around the edges of that unemotional armor. Cold, controlled, but temper nonetheless. "And speaking of names, I still don't know yours."

"Sunny." She clipped off the word, giving him no more

information than she had to. Her temper was warmer than his, and she was glad to see his appear. She'd been as much miffed by the casual way he'd labeled her a trespasser as by the label itself.

"Sonny?" His brow wrinkled. "As in sonny boy?"

"No. I'm not someone's male child. Apparently you haven't caught on to that yet either. Sunny, as in sunshine."

He gave her a long look. "There is nothing whatsoever about you that reminds me of sunshine."

The precise delivery undid her. She fought the laugh but it got away from her.

Though he didn't smile back, he seemed to relax a bit. "Sunny sounds like it might be a nickname."

She nodded, her mood and stance easing. Propping her elbows on the table, she clasped her hands and rested her chin atop her knuckles. "Yes, it is. But something tells me that you don't go by John, Johnny, or Jack."

"Jonathan is preferred, thank you."

Yep. He wasn't difficult to get a handle on. "Well, Jonathan, is that enough proof?"

"Yes, you're not trespassing. You're here with Laurel's permission . . ."

She'd felt her face go blank, and he must've seen it.

"Aren't you?" he asked, eyes narrowing.

She considered him for a moment, and then sat back. Wearily she lifted her shoulders. "It was more her mother's idea," she said dryly.

"And what exactly is it that you're doing here?" His gaze drifted to the hall, then back. "The downstairs rooms are empty of everything but furniture. Are you preparing the house for sale?"

"Uh-huh. You'd agreed to sell it."

"I didn't realize it would be this fast."

"It's not on the market yet," she clarified. "When I'm through clearing out the personal stuff, painters and contractors have to be hired."

"Why you?"

"Why me what?"

"In what capacity are you here? As a friend of the family?"

"Oh." She pursed her lips. "Well, actually—"

"You seem too young to be the real estate agent."

"In fact, I am an agent," she informed him coolly. "And a successful one. You'd be amazed at how grown up I can look when I put my mind to it."

"Excuse me." At her rebuff, his stuffy side made another appearance. "I stand corrected."

She waved it off. "But I won't be handling the sale. I work out of San Francisco and don't know the area here well enough to feel comfortable with it. Mavis Fairly lives here in Chester Beach and works out of Castleton City. She's a family friend and will handle negotiations."

She got up, refilled her cup, then sat down again. "Now I need to know what you're doing here. Do you by chance want to hang on to this place after all?"

"You look apprehensive. Evidently you don't want me to reconsider."

And that thoughtful look of his probably meant that he was reconsidering. Oh, great. One complication after another. She stood and pushed her chair under the table. "Call . . . Laurel, when you make up your mind. And consider the coffeemaker a gift. I'll get my suitcase and be gone."

"You don't have to go, Sunny. You're welcome to stay."

"This place isn't big enough for both of us," she mumbled as she emptied her cup into the sink. Stopping on her way out of the kitchen, she turned back, and tilted her head as if to look down her nose at him. When annoyed, her habit was to annoy right back. "And I can't help but wonder in what capacity you're inviting me to stay, Mr. Corday?"

He stared at her for a long moment, as if mulling over her meaning. Then his eyes closed briefly, showing her he'd caught on. Appearing impatient as well as irritated, he shook his head at the well-worn oilcloth that covered the table. "Are you always this prickly?"

Sunny regretted making the implication. Her peppery side had gotten her in trouble more than once.

"You're not my type," he went on, voice so dismissive his insult topped hers. He managed to give the impression of looking down his nose at her without even looking at her. Then that cool green gaze rose and caught hers. "And I haven't changed my mind about selling. Your commission is safe. I live in Bakersfield." He paused, then added, as if explaining to a child, "No ocean. I wanted to see this place before it was sold. Perhaps I should have contacted Laurel, but I was given a key at the end of probate so I just came ahead. And until you arrived," he said and hesitated, and she didn't miss the hesitation. "I liked it here. If it doesn't interfere with your work, I'd like to stick around. Perhaps we could tolerate each other."

She frowned. "My commission?"

He frowned. "That's the only thing you got out of that whole speech? This is prime oceanfront property. The commission alone will amount to a small fortune."

"Oh. But I told you I'm not handling the sale." She jumped at a sudden strident ringing and then broke into a smile. "Hey, I don't have to stay mad at the phone company." She sprinted to the parlor, grabbed the receiver and spoke into it.

"Hello, doll," said the voice at the other end.

"Ryan. Hi. My phone works."

"That seems a little obvious, don't you think?"

"Oh, shut up. Are you just checking, or what?"

"My four o'clock appointment for tomorrow just called to cancel, and I don't have anyone until noon the next day. If I'm still invited, I can make it by dinner tomorrow."

"Great. Come on up. You have that set of directions?"

"Got it. See you tomorrow."

"Uh, Ry—" But the phone clicked in her ear. She'd explain and introduce Jonathan tomorrow. No big deal.

"Expecting company?"

She jumped, then spun to find Jonathan in the doorway. "Ground rule number one. Don't sneak up on me."

His gaze flitted back down the hall toward the kitchen, then returned to her. "Perhaps we should rethink this. Tolerating each other may prove to be beyond us."

She'd caught the dry tone and realized he had humor as well as temper behind that reserved exterior, and that he was trying to be fair. It wasn't his fault she felt so weighed down with this place and the hovering aura of the missing Franklin Corday, the father who'd unsuccessfully tried to disown her when she was in fourth grade. She'd spent a long portion of her life trying to disown him right back, yet here she was clearing out his house.

"Sorry," she told Jonathan, and formally extended her hand. The least she could do was meet him halfway. "You and I got off on the wrong foot, and we're still dancing around on it. Truce?"

It occurred to her then that telling him her legal name at this late stage might put them right back on the wrong foot again. Well, too bad.

He took her hand. "Truce. Who's Ryan?"

"We share an apartment." As she withdrew her hand she realized she'd invited company without first running it by the co-owner. Oops. "He, uh, hung up before I could tell him about you. And I didn't even think about telling you about him."

"I won't worry about it if you don't." He tilted his head.

"Have you had breakfast? Or, more to the point, do you know how to cook?"

She got the point but didn't respond to it.

"Cook," he repeated carefully. "Do you know how to cook?"

"Apparently you don't."

"I can handle a coffeemaker and a toaster, but that's about it." He looked hopeful.

Another one who liked to eat but didn't know how to operate a kitchen. Odd, but she felt almost grateful. The familiar role of being the cook in a party of two made her feel at home.

"Would you like some breakfast, Jonathan?"

He lost the stuffy look when he smiled, she noted, and she got the sudden urge to make him smile more often.

The vehicle was so big she wondered how she'd missed it, and then realized that since it was directly in back of the house the porch would've hidden it as she'd driven up.

With a nod of his head Jonathan indicated the dumpster sitting off to the side. "That one is empty, but I venture to guess you've filled a couple of them already."

"And you'd be right. That's the third one. When Franklin replaced anything, he didn't throw the old one away. He just put it somewhere. You'd be amazed."

"I can help. But I don't want to, er . . . ."

"Butt in? Give me the impression you don't trust me?" She pulled the door closed. "Don't worry about it. I'm not thin-skinned."

"All right. Quick to react, but not thin-skinned."

She darted a look at him. He'd managed to be straight and direct in getting that aspect of her personality out there, and she found herself wondering just how stuffy that stuffed-shirt persona was.

With a casual nod, she led the way back into the kitchen. "Roberta also thought Franklin might have done some doodling and left some sketches, drawings, whatever, and she didn't want them overlooked."

"Some Franklin Corday originals might amount to another small fortune."

"I guess so. But as an artist, he'd fizzled out a long time ago." As a man, he'd also fizzled out, but she kept that opinion to herself. "He didn't live here anyway. Just used the place as a getaway. He liked noise and people and bright lights."

"Gorgeous getaway."

"Uh-huh. Can't be beat for location. The house was designed and built by his grandfather." She squinted into space. "Who would've been your great-great uncle—three times great? Four?" She shook her head; pinpointing relationship was mind-boggling. "Anyway, that Corday had a head on his shoulders. Franklin inherited wealth as well as talent that he turned into big bucks, but he frittered it away. All he had left was this house and acreage, only because he wasn't allowed to fritter that away."

They ended their tour on the screened back porch. At the rear of the house, it allowed a view of the road leading in from the highway as well as the beach on the other side. The fog had lifted, and the Pacific's blue expanse was visible, but not the white-capped waves.

They slanted looks at each other. Possibly he was also wondering where to go from here. She'd bought two folding lawn chairs during her last visit to Castleton, in order to accommodate Ryan once he got up here, and they leaned next to the wall. She opened a chair, sat down, and Jonathan followed suit.

"You know a lot of Corday history," he said. "How well do you, uh . . ."

"Know the Corday women?" she finished for him.

Okay, Sunny, you're on.

"At times they were as much in the news as Franklin." She decided to start with her mother and then introduce herself. "So you've probably heard that Roberta is a veritable recluse. But she's sharp as a tack. She lives her life as she wants to and makes no apology for it."

"Like mother, like daughter," he murmured, disapproval in his tone, and then his expression tightened, as if he hadn't meant to speak aloud.

She looked at her hands in her lap. "And on what do you base that opinion?" she asked softly.

He didn't answer for a long moment. She continued to examine her fingernails.

"I apologize," he said. "That opinion is based on nothing but hearsay, and there is no excuse for gossip. I'm not proud of that remark."

"Well, let's be honest here. Laurel's made a lot of mistakes. An annulled marriage before her sixteenth birthday, drug rehab before she was twenty, and then a real bona fide divorce. And she'd really earned that one. She'd almost killed the guy."

"Actually, I wasn't referring to any of that." He still appeared uncomfortable, but once he'd opened his mouth, it appeared he wanted to clarify his comment. "I was thinking of her relationship with her father—or lack of one, I should say. When he disappeared, she couldn't have been more callous. The sweet little teenager told a reporter to f-blank off because she didn't f-blank care. She waited the required seven years, then got busy initiating procedures to have him declared legally dead. A warm, loving daughter, she wasn't."

Sunny felt years of bitterness rising like acid. "You have a good relationship with your father?"

He looked surprised at the question, and wary. "Yes. I do."

"Were you aware that Franklin had denied parentage? Laurel was in primary school when her father publicly labeled her illegitimate—or tried to. Roberta proved to have more mettle than Franklin gave her credit for. She forced a paternity test, which proved he was indeed the child's father, and then she won the judgment concerning this place."

She shot to her feet. With jerky movements she collapsed her chair and leaned it against the porch wall. Forcing herself not to bolt into the house as if she were still the rebellious teenager he'd just described, she gave him a long, level look and decided it wasn't necessary to tell him her given name was Laurel. Another week, maybe two, and she'd be out of here forever. Until then, she was a friend of the family.

He stared back, expression impassive.

"They got a raw deal," she said, hearing defense and defiance in her voice. The defense part bothered her because there was no reason for it. "Both of them. If you want to look for a villain in this piece, look at him. That was a man without a heart or conscience."

"His body was never found."

She narrowed her eyes. He didn't seem insensitive, nor was he challenging her, but neither was he backing down. Then, suddenly, she felt tension easing out of her, and she even managed what was probably a weak smile. "I don't scare you, do I?"

He smiled back, but the expression clearly was an uncomfortable one. "I'm not simply curious, Sunny. When my name showed up in that will, I became a part of this."

"Okay," she said grudgingly after a short moment. "I guess I can see that. But I can't tell you anything more. His body was never found. Period. The consensus was, and still is, that the ocean got him. He'd been seen here, or at least in town, then just not seen again. Anywhere. End of story, beginning of . . . what? The seven-year mystery?"

His head turned away. She watched his profile as he stared at the million-dollar view, and then she followed his gaze. She disliked looking at the sea through netting. It protected them from bugs but distorted the view.

"I've got one more question," he said, and her chin wanted to drag on the floor.

"Where's the nearest beach access? I've been here two days, it's my first trip to the coast, and I have yet to walk the beach."

Feeling as if a weight had lifted from her, she broke into a laugh. "Well, that's easily remedied. There is a trail down the cliff, and I'm just the person to introduce you to the art of wading."

"Waiting?" His brow was wrinkling. "For what would we be waiting?"

"Wading," she enunciated carefully. "That's what you do when you take your shoes and socks off and get your feet wet."

His self-conscious laugh made him look five years younger

than she'd previously guessed he was. She hadn't noted his birth date when she'd looked at his driver's license, but she doubted he'd hit thirty yet, either.

Then she added a frown to the look she gave him. "But you look more like a night on the town than a day at the beach. Do you have jeans? Shorts? Tennies?"

"I'll find something."

In her old jeans and gray sweatshirt she was already dressed for the beach, so she waited on the front porch for him. When he joined her, his new attire of khaki shorts, deck shoes and a sporty brown polo shirt was less formal, but just as stylish as his previous garb. Apparently the man didn't know how to be sloppy.

Sunny led the way to the cliff. At the bluff's edge she stopped, hugged her arms against the chill, rubbing her hands up and down the sleeves of her sweatshirt, and let the breeze tug at her hair. She could watch the surf break and swirl all day and not tire of it. One of the mysteries of nature was how the ocean's constant motion carried such a distinct calming effect. Waves built, rolled, crashed, and spilled lazily. The wind carried drops of spray that spattered her face. The color of the water ranged from white to blue to green to sandy brown, depending on where and when the wave struck and how the sun hit it.

"There's more sand here today than yesterday," Jonathan said.

She looked up with a smile. "That's one way of putting it. Tide's out."

He grimaced, then gave her a sheepish grin. "I don't believe I said that." His gaze traveled from right to left. "So where is this path?"

"There." She pointed. They'd passed the slightly marked trail to view the ocean from the bluff's edge, and they stood on the south corner of the horseshoe-shaped cove. "But I wouldn't exactly call it a path."

His eyebrows drew together. "I wouldn't either. I still can't see it."

As she walked back to the scant path, she realized that to him it probably looked more like an indentation in the cliff than a trail. But it was a way to get down. She stopped at the top of it.

"Here," she said.

"Oh." He came to stand beside her, and he looked down at the sandy cove with a disappointed expression. "You were kidding. I thought there really was a way down."

"Oh, for Pete's sake. It is a way down, and it's not that bad. Here, I'll show you."

He grabbed her arm. "Sunny, you can't be serious. You'll break your neck."

"Okay," she said, and caught her bottom lip between her teeth while she surveyed the meager trail with an exacting eye. "I admit you've kind of got to slide down on your rump in a couple places." She pointed. "Like right there, and then again there, just before you reach the bottom. And that last little run there is exactly that. A run. You take a step, and then another, and then you start running, and when it flattens out at the bottom you'll be able to stop."

He squinted at her as if she were speaking a foreign language.

"Jonathan, it's not that bad. Last week I went down with a blanket over my shoulder and a bag lunch." She paused. "Well, I used one of those tie things on the bag to keep it closed and threw it down, but I managed the blanket okay."

"And how do you get back up?" He'd lost some color and his eyes had glazed over.

"That's not as hard as it looks. You see that last slope," she paused and pointed again. "On your way up you have to grab a little root that's there and kind of pull yourself up, finding footholds where you can. Then the rest of it isn't too bad."

He continued to watch her, saying nothing. Then he looked away, rolled his eyes and said something under his breath.

She felt her eyes widen. That had sounded suspiciously like an oath. Did he know how to swear?

"No way," he said flatly. "There is no way I am going to do that. I am not going down there."

"Well, I am. That's why I walked down here. I'm even going to play tag with the waves, but you can stay up here if you want to. Then I'll climb back up and go make lunch. Do you like grilled cheese sandwiches?"

When his level gaze met hers, it told her that this man made his own decisions and did not accept dares. "I should have brought the cell phone," he said. "If you're serious about going down there, we should alert the paramedics."

As soon as Sunny started her descent, she regretted it. Knowing Doubting Thomas was up there watching her made her nervous, throwing her off just enough that she might take a bad fall. Then she got to the slope, took off running and was home free. She looked up and waved, but then wished even harder she hadn't come down. If he followed, he might be the one to fall.

Okay, get back up there. You can go play in the water another time.

She walked back toward the incline, then stopped.

"Oh, no," she said without moving her lips.

He was on his way down.

He was slow, cautious, awkward, long and lanky, but he made it all the way to the final slope without breaking his neck. She took the first easy breath she'd taken since he'd begun his descent.

After the second sliding part he remained on his rump for a short moment before carefully getting to his feet. He took one step and then another, then his eyes opened wide in disbelief as he careened down the rest of the way, unable to control his speed.

As they each tried to avoid the other, naturally they both guessed wrong and moved into each other's path.

She heard a loud crack like a gunshot at the same moment he bowled into her. She felt a burning sensation at her right temple and they both went down.

CHAPTER FOUR

"Are you okay?" Jonathan sounded winded and looked scared.

Sunny was sprawled on her back under him, and the right side of her head felt like a strip of skin had been seared off. "Wha . . . what happened?"

His gaze moved a fraction away as he examined her forehead where it felt burned. "I think you got grazed by a bullet." His head jerked up and he scanned the beach.

The stinging sensation was graduating into a dull throb. "Bullet?" That didn't make sense. She tried to move. "Uh, Jonathan."

"What?" Quickly his attention returned to her.

"You're crushing me."

"Oh." Once he became aware of their positions, he clearly couldn't get off of her fast enough. Then as he knelt at her side his gaze again explored the inside of the horseshoe, the sandy floor to the cliff above, the beach on both sides.

After working herself into a sitting position, she also looked around but saw nothing. She reached to touch her sore forehead.

"No," he said sharply, pushing her hand away. "Yours fingers are dirty. You may infect it."

He got to his feet and then gave her his hand to pull her up. Her knees felt so shaky, she was grateful for his help.

"We need to get you back to the house so we can clean that up," he said.

They walked to the base of the cliff. As his gaze traveled the length of the trail to the top, a worried expression came over his face, but evidently not for himself. He turned to her. "Can you manage that?"

"I'm fine, Jonathan."

"Are you dizzy at all?"

"No." She was more concerned with the shaky knees, but the unsteady feeling had eased once she'd started walking.

"Lightheaded?"

"I'm fine, I said." To prove it, she got a good grip on the root, found her first foothold, and made what might be her best time yet on her way to the top.

She entered the house from the front porch. He'd detoured to his SUV in the back, and he was carrying a first aid kit in a black bag when he stepped through the doorway from the back porch to meet her in the kitchen. She gave him and the kit a look that probably carried doubt. He washed his hands and pulled on a pair of gloves.

"Sit down." He motioned toward a chair without looking at her. She didn't move. He soaked a cotton ball in something with a harsh odor that made her eyes water. When he looked up and found her still standing, he gave her a slow smile. "It's okay. I'm a doctor."

"Yeah?"

"Yes. An ophthalmologist, actually. I admit that gunshot wounds aren't my specialty, but I think I can handle this."

She wet her lips, still staring at him, then pulled the chair out and sat down. She'd give him one try here. One try.

"This is going to sting." He applied the cotton. She yelped and jerked away.

He put his hand on her shoulder. "As you can see, I'm an honest doctor. It really did sting. And I have to do it one more time."

"No way." She made a move to rise.

"One more time, Sunny. Trust me. It's got to be clean."

She looked up, knowing he was right but not liking it. Taking a big breath, she nodded. She sat back, stared straight ahead, set her mouth in a tight line and clenched her fists in her lap.

He laughed and turned away.

Her head snapped back around and she glared at him. "You want to trade places here?"

"I'm sorry, I'm sorry. Excuse me." This time, he positioned his left hand under her chin to hold her head in place. She frowned, but it didn't give her a trapped feeling, and the second application wasn't as bad as the first.

"Done," he told her. "You can start breathing again."

"Thanks. I think."

"You're welcome. You may have a reminding scar, but the way you wear your hair the bangs will cover it. And in time it will fade. You were lucky. I don't want to think about how lucky."

He discarded the cotton and threw the gloves away after it. "Your hair is so blond it's almost white. At first I thought it had to come out of a bottle, but now I'm thinking it's natural."

"It is."

Exhibiting no self-consciousness, he gave her another appraising once-over. "A perfect blue-eyed blonde, complete with pixie face and hairdo. But you're built kind of small. You look like a good wind could knock you over."

"That's some bedside manner you've got there, Doctor."

When his face quickly sobered, she wished she hadn't chided him. She'd liked the lighter, relaxed side of himself he'd just showed her.

He closed the first aid kit. "This incident has to be reported to the police. We can go now. I'll drive."

"Ohh." She dragged the word out. With her elbow on the table, she leaned the unhurt side of her forehead against her fist and briefly closed her eyes. "I hadn't thought about that. Do we

"Seems like a pretty good guy, though maybe a bit on the persnickety side. I'll give Mavis a good report."

At the door, she heard her name and looked back.

"Remember now. He was right, and you were wrong."

"Yes, Tom. I'll remember."

Jonathan stood in the sun, leaning against the SUV's dented fender, and he looked up when she exited the office. She met his wary gaze, but said nothing for a long moment. Then she smiled. "Okay. You were right, and I was wrong. Tom wanted me to be sure and tell you that."

His face relaxed.

Her forehead itched. She started to scratch it, thought better about it, and dropped her hand. "We've lost almost the whole day already, and I need something for dinner. For tonight, and for tomorrow when Ryan's coming. Remember?" Reluctantly, she looked across the street at Beverly's Emporium. "I don't feel like making the run into Castleton. Maybe we can pick up something at Bev's."

He fell in step with her. "What does Ryan do for a living?"

"He's a psychologist. And he has an annoying habit of analyzing everyone he meets. Don't encourage him."

Jonathan's nose wrinkled when he walked into the small store.

"Yeah," she said. "They sell bait, too."

"Emporium?" he murmured, looking at the three short aisles of stacked shelves.

"What did you expect? Chester Beach is so small, it's more like a wide spot in the road than a town." She led the way to the cold storage section in the back. The glass-enclosed counter held a salmon on ice, prawns and scallops. "One thing about Bev. She only sells fresh fish."

"Uh, Sunny."

She looked up questioningly.

"I really don't care for fish."

"Oh. Well, there goes that." She thought for a minute. "I've got a tub of spaghetti sauce in the freezer. Will you settle for that tonight?"

He looked relieved. "I like spaghetti."

Wondering if she'd ever met anyone who didn't like spaghetti, she left that section and went to the packaged meat display and discovered there'd been a better variety at the fish counter. Chicken wings were on special, but she didn't like chicken wings. Neither did she like the color of the hamburger, and the fat content was twenty-two percent. Way too high. She picked up a package of thinly sliced top round that looked okay and thought about what she could do with it.

She glanced up, caught Jonathan's bemused, uncomfortable expression, and resisted the urge to tell him that she'd only led him into a small town grocery store, not ladies' lingerie. "How do you feel about stroganoff?"

"You know how to make stroganoff?" The look he gave her held reverence.

"Sounds like he likes it," said a familiar voice.

Sunny turned, and then gave a hug to the tall, gaunt woman who smelled of tobacco. "Hi, Mavis."

Mavis returned the embrace, then offered her hand to Jonathan without giving Sunny a chance to introduce them. "Hello, Jonathan Corday. I'm Mavis Fairly, and it's good to meet you." Her medium-brown hair was swept to one side on her forehead, fell to her shoulders in a casual pageboy, and was being allowed to gray naturally. Her eyes were emerald-green, bright and interested. "If you're wondering how I fit into the scheme of things, I'm Roberta's best friend. Have been for years."

He shook her hand. "I'm pleased to meet you. You're also our real estate agent. And your last name is the same as the sheriff's."

"That's because I've been married to him for a while now." She looked at Sunny. "Haven't you filled him in on anything?"

"Golly gee, I just met him this morning, Mavis."

The woman lifted the bangs at Sunny's forehead and examined the raw furrow there. Sunny flinched, but allowed the familiarity. The older woman's eyes narrowed. "I don't like that, Sunny. Something like this should never have happened. Too many outsiders coming through here."

Her gaze traveled to the checkout counter where a slightly built teenaged boy stood, waiting for a customer to give him something to do. "If it was an outsider," she added under her breath.

"I heard you, Mavis Fairly, and you're looking at my son. What do you think he did?"

"Oh, Bev, I didn't see—"

"Apparently you didn't. What do you think Matthew did?"

Sunny scrunched her face up. *Criminy, anyway. Why don't one of you write up the headline and the other one can run it over to the newspaper office?*

Bev matched Mavis in age and height, had a head of short dark curls and brown eyes that were presently flashing with resentment. Since Mavis seemed to be having difficulty getting her tongue and brain coordinated, Sunny stepped to the plate. "There was a target shooter out near the house, Bev, but we have no idea who it was. As soon as Mavis gets her foot out of her mouth, she'll apologize. And this is Jonathan Corday. Jonathan, this is Bev Wilkes, the owner of the store. That's her son Matthew at the counter."

Bev directed a brief nod his way, but didn't actually meet his eyes, or Sunny's. Sunny's dry speech had apparently defused the storeowner. Having nothing to dispute, her manner now seemed as strained as her peer's.

Mavis finally got her tongue unstuck. "Excuse me, Bev. I wasn't implying Matthew might've been responsible, so much as I was thinking of those other boys that—"

"Well, I'd believe it of them, too. But not Matthew. He's a cut above them."

Leaving the two women to sort it out, Sunny motioned Jonathan around the corner to the fresh vegetables, where she grabbed a package of mushrooms.

"We need a tub of sour cream, and we're low on milk. You see the dairy section over there?" As he walked away, she added a head of lettuce, a tomato and a cucumber, then went searching for egg noodles, hoping she wasn't going to lose anything on the way and wondering why she hadn't thought to grab a cart on the way in.

Matthew checked their items. He glanced up once at Sunny, but never met Jonathan's eyes. The young boy looked nervous, and she guessed he'd overheard his mother and Mavis.

"Been working all day?" she asked, thinking they might as well get it out in the open.

But either he didn't recognize the gambit or chose not to respond. "Close to it," he said, telling her nothing at all, and totaled their bill. "That comes to twenty-nine eighty-five."

That was way too high for those few things, but she'd known their prices before she'd come in here. She had her wallet in her hand and started to pull out bills.

"I've got it," Jonathan said.

"We'll split it."

"Let me get it."

"Thanks, but we'll split—"

"I'll get it," he said firmly. Though he was polite about it, he elbowed her out of the way. When she stepped on the foot of someone behind her, she looked up apologetically. Mavis held a can of tomato sauce and a loaf of French bread. The Fairly family might also be having spaghetti for dinner tonight.

"Met your match, Sunny?" Mavis asked. "That's twice today."

Curiously Sunny looked at her, then realized Jonathan was at the door and waiting for her. She put her wallet back into her shoulder bag and grabbed the second grocery bag. At least he was letting her share in the carrying out part.

That's twice what, Mavis?

You went up against him twice today, and he won both times, stupid.

Oh, for Pete's sake.

CHAPTER FIVE

"You outdid yourself, Sunny," Ryan said as he placed his fork across his empty plate.

"Yes, that was an excellent meal," Jonathan agreed.

"But note that I brought dessert," Ryan told him. "She doesn't like sweets. If you want it, you provide it." He looked at Sunny, and she looked back. He pushed his chair away from the table. "Note that you also have to serve it."

He rummaged in the cupboards until he found plates, then in the drawers until he found a knife, then in the refrigerator until he found his pie, lemon meringue, then brought everything to the table without dropping anything.

He'd brought back three plates. When he got to the third one, he glanced at her and she shook her head. She got up and put the unused dish back in the cabinet, then worked between the table and sink while the men ate pie.

After scraping his plate free of the last bit of meringue, Ryan turned his attention to Jonathan. "Looks like a neat SUV out there, except for that big dent. New truck?"

"I've had it a couple of months. I was tempted to take it into Castleton and look for a body shop, but then decided to wait until I get home and take it to people I know."

"Yeah, I would, too. Sunny told you not to worry about the Reviler?"

"No. That's your car?"

"My grandmother's. I inherited it. They took her license away when she tried to run over a cop."

Jonathan appeared to be wondering if that was a joke as he picked up his water glass. "How old is she?"

"Ninety next month."

"Sounds like a lively ninety, wanting to drive as long she could."

"Yep. Only thing that scared her was cops. She was driving on borrowed time and knew it. He'd just paralleled and was opening his door to get out. He made her so nervous she misjudged, got too close and took his door off."

His listener flinched.

"She missed him somehow. But she knew she was in trouble when he wet his pants."

Jonathan choked on his water.

"She saw that spreading stain, turned off the ignition and surrendered right then and there. The cop had to park the car for her. Left a wet stain on the seat."

"He's not kidding." Sunny grinned at the look on Jonathan's face. "It really happened."

She glanced back at Ryan. "You want to walk down to the beach and catch the sunset?"

"Definitely." He rose, picked up his plate and Jonathan's, then stopped in the middle of the kitchen as if lost. "No dishwasher? How do you do dishes?"

"I'm it. It's an arrangement that works. Go compare fender dents, and I'll meet you outside in a couple of minutes."

Their voices carried through the screen door. As she worked, she listened to them discussing standard equipment and options, upholstery versus leather seats, rear windows, fold down seats and storage space, and finally she lost interest.

If it's not football, it's cars. It's a guy thing.

A short while later the three of them stood at the top of the cliff path, looking down.

"No kidding," Ryan said dubiously.

Jonathan appeared pleased that someone agreed with him.

"I hope you don't think I'm going first," Ryan said.

"Oh, for Pete's sake." Sunny pushed by them and started down. She stopped and looked back up. "You do understand we go one at a time."

"You betcha." Ryan's head bobbed in an emphatic nod.

He was the last one down. Once safely at the base of the cliff he looked back up, then over at her. "No need to go to an amusement park for a thrill ride when you've got this in your backyard."

Sunny ignored him. She slipped out of her shoes and played tag with the water, most of the time letting it catch her, but neither companion seemed inclined to join her. Leaving them to themselves, she wandered a short way south to a crevasse in the cliff. It was deep, extending inland to a V parallel with the house. On the far side of the ravine, a grove of cypresses stood near the bluff's edge, and she wondered if that was where the rifle shot had come from.

Entering the narrow canyon, she noted numerous beer and soft drink cans. She'd have to come down here and clean the place out. With her foot she nudged one that was dented with bullet holes. Undoubtedly the cans had been tossed down here and used as targets. She shook her head and looked at the cliff high above. Stupid. Reckless. And inconsiderate as hell.

An aged cypress hung precariously over the edge, one long root exposed and snaking halfway down the side of the bluff. It resembled a crooked fireman's pole, or a natural ladder if one were a monkey.

She retraced her steps and joined the men, who were yakking away and paying no attention to her or to the incoming tide that was getting perilously close to them. The sun was also sinking fast, but evidently football was more important. They must've talked the present to pieces because they were now on the past. She watched and waited.

"Green Bay was on top for a long time there," Ryan said. "Those cheesy hats have got a place in history all their own."

"The Forty-niners really earned their dynasty days. They had talent. Montana, then Young and Garcia. And Rice—"

"Hey!"

"What . . ."

They retreated in an awkward backward run, but their shoes still got soaked and their slacks were wet to the shins. Once he got to a safe distance Ryan looked suspiciously at Sunny. "You knew that was coming and didn't tell us on purpose."

She said nothing.

"Don't stand there with that grin on your face. I'm tempted to get you a whole lot wetter than I am."

Jonathan looked up and down the coast. "A person could get trapped in here. We're already cut off from going north or south."

She sat down to put her tennis shoes on. They'd get full of sand but they'd wash out. "You need to be aware of the tide and time of day if you want to go jogging. There's beach access in Chester, about a mile and a half that way." She stopped and pointed. "And to the south the road descends to sea level after about five miles. It's pretty private in here."

He gave her a curious look. "You appear to know both the people and terrain well."

She paused in the act of slipping on the second sneaker. "I used to live around here before I ended up in San Francisco." She got to her feet, aware of Ryan's narrow-eyed look but not meeting it as she led the way to the cliff's path.

The next day Sunny followed Ryan and his suitcase down the porch stairs. The early morning fog danced around them in patches. She wore a baby blue turtleneck over snug black jeans, and she hugged her arms against the chill. He deposited his bag in the trunk, closed it and gave her a pointed look.

"What are you up to, Sunny?"

Staring at the ground, she leaned against the car and folded her arms. She'd gone to bed early last night to avoid this, but she could put it off no longer. "Thanks for not giving me away."

"What are you up to?" he repeated. His disapproval bordered on angry.

"I didn't do it on purpose. It just kind of . . ."

"Let me guess. You were pissed and started talking about Laurel in the third person. Am I close?"

She didn't look up. "Yeah."

"You're playing mind games. I don't like it, and neither will he. When are you going to level with him?"

"He's got a very low opinion of Laurel."

"He wouldn't if he knew he was living with her. He seems like a decent guy, and you seem to be getting along all right. When are you going to tell him who you are?"

She met his eyes. "Okay, okay. You're right." She smiled in resignation. "And I'm wrong." Just like Tom said. "I'll talk to Jonathan."

She kissed him lightly on the cheek, then watched as he got into the car. He still appeared displeased as he drove away.

Inside the house, Jonathan was on his way down the stairs. They paused and looked at each other, as if they each had something on their minds. Once Sunny realized this, she said, "The best way to find out something is to ask." Maybe he'd guessed her identity and this would be easier than she'd expected.

"Is your relationship with Ryan romantic or friendly or both?"

"Friendly." That he might have that question hadn't occurred to her. "But that says a lot. He's the greatest guy I've ever known. If I ever find a better friend, I'll have to marry him."

"That explains the separate bedrooms last night. How long have you and he roomed together?"

"About four years now."

He was standing on the bottom stair. His gaze not leaving her, he leaned against the wall, folded his arms and crossed one ankle over the other foot. "You're using him."

She frowned. "Using him?"

"No one is going to put the make on either one of you if it appears you're already in a relationship."

"Oh. I hadn't looked at it that way. Actually, our rooming situation is coming to an end. He's involved in a romance, and as soon as I'm through up here I'll be looking for a new place."

"Is she a psychologist, too?"

"He's a body builder. He works at a gym."

"I thought he was a psychologist."

"Ryan is a psychologist. Marcus is a body builder."

"Who's Marcus?"

"Ryan's significant other."

After a short silence he said, "Oh." Then a longer silence followed, at the end of which he said thoughtfully, "I saw no sign of it."

"He doesn't believe it's necessary to wear a sign around his neck."

He shrugged, manner casual. "Okay. I don't wear a sign either."

She smiled and motioned that she wanted to go up the stairs. He moved aside and she passed him.

"Sunny?"

She stopped and looked back.

"Why do I have the feeling I just passed a test?" he asked.

"Because you did." She continued climbing, then heard her name again. She stopped on the last stair before the top and looked down.

"If you wore a sign around your neck," he asked, "would it read heterosexual?"

Now, Sunny. Tell him your legal name now.

Instead she kept the flirty moment lighthearted. Assuming his recent pose, she leaned against the wall, folded her arms and crossed one foot over the other. Though his gaze didn't leave hers, she knew he was taking in her whole frame.

"Yeah," she answered. "You?"

"Yeah." He smiled, stepped to the door and went out.

You're being stupid, Sunny. Stupid, stupid, stupid.

Chapter Six

"Jonathan!" Sunny hollered for the third time from the kitchen, impatience and irritation making her voice louder with each yell. Her mood had slid downhill fast during the two days since Ryan's visit.

She was making a feast this morning, but not because she was hungry or wanted to impress anyone. She was working off excess energy. Instead of going with convenient frozen hash browns, she'd peeled and diced fresh potatoes, and she'd fancied up the eggs with crumbled bacon and diced onion and tomato bits. After covering a plate with a paper towel, she scooped the fried potatoes onto it, then forked crisp bacon slices onto the side.

By the way, my nickname is Sunny, but my given name is Laurel.

It was so easy, so what was the problem? She didn't want to claim her name? Her father? Her past?

"Jonathan!"

She scraped the scrambled eggs from the skillet into a bowl and put it on the table. What was taking him so long? She knew he was up; she'd heard water running through the pipes.

"Jonathan!"

Dammit! She stared at the red-checked tablecloth, watching the food get cold, then took a deep breath and marched down the hall. When she reached the bottom of the stairs he appeared at the top.

"Sorry," he said.

"Criminy," she said, and stomped her way back to the kitchen. She sat and filled her plate and started eating before he even got to the table. At the back of her mind she knew she was overreacting, but still she didn't try to rein herself in.

"Oh," he said, reaching for the eggs. "You put something in them."

"I call 'em fancy eggs. They're remarkably better if one gets to eat them before they get cold."

He glanced at her but didn't respond to her crossness. He put the bowl of eggs down without taking any and picked up the plate of potatoes. She noticed, but said nothing. He scraped the remaining potatoes onto his plate, ate one forkful and frowned. "You put something in the potatoes, too."

"Onion and garlic. It's called seasoning. I put salt and pepper in there, too."

"I like simple food," he said apologetically. "Just standard fare. I'll have plain toast and bacon."

Had he not noticed the mushrooms and sour cream in the stroganoff, along with the onions and garlic? Or maybe to him, that was standard. Putting her fork down, she stared at him. "You might also want to skip the toast. I buttered it." Some people might consider it nice not to have to butter their own toast.

He sipped coffee then chose a piece of bread. "Actually, I do prefer it dry, but I'll eat it either way." He looked at her as if he thought she might explode.

Which she did. She took his and her plates and dumped them into the garbage. Not just the contents, the whole plates. She threw in her cup of coffee, still half-full, and the plate of toast. The crash of crockery made her feel guilty, but that fueled her anger instead of easing it.

"You said you know how to operate a toaster, so make your own stupid breakfast!"

Coffee sloshed out of his cup when it hit the table. "What is the matter with you? You were okay until Ryan left. Did you have a fight with him or what?"

He'd hit the nail on the head, which only made her madder. "Oh, no, you don't. It's not my fault you're fussy. And I'll clean the bathroom today. You can wash the dishes."

"Sunny—"

She stomped down the hall.

"Sunny!"

She threw open the front door and almost tripped over the cat on the porch. It was so startled that instead of fleeing down the stairs, it scampered into the corner and cut off its own escape route. As if by magic, Sunny's mood lightened. She knelt. "Oh, kitty, I'm sorry. Come here, kitty." It was trapped between her and the wall of the porch. "It's okay. I'm not going to hurt you. C'mon. Come to me, baby."

Aware of Jonathan coming to stand in the doorway behind her, she looked up. "Be careful. Don't scare it."

When his gaze lit upon the cat in the corner, his expression also eased. "It came back."

"Looks only half-grown, and maybe not completely wild yet. I'd like to tame it if I could."

"You could give it breakfast if someone hadn't thrown it in the garbage."

She was facing away from him. A return of contentiousness hit her, then regret, and then her mind cleared, all in about three seconds. She looked back up. "There's a can of tuna in the cupboard, one of those easy-open tab tops. Would you get it?"

Quickly he returned with it, lid removed, and Sunny put it on the floor and pushed it toward the kitten. The cat's apprehension seemed to ease as it sniffed the air. It crept to the can, hesitating only once for another quick glance at the two people, then started licking up tuna.

Sunny grinned. "Hey, all right."

"It appears you now have a pet. But what are you going to do when you have to leave?"

"Take it with me. I told you I'm looking for a new place. Now I'll have company." She remained kneeling on the porch floor, watching the cat. "It," she repeated. "Don't even know if it's male or female."

"If it will let me close enough once it's through eating, I'll find out for you."

She slanted a look up at him. "Guess doctors are good for something."

His expression turned contentious and stayed that way. "Sunny . . ."

She smiled at the warning in his voice. "It was a joke, Jonathan. Lighten up."

"Me? *I* need to lighten up?"

With a sigh, she stood. "Okay. I've been in a lousy mood and taking it out on you. It's not your fault. I'll try to behave."

"Thank you. I'd appreciate that."

"Wow. Can you ever be stuffy sometimes."

His eyes narrowed as he digested that. The cat nuzzled Sunny's ankle. "Hey." She reached down and picked up the unresisting feline.

"It has a loud motor," Jonathan said. It didn't seem to mind when he took it from her. He held it up, then handed it back. "Give it a girl's name. And she'll make a gentler pet for you."

I could've done that for myself, but thanks anyway.

Sunny stroked the kitten. "Yes, you do have a loud motor. Hope you won't keep me awake all night, cat." She gave Jonathan a fast grin. "Hey, I like that. Why give it a made-up name? What's wrong with Cat?"

He chuckled. "Sometimes you're amazingly uncomplicated.

And other times I couldn't figure you out if my life depended on it."

She walked past him into the house, taking Cat with her.

"Did you mean it about the dishes?" he asked. "The ones that aren't broken, that is."

"No." She nuzzled the feline as she walked down the hall, not wondering about her rapid mood change so much as wondering how easily Jonathan had accepted it.

"Then I'm going to drive into Castleton and leave you and Cat to get acquainted."

"Okay." She turned to face him. "Uh, Jonathan?"

"Yes?"

"Is it okay if I use salt and pepper when I make dinner?"

He frowned, and she smiled.

"Bye," she said.

The front door closed, leaving her on her own. He was taking the long way around to get to his truck that was parked in back. Apparently he'd had enough of her for one morning.

By noon Sunny had finished clearing out the upstairs, with the exception of her room and Jonathan's. But the next floor, the attic, would be more work than the first two floors combined. It was time to call the disposal company to pick up another full dumpster and leave her an empty one.

She took a boloney sandwich and a can of Sprite to the back porch and shared everything but the beverage with Cat. The animal got a bowl of water. When a movement in the yard caught the corner of her eye, her head snapped up.

"Oh, hi, Matthew." She opened the screen door and descended the steps. No car. "Did you hike the beach?"

He nodded. She waited for him to speak, but he said nothing. His manner seemed strained.

"Would you like a sandwich?" she offered. "I just finished lunch."

"No, thanks. Uh . . . I just wanted to say I was sorry about what happened to you the other day. I know you had a close call, and Tom Fairly thought maybe me and some other guys had been target shooting around here. But we weren't, not then."

"Okay." He was looking more and more uncomfortable, but she didn't know how to put him at ease.

"I was wondering if you'd looked for the bullet," he added.

"Oh. No, we didn't. Didn't even occur to us to look for it. It would've imbedded itself in the sand or carried into the water."

"Yeah, I guess so. I looked but couldn't find anything, and then I wasn't sure exactly where you were when you were hit. Except that you were in the cove or near it."

"Why were you looking for it?"

"I was hoping to prove it didn't come from my rifle."

Hoping to? Then there was a chance it did?

She asked, "Where do you and your friends usually hold your target practice sessions?"

Turning, he pointed to the grove of cypresses on the bluff with their misshaped branches, permanently blown inland by wind. "But we haven't been out here since you moved in. At least I haven't, and I don't think they have either."

"Who would they be?"

He looked down at his scuffed sneakers. They weren't expensive designer ones; they looked more like variety store specials. "I don't want to get anyone in trouble."

She relented. He was trying to do the right thing. "If I can't interest you in lunch, can I get you something to drink?" She held up her can of soda. "One of these?"

He hesitated. "I shouldn't take the time. I don't want to get caught by the tide."

But he looked like he wanted one. Hiking the beach was

thirsty work.

"I'll get you one, and you can take it with you." She left, returned with the can and said, "If you don't mind company, I'll walk to the beach with you."

"Sure. And thanks." He held up the drink as if to say cheers.

They fell in step. He had gray-blue eyes and sandy-blond hair, and topped her by no more than four or five inches. She had no trouble keeping pace with him. "How's business been? Does the store keep you and your mom busy?"

"Not really. I spell her when she wants me to, but it's been kind of slow lately. I got a job busing tables at Sal's. You ought to go eat there one day. Good food. That and the hotel are the only places that keep Chester Beach alive."

"Maybe I will."

He polished off the soda before they reached the bluff, so she accepted the empty can to take back with her. He made it down the path as easily as she did. Maybe the smaller you were, the easier it was.

Before she got back to the house, she saw dust rising on the road, signaling the arrival of a vehicle. But it wasn't Jonathan's truck. It was a dented, dated sedan she didn't recognize. This was her day for company.

Cat was outside and tried to run away from the vehicle by running in front of it. Sunny yelled a warning and raised her hand, signaling for the driver to stop. He ignored the warning, and Cat made it beyond the second front tire by a narrow margin. Sunny closed her eyes and blew her breath out.

The car jerked to a stop, and a man got out and stalked around the front of it. "I want to talk to your mother."

"Huh?"

He squinted, possibly realizing she might be older than she looked. "You that Corday woman?"

"My name is Laurel Corday," she said coolly.

See how easy that was, Sunny? Now tell Jonathan the same thing when he returns.

"What can I do for you?" She forced politeness into her tone. "And perhaps you could introduce yourself?"

She caught the odor of alcohol, probably beer. That belly on him most likely had come straight out of a can. A sleeveless undershirt exposed fleshy, hairy arms, but it at least covered his stomach. She'd disliked him on sight because he'd almost killed Cat, and he hadn't even been paying enough attention to be aware of the close miss, and her dislike was growing by the second. She backed up a step, in distaste rather than fear.

"Well, Miz Corday, I'm Langley Bowers and you been spreadin' lies about my two boys and I want you to stop it."

"Who are your two boys, Mr. Bowers, and what lies are you talking about?"

Maybe you shouldn't have put those questions together. He might not be able to handle two thoughts at the same time.

"My boys are Toby and Langley, Jr., as you damn well know."

She gave him time, but he stopped there.

"And what lies are you talking about?" she prompted.

"You damn well know that, too. You told the sheriff they was takin' potshots at you on your beach."

"Listen carefully, Mr. Bowers. A bullet grazed my head when I was on the beach. I reported that to the sheriff. I don't know who fired the bullet, and I told him so. I've never met your boys, nor have I heard their names before. Is there anything else, or are you ready to go now?"

"You Cordays think you're tough shit, just 'cause you got money and a big name and a big house. It ain't enough that your daddy got to steal their mama away from my boys, but now you want to go and blacken their names. And I'm not gonna let you get away with it."

"Excuse me, Mr. Bowers. I didn't understand that part about

60

their mama. Will you run that by me one more time?"

Though he made no menacing move, it occurred to her that she was trading words with an angry drunk who was quite a bit bigger than she was. She backed up another step, putting herself out of his immediate reach, but no more. A show of alarm from her would make him braver. She wished the empty cola can was a full one. If he tried anything, she planned to smash his nose in with it.

"You heard me awright. Your daddy coulda had any woman he wanted, and he wanted a lot of 'em, but he made a mistake when he went after my Louise. She told me the truth, after I beat it outta her. Then she up and left me. It was his doin'. Franklin Corday. That was one sorry man with an unhealthy appetite for what didn't belong to him."

"Well, I'm sorry to hear that. But I'm not responsible for my father and his lack of character or his sins. I didn't even know about this particular one. And I don't hold your boys responsible for anything. I don't even know them. Any problems you've got, you need to take to the sheriff. He'll listen to you."

But he won't listen to your beer talking.

Surprisingly she found herself feeling sorry for the man, and her voice softened. "Really, Mr. Bowers, it's okay. Go home and . . . rest up. Talk to the sheriff tomorrow. If your boys didn't do anything, then they're not in trouble."

He seemed thrown by the change in her manner. He looked like he wanted to bluster some more but had run out of reasons.

"Goodbye, Mr. Bowers. Take it easy on your way home." Leaving him standing there, she went inside and then watched the unstable man from the parlor's window. After about thirty seconds of looking stupefied, head turning in different directions as if he were trying to figure out where he was, he finally got into his car. He reversed it over a geranium bush, turned the vehicle around, and drove away.

CHAPTER SEVEN

Sunny was headed for the shed in the backyard in search of a ladder to climb into the attic with when she heard Jonathan's truck returning. But instead of driving around to the back as he usually did, he parked in front and sounded the horn. When she walked around, she spied him standing at the rear of the SUV with its door down. His arms were wrapped around something big, and he was looking up at the porch.

"Oh, there you are," he said, jerking his head her way. "Can you open the front door?"

As she got closer, she realized the object he embraced was a portable TV.

"Sure." She took the three stairs in two steps and held the door open. When he backed up, the TV's cord dropped to drag along the dirt. "Hold it," she warned, then jumped to the ground, stooped to pick up the cord, and tucked it between his elbow and the television. "Let me guess. Monday night football."

He grinned and mounted the stairs, his head craning around the set so he could see each step. "I got a good deal. It was a discontinued floor model."

"Maybe you should've looked into renting one instead of buying one."

"I want another one at home. I hadn't gotten around to shopping for it yet, and this seemed like a good time."

She followed him into the house and pulled the screen closed. "Do you room with someone, too?"

"No. I've got my own place."

He carried the set into the parlor while she thought that over. "One person needs two TVs?"

The faded and scarred end table that belonged next to the overstuffed chair was now against the wall just inside the parlor door, and that's where Jonathan put the TV. The lamp and phone that used to be on the end table had found new homes on the coffee table in front of the sofa. She'd passed by the room several times today but hadn't noticed the new furniture rearrangement.

Gee, Sunny, I never noticed how observant you are.

"I've got one of those wide screens in the living room," he explained. He stepped back, surveyed the set, then moved up and adjusted its position. "And I want a smaller set for the bedroom."

If you had company in bed, you wouldn't need a TV.

"We don't have cable," she said doubtfully.

"An antenna is still on the roof, and the wire's over there in the corner." He nodded his head toward it. "So a television was in here at one time. I also bought a digital converter box. I should be able to work it out."

"Yeah, there was a TV in here." With the help of a dolly she'd gotten it outside to the dumpster, but she hadn't been able to heave it up and get it inside. The driver of the truck that picked up the dumpster was nice enough to take it anyway. "It was the first thing I tossed. Completely dead."

But she hadn't been careful disconnecting it, she remembered, and she hoped now that she hadn't killed the antenna wire. She decided not to mention that possibility.

He glanced at her. "How long before dinner?"

"How long do you want?"

"Couple of hours?"

"Okay. Need any help?"

"No, thanks." His eyes were studying the wall behind the set, the floor between it and the corner, then he frowned up at the ceiling.

Cars, football, and TV hookups. Doesn't take too much to keep a man happy.

Jonathan was good at estimating the time it would take to complete a task; evidently he'd had some practice at this kind of thing. And evidently Sunny hadn't killed the antenna wire. He had five minutes left when she heard him call her, and familiar music sounded at the same moment she heard her name. She turned the stove off and joined him in the parlor. He stood in the middle of the room, gaze on the set and remote in his hand. She went to stand next to him.

Yep, he'd caught an *I Love Lucy* episode. Together they watched Lucy as she sampled an energizing vegetable brew that carried an alcoholic content. From the look of him, Jonathan was also enjoying Lucy's wide-open eyes, slurred speech and limp elbow on the counter as the brew took over. This segment was filmed before either of them had been born, yet it was more entertaining than much of the new fare presented each fall. The episode was interrupted for a run of commercials.

"Your time's up," Sunny told him. "If you don't want dried meat and mushy potatoes, we need to eat now."

With the remote he switched the power off. "When you use this, make sure you return it to the top of the set so we can always find it."

She nodded dutifully. "Yes, Jonathan."

"And you can no longer operate the lamp with the wall switch. You'll have to turn it on manually."

"Okay." She didn't ask why. Ryan loved long, technical explanations that drove her to distraction. All she needed to know was how to turn something on and off, and the remote was right there on top of the TV.

"And—"

"Jonathan, there's nothing worse than well-done London broil. Get a move on."

Carrots and scalloped potatoes accompanied the slab of meat. She usually added thinly sliced onion to the potatoes, but tonight they were plain. She'd added nothing to anything and was determined to eat everything exactly the way it was.

He cut a bite of meat and looked thoughtful as he chewed. He speared a few carrot slices and sampled them. He ate a forkful of potato, then put his fork down and stared at her. She ate quietly, aware of his gaze but not looking up.

"Have you made your point, Sunny? Are you going to be back to normal by tomorrow?"

She tried to put innocence in the look she gave him. "What's normal?"

After a long stare that she refused to return, he got up to get salt and pepper then liberally sprinkled each over the food on his plate. "I wish to hell I knew," he said under his breath.

You're a bad influence on him, Sunny. You've taught him how to swear.

After dinner he again gave her a wide berth, though he only went upstairs this time, not all the way to Castleton. She was rinsing the broiler pan when he turned the bathtub faucet on. Not getting even half enough water to rinse the sudsy pan, she made a face and turned the spigot off. He couldn't have waited another thirty seconds?

She dried the dishes in the drainer, cleaned the table and stove, even wiped off the handle of the refrigerator. Finally the bathtub was full enough to suit him and he turned the faucet off.

"Thanks," she muttered, finished the pan and put it away, and headed down the hall to sample the new TV. She punched the set on with the remote and checked the newspaper listings

65

while waiting for it to warm up. Cat purred around her ankles, probably waiting for her mistress to sit down so she could jump into her lap. The kitten had enjoyed the London broil, cut up into tiny pieces, even without seasoning.

Sunny looked curiously at the TV. It wasn't doing anything. She retrieved the remote, lined it up exactly with the set, punched it off and then on again and still got nothing. Well, it was an ancient antenna up there. The breeze may have moved it just enough it'd lost the signal.

She flicked the wall switch to turn on the lamp so she could read, but that didn't work either, and she swore under her breath. He'd only spent two hours in here today and now nothing worked. Maybe he was one of those fiddlers who didn't know how to fiddle.

Impatiently she again picked up the remote. While she waited for the TV technician to get through with his bath and undo whatever he'd done to the lamp, she could try to get reception on other channels and check the audio as well, which would tell them that the problem was a faulty picture tube. But as she punched up the volume, she sheepishly remembered him telling her that the lamp had to be turned on manually. As she turned to reach for its switch, the sudden blast of sound behind her jolted conscious thought right out of her.

With a loud yelp she jumped and came down hard on Cat's tail. The animal screeched, then lit out for the hall by way of the coffee table and knocked the lamp over. It clattered to the floor, made a couple rattling spins before it shattered, and the crescendo behind her continued. She whirled toward the TV. Color, action, sound. Lots of sound.

Feet thundered down the stairs. Jonathan grabbed the newel post and swiveled around, on full alert and gaze flitting everywhere. Coming to a skidding stop in the parlor doorway he stared at her, and she stared back. Soapy water drained down a muscular chest and hairy legs. Bare chest . . . bare legs . . . bare everything.

"Are you okay?" His gaze again shot to the closed front door, down the hall, back to her. "What made you scream? What happened?"

She said nothing. He stepped into the room and reached toward the TV, probably for the remote that wasn't there. It wasn't on the coffee table where she'd put it, either. Then he found it in the wreckage of the lamp, picked it up and turned off the blaring television.

"You don't have to tell me," he said, returning the remote to where it belonged. The all-knowing male shook his head at the shortcomings of the unknowing female. "I know exactly what you did. If you'd listened when I tried to explain, you would've understood that the wall switch now operates the TV, not the lamp." He added something that sounded like, "Save me from," but that was all she caught.

He looked at her and she looked at him, but she wasn't looking at his eyes.

It was his turn to jump.

"I—oh, I—hey—uh . . ." He looked madly around as if for a foxhole to dive into. She handed him the newspaper. He covered himself with it, circled around her and backed out of the room. He ascended the stairs with all the dignity a naked man in his position could muster. Three steps from the top, he must've realized that since he was walking away from her it was his backside he should be shielding with the newspaper.

The bathroom door closed.

Sunny realized she was standing in the puddle he'd left on the hall's hardwood floor, yet she couldn't exactly recall leaving the parlor to track his exit. She should mop up the water before it spread to the parlor rug. She also needed to clean up the broken lamp pieces and apologize to Cat. But she remained

still, gaze glued to the closed bathroom door.
Is that what hung like a horse means?

CHAPTER EIGHT

In deportment, on a scale of one to ten, Jonathan was an eleven.

When he appeared downstairs after his bath, he seemed somewhat stilted, but Sunny had already figured out he'd been born that way. Wearing a sea green sport shirt that very closely matched the color of his eyes, along with dark slacks and polished black shoes, he stood in the parlor doorway and waited to meet her eyes.

"Excuse me," he said formally.

"Of . . . course," she said.

He then entered the room and settled in the other armchair to watch the action film Sunny had found. He sat ramrod straight, never looked her way, and absolutely no comment, wiseass or otherwise, occurred to her.

The image of a naked and magnificent male was imprinted in her memory cells. Nothing either of them could do about that. But also impressive was his instant reaction when he'd heard her scream. With no thought for anything other than that something was wrong downstairs, down he had come.

As she sat there and watched the few minutes of movie in between the several minutes of commercials, her respect for him grew. Odd, but she could think of very few men, other than Ryan, whom she respected. And none, other than Ryan, she'd ever felt she could count on.

She swallowed hard and realized she'd lost the thread of the movie. It was disconcerting to discover how unaccustomed she was to thinking about issues of trust and how accepting she'd been to having so few people in her life worthy of it. The kind of single-mindedness that brought a man stampeding down the stairs when someone screamed was close to incomprehensible.

It was silly, if one wanted to look at it from a clinical angle, that Jonathan had come racing to her rescue because the TV had startled her after she'd jacked up the sound. Yet it still made her feel . . . funny inside. Quivery, unsettled, wistful. Yeah, funny. The word fit.

Early the next morning they got back to work. The trapdoor allowing access to the attic was located in a recess off the upstairs hall, and Jonathan carried the stepladder they'd found in the shed up the stairs while Sunny let Cat outside to roam. The kitten was lightning-fast and could climb anything, and Sunny didn't want to contend with the animal while they explored the attic. Nor did she want the cat to decide she liked it up there and not want to come out.

The ladder was in place when she joined Jonathan. Though he wasn't exactly sloppily dressed, neither was he his usual natty self. He wore faded, serviceable chinos she could tell he'd actually done physical work in. Though they looked clean, they were permanently soiled. Evidently he worked on his truck himself and had packed his workpants just in case. Her jeans were the oldest she owned, one leg torn at the knee and the hems frayed.

She noted that the trapdoor was laid back as she ascended the stairs, so he'd already been up there, but he was politely waiting for her before proceeding further. As she climbed toward him, the image of him at the bottom of the stairs in all his glory crossed her mind. She just let it cross and took hold of the ladder.

"I should go first," he said quickly.

Mavis wore a skirt and jacket combo in light-green linen. Her attire didn't stop her from following suit, however.

Near the water's edge, a woman and young child were building castles in the damp sand. An older couple, possibly in their fifties, walked hand in hand. Further down the beach a man and a dog played with a Frisbee.

Sunny remained quiet for a long moment, staring at the ocean but barely aware of it. She asked, "Did my mother know?"

"I don't know. I never told her and doubt that Franklin would have. It was after their divorce, a long time after. But that doesn't excuse anything," she added. She stubbed the cigarette out in the sand, put it in her cupped left hand and closed her fist over it. "It was the last time he was up here."

"How about Tom? Does he know?"

Still looking at her closed fist, Mavis nodded. "I told him. I had to." Her gaze moved to a trash receptacle sitting where the sand met the cement walk. She got up and walked over to discard the cigarette butt. Before returning, she slipped her shoes off to carry back, one in each hand. She sat down, leaning on her left hip, arm and hand supporting her weight. Though she faced Sunny, she was looking beyond her. She didn't appear to be looking at anything in particular, however, just staring into space.

"It was a bad time," Mavis said, speaking in a monotone. "I was at a really low point. I can't explain it, even to myself, so I don't expect anyone else to understand. Tom was . . . furious. And not just hurt. Injured. So much so that I wondered if I was only adding to the wrong by telling him. But I thought then, and still do, that hiding unfaithfulness only compounds it. I had to face up to it, be honest with him."

The Frisbee sailed by, careening away in an arc. The blond lab snagged it in the air and loped back to its master. Mavis watched with incurious eyes. She picked up a handful of sand, let it run through her fingers, and looked out over the water. "For a while it looked like I might lose Tom. But he accepted it. In time he even forgave me. I know what kind of man I've got. If I didn't before, I learned then. But I don't know if I'll ever be able to forgive myself. It wasn't exactly an affair. It was . . ." She stopped and looked down at the sand. "A one-night stand," she finished in a near whisper.

She picked up another handful and watched the grains dribble through her fingers, took in a long breath, let it out and then tonelessly went on. "Tom was out of town. Had been for a long time. He'd called that afternoon to tell me it would be at least another week, grew impatient with me when I got impatient with him. I went out to dinner alone, feeling sorry for myself, ran into Franklin, drank wine with him, walked the beach . . ."

Suddenly, angrily, she made a fist and struck the sand. Grains spit out in an uneven, explosive design. "It happened, Sunny. I don't excuse it, don't expect anyone else to, and I don't want to talk about it anymore. I can't, really can't."

Jerking to her feet she walked away, angry regret and pain evident in every step she took. When she reached the sidewalk, she balanced on one foot and then the other as she slipped the shoes back on. She never turned to look behind her. Sunny watched her for as far as she could see her, then she got to her feet and began the trek for home.

It was nearing 4:00 P.M., and the relentless sun bore down on Sunny as she approached the old Victorian. No official vehicle was in sight, and the shade of the porch should have beckoned her, yet dread slowed her steps. When she entered the house, the bathroom door was open, and she heard a broom swishing across the floor. She called Jonathan's name from the stairs.

He came to the door, holding the straw broom. "Hi."

She paused and looked at him. "Why?"

When he appeared not to have a ready answer, she grinned. "Ah, chivalry. It rears its head." That was nicer than asking him if he really thought he was more capable than she. Because of course he did.

He frowned, but she caught a look of sheepishness behind the frown.

"I can handle my own spiders," she told him. She climbed into the dark hole, waved one arm above her to search for the chain to the light bulb, took another step up and waved again, came in contact with it and yanked.

"Not much wattage," Jonathan said dubiously, watching the swinging bulb.

"We can always get a bigger bulb. Uh, stronger, I mean? Brighter?"

"I get the idea."

Wattage, Sunny, wattage. He already said it.

She eased over to sit on the edge of the attic floor, checking first for anything that might be crawling there, then maneuvered her way off the ladder and into the attic proper. The attic was A-shaped, perhaps six feet high in the center and tapering to about five feet in height at the walls. Its circumference was slightly less than the size of the house itself, and it was chock full of stuff. This was going to be a job and a half.

She turned back. "Your turn."

His head quickly appeared in the opening. The initial drudgery she'd felt regarding this chore had been replaced by a sense of adventure that he apparently shared. Possibly because they were sharing a heretofore unexperienced experience.

The bulb was still swinging, distorting their shadows. She could do without that part of it. It was just a little too creepy. She stood upright and stepped back, allowing him room.

"We'll both have to stoop to get around near the walls," she said. "But even you should be able to stand up straight in the center."

Then she turned in a slow circle, taking inventory. "Old suitcases and trunks, boxes, lots of them, some small pieces of furniture—" Her breath caught in a gasp.

"What?" He whirled her way.

"Ohh." She felt deflated as the sudden shock receded. "It's a dressmaker's dummy."

He chuckled. "Headless and armless. Not too pretty, is it, especially with that weird, swinging . . ." He grabbed the bulb's chain and held it, and the shadows stilled.

"Thank you," she said formally.

"You're welcome," he said, imitating the same staid manner she'd used. Then, making her grin, he switched to the flippant way she usually talked. "But I remind you that you said you could take care of your own spiders."

"So what do we tackle first?" she wondered aloud, gaze wandering from box to crate to piece of junk. "You want to get back down there, and I'll hand stuff down to you?"

"Maybe we should do that the other way around," he countered. "You'd have the wall and stair railing to help support the heavier pieces."

Yep, that handy dolly wasn't going to help her out up here. "Okay," she said. "But that means you're on your own when you get to the spiders."

He slanted a sideways glance at her. "Sunny, I find it happening more and more often that I get a terrific urge to put you in your place."

Did that have a sexual edge to it, Jonathan?

Don't go there, Sunny.

"So what's first?" she asked. "Once we get rid of the lighter stuff, the furniture will go faster."

"Agreed."

Her eye caught a dismantled crib leaning against the wall behind a dusty duffel bag. Its position indicated it was one of the last pieces stored. "Must've been mine," she murmured.

"Excuse me?"

"Nothing."

Well, that was an excellent opportunity you just blew, Sunny. Are you a coward or an idiot, or both?

Oh, shut up.

She grabbed the duffel bag. It was surprisingly light, so she also took the garment bag that lay over the top of a trunk and placed both pieces next to the trapdoor. "I'm going down with these. You can hand me down whatever comes next."

The hall quickly became littered with boxes and bags. They laughed over several paper bags of used Christmas wrap, folded neatly and stored away to disintegrate over the years.

"Sunny, I think I just found something," he hollered down to her. "It looks like an authentic Victrola. It's even got the trademark of a dog listening to a gramophone."

"Yeah?" She grinned up at the opening.

"It's a cabinet, covered with an old sheet. Let's take it down last. We'll have to take special care—oh, there you are."

He removed the sheet he'd just replaced. "Look. The cabinet doors open all right. Kind of squeaky, and it needs cleaning. But it's quite a find."

"Yeah." She reached to touch it, then quickly drew her hand back, thinking about oil from her fingers. "Mavis knows some people who deal in antiques. We could talk to them about it. I doubt that even Roberta knew this was up here."

"Well, it's been here long enough it can stay a little longer. I doubt you and I could get it down by ourselves without damaging it."

The dim and cramped room was heavy enough now with dust that it was getting hard to breathe. "Let's call it quits," she suggested, "and work on sorting what we've got. We can get back up here tomorrow."

He clearly wanted to keep going. But she figured they had enough to keep them busy for the rest of the day, so she bribed him with tomato sandwiches for lunch. She'd discovered he loved tomato and onion sandwiches slathered in mayonnaise and covered with salt and pepper. She'd refrained from inquiring why it was okay to mix onions with tomatoes when it wasn't okay to mix them with breakfast potatoes.

After lunch, they carried the stuff in the upstairs hall down to the utility room off the kitchen and sorted it there. Though Jonathan seemed to quickly grow bored, he didn't grumble, and he stuck with the job.

She was also on the bored side. Kneeling on the floor, she blew a breath out with a weary, resigned sigh, pushed the steamer trunk she'd just emptied away, and reached behind her for the duffel bag. It was light, but something clattered when it hit the floor. She unzipped the bag. It held one item, an ordinary baseball bat. She was beyond wondering why anything had been saved. Then she looked closer, and recoiled.

"Uh, Jonathan, that's . . . is that . . ."

He looked up from a box of old shoes. "Is what?"

"Blood," she said, staring at the bat. "It's got blood on it."

He came over and knelt next to her. "Blood and hair," he said, voice subdued.

Tom Fairly looked at the bat, still residing within the duffel bag, for a long time.

"Well," he said, "the lab will tell us for sure, but I'm gonna be one surprised citizen with a badge if that isn't human blood and hair." He looked at the two citizens who'd brought in the bag. "You didn't touch it?"

"Not the bat," Sunny said. "But both Jonathan and I handled

Her gaze moved to the stepladder in the alcove.

"No," he said. "No more grisly discoveries. You can rest easy."
Remaining in her spot halfway up the stairs, she turned sideways to lean against the wall and drew in a relieved, easier breath. But there was more to come. It would be a long while before she or anyone else could write an end to the legacy of Franklin Corday. Unzipping that duffel bag had been like opening Pandora's box.

Jonathan stood still for a moment, watching her. Then he leaned the broom against the doorjamb and started to descend the stairs. She straightened to make room for him to pass, but he came to a stop with one foot resting on the stair lower than hers so that his head angled only slightly higher than hers. He put his knuckles beneath her chin to raise her face to his.

"It's okay," he whispered. "It really is okay."

"Oh," she said, incapable in that moment of uttering any other word. The clear green eyes looking into hers were close to mesmerizing. His nearness, and the touch of his hand on her chin, chased everything else out of her mind. Franklin, adulterous affairs, the attic and the bloody bat all wrapped together and floated away like a ball of dust in a breeze. "Oh," she repeated.

Leaning in, he brushed his mouth across hers. It wasn't exactly a kiss, more like a sweet, friendly gesture. Just one set of lips barely touching the other, but it was incredibly sexy and arousing. When he pulled back, her eyes searched his. Had he been as moved as she?

Tenderness and gentle concern were evident in his return gaze . . . and something else. Surprise. Yes, that was it, almost a mirror of what she was feeling. But was it pleasant surprise, or the kind that says *hey, wait a minute. What's going on here and how do I get out of it?*

She didn't have a chance to figure it out before he cleared his expression. He repeated, again in a whisper, "It's okay." And then he climbed back up the stairs.

She drew in a breath, not realizing till then that she'd forgotten to breathe. She wet her lips and tried to make her face relax. As Jonathan reached for the broom, he looked back down at her. In the instant that his eyes first met hers, she got the impression he was weighing something in his mind. Then again his expression smoothed out. The man would make an excellent poker player.

With one hand placed over the other atop the broom, he rested his chin on his knuckles. "We opened every box and trunk, checked every conceivable hiding place, and the only thing Tom discovered up there was the exact allowable height in every corner." His face creased into a smile. If Jonathan had been thrown by that kiss, he'd quickly recovered. "That man is a slow learner. He banged his head every time he moved. And his vocabulary has even more color than yours."

"So we wait for the results of the crime lab tests," she said, and he nodded. Their conversation seemed to clear the air of the effect of the kiss. Almost. It had merely been a simple gesture of comfort which had taken each of them by surprise, she told herself, and she pushed away from the wall.

"Sunny?"

She looked back.

"Ryan wanted to visit again when he had more time. Now that we've got the TV, I was thinking about inviting him up for Sunday football. He could stay over for the Monday night game and could help get those heavier pieces down from the attic. Does that sound all right to you?"

"Sure."

"Do you want to call him, or should I?"

Her laugh made her feel normal again. "If I invited him up

here to watch football, he'd think I was delirious and get worried."

"I don't have an objection to him inviting Marcus if he wants to. But I don't know how to tell him that."

Leaning against the wall again, she folded her arms and grinned up at him. "Same way you just put it to me should work."

A slow, sheepish smile spread across his face. "Yes. We do build our own mountains out of mole hills, don't we?"

When he started back to his chores, she remained on the stairs, and he turned back and gave her a questioning look. "Something else?"

"Just wondering about dinner. I've got a package of ground round, but I don't know what I want to do with it."

"I like meat loaf."

She looked up. "Baked potato? Mashed?"

"Mashed."

"Vegetable preference?"

"Peas are good."

"Thank you, Jonathan. It's a treat cooking for someone who knows what he wants."

At the bottom of the stairs she realized what she'd said, and she broke into a smile that lasted all the way to the kitchen. She'd once thrown their breakfast into the garbage because he'd known what he wanted and had told her. But if he'd also noticed the contradiction between then and now, he'd said nothing about it.

Smart man.

And one hell of a kisser.

Stop it, Sunny.

The next morning Sunny sat alone at the kitchen table and stared with growing irritation at the skillet on the stove, nothing in it but a dab of margarine. She was making an omelet, one big one they'd split between them, but she couldn't pour the egg mixture into the pan until Jonathan was up. And, instead of staying warm in the oven, the hash browns were well on their way to drying out in there.

Yesterday's search had left the attic in a mess. She wanted to get back up there, but half the workforce was still in his bed, and apparently he'd grown immune to the sound of her voice. Hollering his name had gained her nothing but a tired throat.

She got up, walked the hall and mounted the stairs. His snores grew louder as she neared his room. Not bothering to knock, she opened the door. He was flat on his back, eyes closed and mouth open. She dashed to the bed, jumped on it and straddled him, gripped his shoulders and shook. His mouth closed and his eyes snapped open. She hopped off the bed as quickly as she'd hopped on.

"Breakfast is ready."

She left, no longer irritated.

The omelet slid neatly out of the pan onto a plate the same moment he entered the kitchen. When she looked up she caught annoyance in his eyes and the set of his shoulders. She also detected challenge, which made her study him for an extra second. And he was unshaven, which made her realize she liked him with beard stubble. *Hmm.*

"I hope you appreciate my restraint," she said with a straight face, then replaced the skillet on the stove, walked around to her chair, sat down, and put the platter on the table. "I thought about adding cheese to the eggs, but wasn't sure you'd like it." She helped herself to potatoes, cut away a third of the omelet and put it on her plate, then half rose out of her chair to put the platter next to his place setting. "Do you like cheese omelets?"

He sat down without answering.

"As you'll note, there's no butter on your toast." She picked

86

up her knife and proceeded to butter hers. "And we need to go shopping. This is the last of the potatoes. We're also out of bacon and I'd like to get some sausage links. Do you like sausage?"

No answer. He picked up the egg platter.

She tested the omelet, found it a little plain, but not bad.

"Sunny?"

"Yes?"

"It's only fair to warn you." He appeared to have worked through his annoyance because his voice held a casual note. His manner was precise, but not stiff, as he slid the remainder of omelet onto his plate. "If you ever do that again, jump on top of me in bed, you need to understand you will not be getting out of that bed until I'm ready to let you go."

Well. That kind of plain speaking, from a man as reserved as Jonathan, required some thought, especially because of the unexpected yet undeniable dare. She took a bite of toast and chewed it as she watched him. As composed and unruffled as ever, he cut into his omelet and watched her right back.

Not once in her life had Sunny not responded to a challenge.

"Oh, yeah?" she said, quite originally.

"Yes," he said politely. "Consider that a promise."

Chapter Ten

September seemed determined to leave an impression. When the temperature gauge that seldom rose to eighty started to climb toward ninety, Sunny and Jonathan were forced out of the attic and to the beach.

Quite willingly, Sunny left grisly discoveries and guilty confessions behind her. But she found that memories of comforting gestures that went straight to the sexual gut were more difficult to leave behind. And, although Jonathan Corday had a stuffy side, no one wore soapsuds better than he did.

They wore nothing more revealing than shorts and tank tops as they played on the beach, however. And the physical, sexy horseplay one might expect between two attractive and healthy people of opposite sexes—which could lead to sexy play of a heavier nature—never became an issue. Not because they consciously avoided it, but simply because Jonathan wasn't the kind of man who was inclined to toss a woman over his shoulder and into the ocean. Sunny found she appreciated that. She was able to enjoy his company without male slash female sparring.

Well, almost none, she thought as she washed dinner dishes. That speech of his after she'd jumped on top of him to wake him up a couple of mornings ago was as suggestive as it was challenging. It'd been as uncharacteristic for him—and she'd thought she had a handle on him—as it was unusual for her to be backing off. And backing off she was, though she didn't like admitting it. They'd changed roles, it appeared, which was as surprising to her as her recently found prudence. Maybe Mavis was right. Had Sunny met her match?

Sunny frowned at the dishwater. Then decisively, she upended the pan and finished up so she could go run a bath and wash the day's heat and sand off herself like she'd just washed food off the plates. Too bad her nagging musings couldn't also be scrubbed off in the bath and disappear down the drain.

The next day was another warm one, and Sunny chased shade around the house while she worked in the geranium beds. Though she'd had little experience in gardening, she was discovering that the smell of freshly turned earth and the vanquishing of weeds was an excellent way to soothe one's soul. It compared quite well with meditation—was even superior to it because she'd never been able to sit still long enough to meditate.

Cat kept trying to dig a hole, and Sunny kept brushing her away while she tilled around the stalks Langley Bowers had killed. Hopefully the joint of a healthy plant would root itself and fill in. Gorgeous colors: rich reds, purples and plums, and a delicate strawberry pink she took extra time with. As she worked, she realized she'd gone beyond the deal she'd made with her mother to clean out the old Victorian and ready it for sale. By tending the flowers, she was nurturing the place.

She paused, wrinkling her forehead as she caught an unpleasant smell. Cat had managed to dig her hole after all and now sat above it in a natural, unmistakable pose.

"Oh, shit, you stinky cat. You had to do that? Right now, right there?"

When she started to rise, she became aware that Jonathan was behind her. He grasped her elbow, and she allowed him to assist her to her feet.

"Yes, it appears she has to do that, right now and right there." He slanted an amused, fond look at the half-grown cat and its regal pose. Then he directed the same easy look at Sunny. "Some things never change. I became aware the first time I met you that you had a mouth on you, and this still holds true."

Her brow furrowed as she tried to remember what she'd said. She had good recall of her language—which she didn't think was that bad—during his unfortunate encounter as opposed to her fender bender, but what had she just said . . . oh. Okay.

"Yes," she said in the prim, professional tone reserved for schoolteachers and octogenarians. "I used a very crude name to refer to a perfectly natural substance. How rude of me. Do you think you can find it in your heart to let it go this time?"

His gaze moved to her lips and stayed there. "Yes, quite a mouth," he said softly, then lowered his to hers and claimed it.

She'd seen the kiss coming, met it and him halfway, and then she let the heat build—liking it, savoring it, and giving it right back. To hell with prudence. When he drew away she noted his bemused expression. If he'd been testing her, he now had more questions than before he'd kissed her.

Sunny peeled her gloves off, patted them against her leg. "We've been dancing around that for quite some time now," she said conversationally. She knew how to be cool, too.

He waited a beat. "And?"

His eyes weren't just green; they were the color of the greenest grass. "Well, if you're going to be staid, then be staid," she said. "If you're going to be sexy, be sexy."

"Staid," he echoed. His lips pursed as he thought that over, his gaze going off to the side. She noted that was the only adjective he was questioning. He looked back. "I believe I heard two unspoken words in that speech. Predictable. And unpredictable."

She thought over his statement, nodded. "Okay. That, too."

"You're about as unpredictable as unpredictable can get. That might be one of the few things we have in common."

"Might be."

He waited a longer beat. "I'm thinking some exploration might be in order."

Not wanting to let him know he'd thrown her, she tried not to let her eyes narrow or her brow to wrinkle. He was doing it again. Another provocative statement from a person from whom she did not expect provocative statements. Romantic exploration was in order?

Then with his eyes and a nod of his head, he indicated the grove of trees across the grassy field. "I want to explore over there. Would you like to join me?"

Exactly . . . what . . . did he want to explore over there? He was inviting her.

Was he too innocent, or was she too suspicious?

Okay, until further notice, take him literally.

She looked down at the row of geraniums, one end neat and the other not, and she decided to think about his guilelessness—or lack thereof—and her skepticism later. "Thanks, but I want to finish up here."

He walked away in that precise, straight-backed stride, and Cat followed. As she watched him, she pursed her lips. Maybe it hadn't appeared so at first, but that man had more than his share of sex appeal.

So, Sunny, what are you going to do about that?

She pulled her gloves back on, knelt, and got back to work.

Finish this flowerbed, that's what.

The sun's heat finally let up the next day. Sunny rose early, let Cat out, and then she couldn't resist letting herself out as well. The day was brisk, clear sky, no fog. Sweatshirt weather. She ran upstairs to get it and pulled it on over her white tee. Halfway back down the stairs, she paused and looked up. Cupping her hands around her mouth, she hollered, "Good morning. I'm going for a walk. You've got a half-hour. Tops."

She continued down, out the door and on to the beach. Cat caught up and then led. The kitten kept her distance from the water, but the rest of the beach was her private playground. Sunny didn't keep her distance from the surf; that was her playground.

Arriving back home she kicked the sneakers off and rinsed her feet and shoes with the backyard hose. Entering the kitchen, she yelled, "I'm back. If you're not up, get up."

She pulled the sweatshirt off, started coffee, and decided on oatmeal and cantaloupe for breakfast. The cereal was ready before he was so she turned the flame off, put a lid on the pot, yelled again, poured more coffee and sat down to wait. After that unorthodox awakening of hers last week he'd been tuned to the sound of her voice. He'd show any minute.

She gave the red-checked oilcloth a critical look. *This has gotta go. A peachy print would be pretty, just simple cotton, nothing fancy.*

She eyed the faded yellow cabinets. *A deep peach there, off-white walls, and—*

Catching herself, she smiled. No way. The new owners could do their own decorating.

Then the smile vanished. Enough time had passed that she gave the empty hallway an irritated scowl. "Jonathan! Get down here or go hungry!"

Silence. She drew in a breath, blew it out, and drained the last of her coffee.

Pour a cup for him, take it upstairs and douse him with it.

But she walked the hallway empty-handed and climbed the stairs. No snoring this time. She knocked, got no response, so went ahead and opened his door. His mouth was closed as well as his eyes. Covers were pulled up to his chin.

Don't even think about it. He wasn't bluffing.

She remained in the doorway.

No, Sunny.

She didn't budge.

Okay, you're not a coward. But you are an idiot. An absolute idiot.

She moved fast, but his arms closed around her the instant her knee touched the mattress. She didn't have a chance to straddle him as she had before, so he helped her into position. She was on top, but he was in control. His green eyes were smiling and smug.

"You weren't asleep," she accused.

"And you knew it."

"You set me up."

"And you knew it."

His face was too angular to be storybook handsome, but he was easy on the eyes. His hands moved lightly up and down her waist, then slipped beneath her t-shirt. Her skin tingled. She wondered if he noticed, and then he smiled. He'd noticed.

He was bare-chested. She guessed the rest of him was just as bare. Her breathing speeded up a notch.

"You're not struggling," he observed.

"No, I'm not," she agreed. With her palms resting on either side of his pillow she leaned down and kissed each eyelid.

He made a groaning sound. "Are you sure about this, Sunny?"

No, I'm not. But I'm gonna do it anyway.

Beneath her cotton tee, his hands teased their way up her back. She kissed his lips, chin, neck, then returned to his mouth for a longer time. His response made her wonder who was kissing and who was responding. She felt fingers playing with her bra strap.

When she realized his facial skin was smooth, she raised her head. "How did you manage to shave without my knowing it?"

"I'm talented."

"And well-planned. And devious."

"Thank you."

Her bra became unfastened. The palms of his hands smoothed her back, spreading until his thumbs rested feather light at the outside swell of her breasts.

"Think about this, Sunny." His voice was husky, eyes smoky. "It's not too late yet, but we're getting there."

"Looks like you're the one who's struggling." She continued to play around his mouth with hers.

Fingers trailed down to the hem of her shirt, teasing her skin as they moved. He bunched the fabric in his hands.

"I'm sure," he whispered. "But I also want you to be sure. I don't enter relationships lightly."

That gave her pause. She didn't pull away, but her hesitance must have communicated itself because his hands moved to her waist again, a safer positioning, yet still holding her in place.

"I didn't say that because I wanted to talk you out of it," he said softly. "I don't want you to change your mind."

She leaned down. With her lips touching his, she whispered, "I don't want to change my mind either." Then she straightened and allowed him to pull the t-shirt off over her head. The bra went with it.

"You're beautiful," he whispered.

She swallowed hard. "I already got a pretty good look at you once. And I kinda liked what I saw, too."

"You haven't seen anything yet," he murmured, and changed their positions in order to help her out of her jeans.

CHAPTER ELEVEN

Sunny and Jonathan went out for breakfast. Congealed oatmeal and dried-out cantaloupe lacked appeal. At a nod from her, he guided the SUV into the parking lot of the first restaurant they came to on the outskirts of Castleton. As Sunny alighted from the truck with a bounce in her step, she realized that for the first time in a long time her mood actually matched her name.

The hostess led them to a table, and Jonathan pulled a chair out for Sunny. She sat, looked up at him, and then down at her hand resting comfortably on his larger one on the arm of the chair. She liked the way it looked there.

The hostess smiled. "Newlyweds?"

"Huh?" Sunny's head jerked up. Holding the smile, the woman walked away.

Jonathan grinned as he sat down. "It shows."

Her face warmed. "Something shows." She buried herself in the menu.

"My dear Sunny, I do believe I'm seeing a side of you I never saw before."

"Oh, shut up."

"I suggest you get used to the feeling because the activity which caused it might be happening again from time to time."

His words gave her such a delicious—and impish—feeling that she gave him a look over the top of the menu that made his face go slack. He hitched in a breath. "Eat fast."

They ordered waffles. His was plain and hers was smothered

in enough strawberries and whipped cream that she had to search for the waffle.

Sated, in more ways than one, Jonathan pushed his empty plate aside. Sunny had finished a long time ago, having barely made a dent in the plate's contents. His gaze moved to something beyond her, and his eyes dulled. "Great. How far do we have to go to get away from the good citizens of Chester?"

Sunny turned in her chair. "Oh, hi, Tom. Aren't you out of your jurisdiction?"

Tom pulled out a chair and sat down without being invited. "Still my eating jurisdiction. They make good chili here."

"For breakfast?" Jonathan looked appalled.

"It's almost noon." Tom gave him a curious look.

"Oh." The younger man appeared slightly nonplussed. "Of course it is." He rested his left elbow on the arm of the chair and managed a surreptitious glance at his watch.

Tom directed his attention to Sunny. "Glad I ran into you. I got the report back on that baseball bat, and the blood type isn't the same as your—oh, hi, Millie."

"You ready yet, Tom?" The waitress put one check facedown in the middle of the table, and then poised her pencil above her ordering pad.

"Your biggest bowl of chili, nuke it with cheddar and onions, and bring me a box of crackers to go along with it. And a glass of water and ice, leave the pitcher."

"I could write this one on my own and bring it with me. But if I did, you're just ornery enough to order something else."

Tom guffawed.

Although her gaze was on Millie as she walked away, Sunny spoke to Tom. "You were saying the blood type isn't Franklin's."

"Nope. Isn't."

Once Millie rounded the cashier's station, she was out of sight, but Sunny's gaze remained on the corner of the stand.

She asked, "Then whose?"

"Now that is the question. A really good question. All indications point to the fact that the bat walloped somebody real good. And the prints on the base—there were two good ones—don't belong to old Franklin either. He was neither the victim nor the one wielding the weapon, but it was found in his attic. When you figure that one out, you let me know."

"Then someone else is missing besides Franklin," Jonathan reasoned. "Somebody's going to have to go digging."

Tom hesitated, gave him a squinted, are-you-serious kind of look. Sunny had also caught what was most likely an unintended pun, but she was too preoccupied to respond to it.

"What's next, Tom?" she asked. "What do we do now?"

"Check the missing person's file," he paused and gave Jonathan another squinty look. "And try to date the, uh, tissue on the bat. But I don't mind sayin' we got more questions right now than answers."

"But as far as we're concerned," Jonathan said, "it's . . ."

"Yep. Business as usual. Whatever that is." He gave each of them a thoughtful look. "Whatever that is," he repeated. "Anything going on I should know about? Something different about you, both of you, but I can't put my finger on it."

Sunny stared at him. *No way can it show that we just got out of the same bed. No way, no how.*

Then she reached for the check the same moment Jonathan did. The touch of his hand on hers ignited sparks, and she drew back. A defensive reaction, under the circumstances, and he must've caught it because his mouth turned up at the corners as he put bills down to cover the check.

She stood. "Bye, Tom. See you around." She managed not to give the deputy sheriff a direct look.

Jonathan walked beside her on their way out, and she also refused to look at him. *You laugh, and I'll kill you. I swear it.*

But once they'd climbed into the SUV, Jonathan sat behind the wheel without inserting the key for a long enough time that she had to look at him. When she did, she broke up, and they laughed until they had to wipe tears of glee from their eyes. Sure, they had some thorny problems, like a bloody bat and a missing and unidentified body, but hey, they were only human.

Later that week, the phone rang when Sunny was halfway up the stairs with a basket of clean laundry. *Criminy. It never fails.*

Carefully she balanced the basket on a stair, hoping it wouldn't tip and spill sheets and pillowcases out to cascade down the steps, and she raced to the parlor.

"Hi, doll," said the voice at the other end.

"Ryan." She perched on the arm of the sofa and cradled the phone at her ear. "Hi."

"When Jonathan called, I told him that we couldn't make it up there until next week. But Marcus finagled the time off, I just cleared my calendar, and we've got the weekend free until Tuesday. We can be there Saturday for dinner if you'll cook it."

"You're on."

"Speaking of such, Marcus wanted me to tell you how much he likes that chicken dish you make with mushrooms and tomatoes and rice."

"He did, huh?"

"If you'll cook the chicken, I'll bring the wine. And dessert."

"Deal."

"Bye, doll."

She hung up, still smiling, then tracked Jonathan down in the backyard where he was toweling dry his truck. Cat sat at a safe distance from the dripping vehicle. She groomed herself, watched a while, then groomed herself some more.

"Company's coming," Sunny announced. "Day after tomorrow. I've gotta go shopping. Wanna go with me?"

He seemed pleased to be invited. She made a list while he finished the car. Since she was the cook, she was also the shopper and she paid the bill. But he snagged the receipts and split every one right down the middle. She figured anyone that precise needed to be that precise, so she let him handle it his way without argument.

Pushing a grocery cart down the aisle with Jonathan at her side felt almost like an intimate act. Though twice married, she'd never before shared this chore, and suddenly it wasn't a chore. Adding a six-pack of Sprite to the cart, she eyed the wine section across the aisle.

She tapped a bottle of Korbel Brut with her fingertip and slanted a look at him. "We could take this and a blanket down to the beach tonight and catch the sunset. What do you think?"

In response, she got a slow smile.

She returned it. "I promise not to let the ocean ambush you again."

"Have you ever seen that classic with Burt Lancaster and Deborah Kerr? Maybe we could let the water catch us on purpose."

A bored, middle-aged woman who looked tired checked their groceries. Jonathan was reading the *TV Guide* that had already passed over the price check scanner. The clerk came to the champagne and held it up. "ID?"

"Oh, yeah," Sunny said. She fumbled in her oversized shoulder bag. Whatever she wanted was always at the bottom, and she looked up apologetically. The woman smothered a yawn, waiting to ring up the total.

"Never mind. I've got it," Jonathan said.

The clerk shook her head. "She initiated the sale, she concludes it. She doesn't have the ID, the bottle goes back on the shelf."

"But if I pay for it—"

"Stuff it, Jonathan. You're being fussy again. Here. I found it."

The woman looked at the license, then back up in surprise. "Twenty-six? You sure don't look it, Ms. Corday."

"Yeah, I've heard that before." She reached for the license, but Jonathan snatched it out of the clerk's hand. Startled, Sunny stared at him. Then she recalled the woman's words.

"Oh," she said. There was nothing else to say. "Oh."

CHAPTER TWELVE

"Laurel Frances Corday," Jonathan read tonelessly. "Surprise, surprise."

He flipped the license onto the counter without looking at Sunny then exited the store.

The clerk watched the automatic door closing behind him. Her gaze darted to Sunny. "I'm sorry. Did I . . . ?"

"No. It wasn't your fault." Sunny's tone was as flat as Jonathan's had been.

The clerk, who now seemed wide-awake, appeared both confused and interested. Finally groceries were bagged and in the cart and the doors slid open for Sunny on her way out. She wondered if the truck would still be in the lot. Jonathan might've been angry enough to take off. If so, she'd find an ATM to get enough cash to pay cab fare out to Corday Cove. Then she'd put herself and her suitcase into the Reviler and get herself back home to San Francisco.

But the SUV was still there, Jonathan seated behind the wheel. He motioned her to the back and the window rolled down. She loaded the bags by herself and returned the cart to its storing area. Once she'd climbed up onto the seat he started the engine, backed up and pulled out, giving her nothing but his profile.

"I'm sorry." She made her voice as matter-of-fact as possible. Excuses would get her nowhere, and she wasn't a whiner anyway. "It's inexcusable that I didn't properly identify myself before now. You have a right to be angry."

He pulled onto the freeway and the truck's speed increased.

"It was a lie by omission, yes. But I didn't actually tell you a lie." She was splitting hairs, but this was the truth. "Though Laurel is my legal name, no one ever uses it, not even my mother. If I hadn't changed my last name back after the divorce, you still wouldn't know who I am. What difference would it make?"

When she still got no response, she gave up. She wished he'd turn some music on. Anything would be better than this loud silence. If she knew what knobs controlled what, she might do it herself. But he'd put an effective wall up, barring her from him, and most likely from anything that belonged to him.

At the house he parked in back and then helped carry bags of groceries inside. Cat seemed happy to see them. After locking the truck, Jonathan disappeared down the hall. When Sunny heard his bedroom door close, it carried a final sound.

She'd never gotten the silent treatment before. Not from her mother, the two men she'd been married to, nor Ryan. She knew what rage was—wow, did she ever—and she knew what strained feelings felt like, but she'd never encountered total silence. She didn't like it.

While putting groceries away she came across the Brut. A strong desire to cry arose, yet she also wanted to grip the bottle by the neck and bash it in the sink. She pushed it into the corner of the counter.

Cat's cheery greeting was turning into complaining mews. Sunny used the new red feeding bowl she'd just bought to introduce the animal to her first can of cat food. She didn't like the smell, and Cat didn't seem to appreciate it either. The animal backed away, still meowing, and tried to wrap herself around her mistress's ankle. Sunny relented, cut up leftover spaghetti and gave that to her. Cat gobbled it down and Sunny laughed softly. "Well, that'll be easier on the budget."

She went to the back porch, stared at the ocean through the screen, then stepped outside. She hadn't planned on watching the sun set by herself, but it was too airless and unfriendly inside the house. Cat followed her to the bluff's edge.

Sunny stood at the top of the trail, not sure if she wanted to descend or not, and watched the kitten scamper down. Then Cat stopped midway and her ears perked. At the same instant, Sunny became uncomfortable. Quickly she turned, making a circle as she surveyed the area. No movement near the trees, on the bluff in either direction, at the house or on the beach.

The tide reached only halfway up the sand. The fact she couldn't see anyone didn't mean a person couldn't be down there, sheltered by the overhanging cliff on either side. Even if someone was there, as unusual as that would be, it didn't necessarily mean menace. But her unease remained.

Cat was still poised halfway up and halfway down. She'd be more alarmed by a stray dog than a person, and dogs occasionally roamed the beach. That was probably all it was. Sunny patted her leg to capture the pet's attention. Paranoid or not, she didn't want to draw notice to herself by calling the animal. After Cat bounded up the incline, they returned to the house. Sunny felt foolish doing it, but she kept checking behind her as she walked. Though it was probably just anxiety built out of her unsettled mood this evening, she couldn't quite rid herself of a sense of fear.

Cat woke Sunny the next morning by nuzzling her cheek. Sunny was back in her old bedroom. After her return last night, Jonathan had gone out for his own long walk and hadn't invited her. He hadn't spoken to her since they'd been inside the supermarket.

"Umm," Sunny said, moving into the nuzzling instead of

away from it. She opened her eyes, but it wasn't Cat. It was Jonathan's hand. The first time he was up before her, and even more surprising, she hadn't heard him.

"Good morning." His tone was quiet, face sober, mood reflective.

"Good morning." For the life of her, she couldn't think of anything else to say.

"I was angry last night."

"I . . . noticed."

"I thought you'd been dishonest with me, deliberately led me on, even into an intimate relationship. But I didn't have the foggiest idea why. I didn't see where you had anything to gain. Nothing made sense. I also felt like a fool, and that is rough on anyone's ego."

His fingers were warm and soft next to her cheek. She felt mesmerized by his eyes, voice, the touch of his hand.

"But when I looked at it from your point of view," he went on. "It made sense."

"How's . . . that?"

"On that first day I'd made some unkind remarks about Laurel." He paused, the corners of his mouth turning up, and then he chuckled. "You've even got me doing it. I'm talking to her, yet I'm still talking about her."

Their gazes became level when he knelt next to the bed. She smelled his aftershave and realized that sounds of his shaving hadn't even awakened her. Apparently she'd grown accustomed to him and no longer heard him. She touched his smooth cheek, drawing him in with all her senses except taste. Turning her face into his hand, she lightly closed her teeth on his palm.

"Hey," he whispered, eyes softening and growing vibrant at the same time. "Are you going to let me finish explaining? Or what?"

"Please." Her voice was as soft as his. "I think you'd just

made some unkind remarks about Laurel."

"Yes," he said formally. "At which time you handled yourself and the situation without confrontation. And then it would have been difficult, and may not have seemed necessary, to reintroduce yourself and go back and start all over again. Once we'd made love—which I'd planned, not you—it must have become next to impossible for you to say, *hey, guess what?*" He paused. "How am I doing? Am I right so far?"

"Uh, yeah. Keep going. Please."

"There really isn't anything else to cover." He gave her an exaggerated frown. "Is there?"

"No. No, I'm not harboring any more secrets."

He brought her hand to his mouth and kissed it, continuing to hold her gaze.

"Jonathan?"

"Hmm?"

"How can you do that? How is it possible for you to explain me better than I can explain myself?"

He just smiled. "Sunny?"

"Hmm?"

"Do you think both of us can fit in that dinky bed?"

She scooted over to make room. "Come on in, and we'll see."

"I'll be adding mushrooms and tomatoes." Sunny paused, fork poised over a piece of frying chicken as she concentrated on ingredients. "And onion, green pepper and garlic. I think that's it, but since you like my spaghetti sauce, all of that should be okay."

"That's fine," Jonathan assured her, looking up from where he knelt on the floor while he entertained Cat with a piece of string.

"But the rice is cooked and served separately."

"That's good."

"And I splurged on asparagus. My favorite."

"Sunny, that's fine."

"And . . ."

"Sunny, are you nervous?"

She turned the flame down under the browning chicken and then looked over at him. "Well, now that you mention it. Yeah, I guess I am."

"Why?"

"I don't know."

After covering the skillet with its lid she crossed to the refrigerator. "Yes, I do too know. I'll be sleeping in my own bed this weekend."

"Oh." That gave him pause. "Well, of course you're going to sleep where you want to. But I'd rather you put tomatoes in the scrambled eggs again instead."

She turned to smile at him, but she knew it was a weak one. "I . . . just feel uncomfortable. Okay?"

"Why?"

"I don't know why." She withdrew a bag of mushrooms, rummaged for garlic. "Jonathan, I don't always make sense even to myself. There's no reason to expect me to start making sense now." A yellow onion and a green pepper joined the array.

"I understand that," Jonathan said, looking thoughtful. "And that's scary. Is your sense of logic contagious?"

Apparently growing tired of waiting for her playmate, Cat leaped for the string. Jonathan lost it and the animal rolled under the table with it. She looked like a living, furry ball. Laughing, Sunny put the vegetables aside, then knelt next to Jonathan and reached out to the kitten. It forgot the string and attacked her hand with teeth and all four feet but not aggressively enough to leave scratches.

A red rubber ball lay under the table that the cat must have left there during a previous play session. Sunny rolled it down the hall and Cat passed it up in her eagerness to catch it.

Still kneeling, the two people on the kitchen floor looked at each other. Then they shared a gentle, chaste kiss.

"Do you realize how much time you're talking about?" Jonathan asked.

"We're both adults. We can handle it."

"That's tonight, tomorrow night, and Monday night. On Tuesday, you might as well make sandwiches and we'll take them upstairs with us. I don't think we'll be getting out of bed all day."

"You're very funny, Jonathan."

"That's not exactly the adjective I'd use, but we can talk about it again on Tuesday."

Their guests brought a banana cream pie and a bottle of Chardonnay with them. Marcus had a stocky build, dark hair and eyes, was more reserved than Ryan, and had a quiet sense of humor. Sunny had liked him at their first meeting. She sensed a strain among the three men at first, but it was the simple awkward moment between strangers who were still strangers. When they went to visit the relatively new SUV in the backyard with its sizable dent in its front fender, Sunny knew they were okay with each other.

The men had taken their wine with them and Sunny followed them with her glass. Dinner was taking care of itself and needed no help from her for at least five minutes. She leaned against the house wall and sipped chilled Chardonnay. Catching Ryan's gaze on her she gave him a questioning look. But he gave her no clue to his thoughts; instead he directed his attention back to Jonathan.

"The salt air up here could be murder on that paint job," he said.

"I wash it every day, hoping to keep the effect as minimal as possible."

I can vouch for that. He also cleans the bathroom every day.

Marcus was testing the seating comfort in the rearmost seats. Cat was staring at the closed passenger's door as if waiting for someone to open it for her, but the animal wasn't allowed inside the vehicle.

"No, Cat," Sunny said and gently nudged the pet aside. She joined Marcus and they clinked glasses.

"If we spill any of this in here," he said. "He might kill us."

"Might," Sunny agreed.

"Seats eight. Nice, really nice. But only kids could sit for very long back here."

Despite the limited space, she managed to cross her legs, then when she looked at him she realized he wouldn't even be able to change position until she got out of there. "Hmm. Body builders who practice their art have difficulty fitting into small spaces."

"And little girls who barely tip the scales at three whole digits can fit anywhere."

"Do me a favor?"

"Sure."

"Dinner's ready. Since you're bigger than I am, will you hogtie those two and get them to the table?"

Everybody but Jonathan put their chicken atop their rice. He also was careful to keep his asparagus in its own place, and he ignored the Hollandaise. Nothing touched anything else on Jonathan's plate.

Sunny and Marcus watched the other two diners using forks and knives to cut into their chicken and then looked at each other and shrugged. They picked up drumsticks in their fingers and ate the way they wanted to. They helped themselves to extra napkins and paid no attention to how smudged their wine glasses got.

When she reached for the creamer she'd put the Hollandaise

in, she again found Ryan's gaze on her, and she doubted his attention had anything to do with her table manners. He seemed to be studying her, and that made her uncomfortable. In order to keep herself busy and him occupied with food, she served dessert. But after dinner he insisted on helping with dishes. She wished he'd go find somebody to talk about football with.

As he applied dishtowel to salad bowl, he glanced at her. "What are you so nervous about?"

"I'm not nervous," she said more sharply than she intended. Then she frowned. "Excuse me. I'm just tired. Once I finish this I'm going to bed."

"Where does this go?"

She pointed at a lower cabinet. He put the faux wooden bowl away, straightened, and picked up a platter. "Jonathan seems like a good guy and I think it's great you found someone. You've been celibate for much too long."

The pan she was working on slipped out of her hands. "Oh, for . . ."

Am I wearing a sign around my neck, or what?

She looked at him, then quickly away. She stared at the drainer, the cabinet, the sink. "Criminy, Ryan. What makes you think that . . ."

He chuckled. "Relax. Like I said, it's the best thing that could've happened to you." He paused, looking thoughtful. "He strikes me as a tad more conventional than you, however. Let me guess. You dared him, right?"

She glared at the soapy water, then at him. "For your information, Mr. Know-it-all, *he* dared *me!*"

Ryan laughed so hard he had to put the platter back into the drainer. He gripped the counter with both hands and roared.

"Oh, for . . ." Sunny grabbed the dishtowel, dried her hands and then threw it into the sink full of water. "That does it! You can do the stupid dishes by yourself!"

She stomped down the hall and stopped in the parlor doorway long enough to tell its occupants, "Goodnight!"

Jonathan and Marcus frowned at her and then each other, clearly wondering what they'd done wrong. She climbed the stairs. At the top she hesitated, then rounded the banister's railing and went to Jonathan's room. Abstinence now seemed absurd, and she'd probably left her nightgown in there anyway.

Come on, let's be honest here. That cover-up-everything garment hasn't seen the inside of his room yet.

She backtracked, grabbed her nightgown from her room and took it to his.

And now what are you doing, Sunny? Is that flimsy piece of pink nylon supposed to be a token of propriety, or what?

Oh, shut up.

CHAPTER THIRTEEN

Everybody slept late the next morning. Which meant that by the time breakfast was over, opposing teams in colorful uniforms were already fighting over a football somewhere, and it was being televised! The men quickly found loge seats in the parlor. Sunny had no help with the dishes, which was fine with her. Cat kept her company. She loved the sausage her mistress had saved and cut up for her but ignored the pancake.

Once dishes were put away, Sunny grabbed a plastic grocery bag and headed for the beach. Because she figured she'd be back before anyone missed her, she didn't bother announcing she was going out. The day was shaping up to be a nice one. The sun had chased the fog away, but it wasn't too warm. Comfortable in cutoffs and a pullover and flip-flops, she pushed her sleeves up to her elbows as she walked, savoring the crisp morning air that was salty with ocean.

Cat led, trailed, foraged, and leaped after butterflies. Sunny watched her scamper down the trail to the beach and disappear, but she didn't follow. Instead she made her way past clumps of reeds, many as high as her shoulders, and came to a stop above the deepest recess of the horseshoe. Berry vines grew in abundance all the way down the cliff, and she wanted to gather a bag of berries to serve over vanilla ice cream for tonight. Even she liked ice cream. The slope at the base of the incline made access to the vines difficult from that point.

At a sharp sound she snapped her head up and her gaze

darted toward the grove of cypresses and their windblown branches. She saw no movement, but heard another rifle report. The shot that had grazed her had been louder and closer, so most likely hadn't been a stray from the trees as she'd thought. The boys must've wandered out that day and were taking pot shots here and there, perhaps into the canyon, and then had run scared when they realized what they'd done. But evidently they were now over their scare.

She continued watching the grove with a mixture of apprehension and annoyance. She was going to talk to Tom about this again, and Matthew and Bev, and the Bowers boys and their father. Better yet, when she returned to the house, she'd ask the three men to go talk to the boys. The message might leave a longer lasting impression if delivered on the spot by three strapping males.

Damned kids. If they kill somebody they might finally start using their brains. But that'd be a little late for the dead guy.

She sensed movement behind her but had no chance to turn before hands planted themselves in the wide part of her back and pushed. She was close enough to the edge that she literally flew into space. Her foot tangled in a vine that wrapped around it, and for an instant she dangled head down in the vines. A flip-flop slid off and batted her in the face on its way down. Desperately she closed her hand around a mesh of stems as thorns lacerated her ankle, feeling like barbed wire, and then the vine around her foot snapped and she plummeted all the way down.

Her handful of trailing plants had held her long enough for her legs to swing around, and that probably saved her from breaking her neck. She hit on her left shoulder, rolled, hit again on her hip and then finally came to a stop on the sand.

She heard someone scrabbling down the trail but she couldn't move; it hurt to breathe. She'd landed on her side, facing away from the trail, and she sensed someone standing over her. Out of self-defense and necessity, Sunny remained still. Then she heard voices rapidly growing near, and next she felt a swish of air as someone walked past her head. After more noise that indicated another descent down the cliff, someone, two people, knelt beside her.

Hands moved over her, but in a professional way rather than invasive. Jonathan?

"Is she breathing?" That was Ryan's voice, from in front of her.

"Yes," Jonathan said tightly, behind her.

"Sunny, sweetheart. Talk to me."

"Don't touch her," Jonathan warned. "Don't move her."

"I know that, dammit. Sunny, talk to me."

Though she still couldn't communicate, she managed to get her eyes open. Ryan was kneeling, his gaze directed over the top of her toward Jonathan. "Is anything broken? Is she wounded? She's bleeding all over."

"I don't see an obvious break, but I can't tell for sure." Jonathan sounded both professional and scared. "We'll see what she can and can't do when she comes to. I don't see a bullet wound, no gushing blood. She's covered with scratches from the thorns so that might account for the blood."

"Ohh, shit." She'd found her voice. It was raspy, but audible.

Ryan sagged and let his breath out in a long-winded, "Whew."

Jonathan gave no reaction. His face lacked expression when she rolled onto her back and looked up at him. "Were you hit?" he asked.

"Not by a bullet."

Ryan held up both hands. "I'm holding up two fingers from each hand. Can you count all four fingers?"

She looked at him and his hands, then at Jonathan. "Is he supposed to give me hints like that?"

"She sounds all right to me," Marcus said. He was out of her line of vision, so she turned toward his voice. Her neck didn't immediately execute the movement, which gave her concern, but then it cooperated. He'd climbed the slope and was standing at the base of the horseshoe, within the vines themselves and was looking upward. "She must've taken a header from up there. The vines scratched her up, but also cushioned her and may have saved her life."

"Sunny," Jonathan said. "I want you to sit up if you can, but take it slow. We need to find out what hurts."

"Everything hurts." She worked to get her limbs coordinated, and finally she managed to sit up. The simple act took so much out of her that once she got her torso upright, she had to lean against Jonathan. He'd not helped her, but she'd caught several aborted moves. As he'd said, they needed to know what she was capable of on her own. The rigid line of his body communicated his tension.

"What?" he asked quickly when she slumped against him. "Are you going to pass out again?"

"I never lost consciousness."

"You weren't conscious when we—"

"Yes, I was. I heard you coming down the cliff, but I didn't know who you were, and I was scared. Then I had to find my air before I could talk anyway."

"Why were you afraid? Whom did you think we were?" That was Marcus again. He seemed to be zeroing in faster than anyone else.

Her gaze traveled up the berry vines to the top. Panic returned, and she battled it back. "I didn't fall. Someone pushed me."

The vines stirred, then shook more aggressively as something moved through them. Marcus whirled to face the threat, and Sunny lost her breath again. Then Cat appeared, leaped to bat at a trailing vine and got them all vibrating again as if a gust of wind had blown through. Then calmly she sat back on her haunches and started grooming.

Each man sagged. Someone called the cat a bad name.

Sunny put a hand on Jonathan's shoulder. "I'm going to stand up. Hopefully under my own power, but I can guarantee I'm gonna lean on you." Then she laughed weakly. "I still have one shoe on. Slip it off before it trips me up, will you?"

He did.

"Who pushed you?" Ryan asked. "One of the rifle shooters?" Though he appeared cold and dispassionate, hot anger emanated from him in waves.

"I was pushed from behind, couldn't see who it was. Someone came down the trail but stayed behind me. You guys arrived pretty fast. You didn't see anyone?"

"Once we saw you sprawled out like that, we never looked." Ryan walked to the mouth of the cove and stared for a long moment in both directions. When he returned, he said, "South is clear. Going north, toward Chester, it takes a curve to the inside. Someone might be able to hug the cliff and stay out of sight that way but would be long gone by the time we got up there."

"Ryan, come here a minute," Marcus said. Ryan looked over, then walked away.

"Can you stand without my support?" Jonathan asked.

She nodded. When he let go—careful to stay within catching distance she was glad to note—she took a couple of practice steps. She was shaky and sore, but okay. "How come you got here so fast?"

"You got a phone call, and I couldn't find you. When I looked outside and heard a rifle shot, we all came running."

"Jonathan, Sunny. Come look at this," Ryan said.

Jonathan glanced that way, then back at Sunny with a frown.

He appeared dubious about the prospect of her walking that far. She waved his concern away. "It's okay. I can manage."

As she took cautious baby steps, he hovered a step behind her. It wasn't necessary to climb the hill of sand, though. They could see what had grabbed their companions' attention from the base of the mound. Either Marcus had dislodged a piece of driftwood embedded in the vines or Sunny had done it in her fall. He stood next to a piece of rotted wood, maybe twelve inches long and as wide as a telephone pole, with its underside darker than the sun-dried side. When they approached, he pulled a layer of vines back so they could get a better look at an exposed white bone.

No, several small bones.

A breath lodged in her throat. It was a skeletal human hand, exposed to its wrist.

Marcus said, tone subdued, "Looks like someone might've taken the same fall Sunny did, but wasn't quite as lucky."

"Or it's the missing victim," Sunny whispered, gaze glued to the grisly find.

Ryan gave her a sharp glance. Looking at Jonathan, Sunny nodded, silently encouraging him to take over. He explained the baseball bat-cum-weapon found in the attic, succinctly and unemotionally, but the two men who stood atop the small hill seemed to grasp the same sense of menace that had grabbed Sunny and Jonathan when they'd first looked inside the duffle bag.

"You mean we're talking about murder, not an accident?" Ryan asked.

"We can figure out what we're talking about after we get Sunny to the hospital," Jonathan answered.

She shook her head, her attention again riveted on the skeletal fingers. "I don't need a hospital. Nothing's broken. I'm just bruised and sore."

"You need X-rays and an examination by someone qualified," Jonathan said evenly. "I don't want any surprises tonight or tomorrow."

"I said I'm fine." Again she shook her head, but this time in annoyance. "I'll show you." She wasn't looking forward to climbing the cliff but knew she had to. And an almost desperate desire to get away from those bleached white bones was building fast.

When she turned toward the trail, Jonathan caught her arm. "Are you serious?"

"How else am I supposed to get up there?"

He continued to stare at her. Then he broke eye contact, and his manner turned businesslike as he turned back toward the hill. "Marcus, will you go to the house and call the paramedics? They'll either have a rescue unit that can traverse the beach or will know who does."

"Oh, for . . . I don't need—"

"Shut up, Sunny." Ryan jumped down from the mound of sand. He walked up to her and then rested both hands on his thighs and bent his knees until his eyes were on a level with hers. "Look at yourself. You're already turning different shades of purple, and you'd be hard put to find a whole square inch of skin that doesn't have blood on it. You need to see a doctor. For once in your life, put a lid on that contentious side and do what you're supposed to do."

If she had an injury that was in need of medical attention, she'd know it, but neither man seemed inclined to let her make that call. Marcus was already at the top of the path. From the look of her two companions, if she attempted to follow him, she'd be stopped. So okay. She turned toward Chester and started walking. But they didn't like that either.

"Uh, Sunny . . ." from Jonathan.

"Sunny!" Ryan's voice.

"Cool it," she warned without turning around. "You won one, don't push for two."

The worst physical threat she faced right now was her muscles freezing up. So a slow walk would serve her better than sitting and waiting. But she didn't feel it necessary to explain that to her self-appointed guardians. She'd noted how quickly they'd joined forces and was wondering if in the long run that boded well for her or not. Then, with no more argument, they caught up and fell in step. Well, that was one mark in their favor.

At the hospital, Sunny spent two long hours being peered at, prodded, X-rayed, and bathed in antiseptic. Her eyes stung, and she feared her nose might permanently be wrinkled from the acrid odor.

Then at long last the doctor followed her to the waiting room and cheerfully made his report to her escorts. He was gray-haired, age-wrinkled, thorough, and in a good mood. "She's got bruises and abrasions, looks like she put in some heavy overtime as a scratching post, but she's got no breaks and doesn't need stitching up. Couldn't even find a decent sprain." He slanted a sideways, awe-struck look at her. "Takes a header off a fifteen-foot cliff and all she does is roll around in the sand. Never figure out how she did it."

She'd asked him to personally pass on his findings because she doubted her companions would take her word for anything.

"Okay?" Sunny asked her guards. "Can I go now?" Oh, boy, did she ever want to lay into them. The few parts of her that hadn't hurt before all that prodding and pushing were sending out steady streams of hurt now.

Jonathan and Ryan exchanged glances, looked at Sunny, then to the doctor, and again at each other. She rolled her eyes. *Oh, come on, would you really feel better if I'd broken a leg or concussed myself into a coma?*

When she noticed the doctor writing on a prescription pad,

she frowned. He tore off the prescription and handed it to Jonathan, one man with a medical degree to another. "She's already stiff and sore and it's going to get worse. That'll help her to sleep."

"No," Sunny said. "Give it back to him. I'll take Advil."

"We'll fill it anyway," Jonathan said. "It's a mild painkiller. About midnight tonight you'll be glad you have it."

Ryan took the prescription from Jonathan and gave it back to the doctor. "She'll take Advil, like she said."

The doctor looked at him, then Sunny. He asked softly, "Do you have a drug problem, Sunny?"

She returned his gaze without flinching. "Not presently."

He nodded, his expression now sober and displaying respect. "I never met you before today, but I feel like I have a personal stake here. Take Advil, Sunny."

She had a sudden desire to cry, but fought it off.

Next was Tom's office. She'd prefer to put off filing a report, but she couldn't get her mind around the fact that someone had deliberately pushed her off the cliff. As much as she wanted to explain it away, no innocent interpretation occurred.

Tom winced when he saw her. "Sunny, whatever you do, don't pose for a portrait today."

"Thanks, Tom." Her grin drew a protest from scratched and bruised cheekbones.

She eased into the visitor's chair, wondering if she could manage without having to ask for a pillow. She noted that neither Jonathan nor Ryan seemed to appreciate the deputy sheriff's humor, which only served to amuse her more. She was feeling punchy.

"Maybe you two guys should go check out the deli at Bev's," she suggested. "Sometimes she has roasted chicken and ribs in that hot case. It's either that or get back on the highway until you run into a fast-food franchise."

The only pillow in sight lay atop the cot inside the open cell, and she didn't think she wanted that one. Deciding to rough it without a cushion, she managed another grin for Tom once her two guardians had left. "Okay, now it's time for you to tell me you'll make this report as painless as possible."

He chuckled. "I like you, Sunny. You're like a breath of fresh air."

Then he sat forward, placed his palms on the desk, and his expression sobered. "But I don't like what I heard. Who was it that called me? Mark?"

"Marcus."

"I have to get this straight from you. Did somebody push you off that cliff?"

A very cold feeling sprang up very quickly in her gut. "Yes."

"Think about this carefully, Sunny. I'm not trying to feed you, or lead you, but stray dogs are known to roam the beach. Could—"

"It have been a friendly mongrel that jumped up to say hi?" she finished for him. "I already thought about that. My impression was, and still is, that it was a person. Not an animal."

He sat back and stared at her. Clearly he hadn't liked hearing that any more than she'd liked saying it. "Then we need to assume the only thing accidental about that bullet crease in your forehead is that it didn't kill you. Who wants you dead, Sunny? And why?"

"Sunny?" Jonathan's voice again, calling hesitantly through the closed bathroom door. He'd been hovering out there off and on since she'd come in here.

"I'm okay, Jonathan. Just give me a little longer." Hot water had never felt so good. This was her second bath today, and she'd probably be back in here again before bed.

They'd eaten chicken and ribs and French bread for dinner,

listening to traffic sounds outside their front door. The skeleton had a lot of company down there on the beach. Tom had popped in and out a couple of times, but she'd been in the tub. She'd caught a glimpse of him once from the top of the stairs as he'd exited the front door gnawing on a drumstick.

She hadn't called to him. Another conversation would only add to the sick feeling in her gut. Tomorrow was soon enough to meet the world again.

But some things she had to meet tonight. There had been tension at the dinner table. Ryan had been both wounded and pissed that she hadn't told him about the bullet crease in her forehead, and she felt bad about that.

"I was here the next day, Sunny, the very next day. But it didn't make enough of an impression on you to tell me about it? If it had gone in the middle of your forehead and out the back of your head, would you have told me then?"

She needed to make amends. But right now, she needed to sit in the water for as long as she needed to sit in the water.

"Sunny?"

She leaned her head back and stared at the ceiling. Jonathan couldn't possibly be a better ophthalmologist than he was a mother hen. "Okay, come on in."

He entered and came to kneel next to the tub. As he looked her up and down, the distress that spread across his face could've matched the hurt throughout her body. "Oh, Sunny."

"Yeah, I know. Wish I could say it isn't as bad as it looks, but the truth is I hurt all over."

With his gaze meeting hers, he put his fingers lightly to her cheek. "Tomorrow will be the worst, then you'll improve a little each day." He paused, smiled. "And, for what it's worth, you're still beautiful."

She smiled back. "Thanks anyway, but you're prejudiced." Her expression sobered. "Guess I better get out of here and go downstairs. Ryan still mad at me?"

"He's okay. Stress brings out the best and worst in a person. That man loves you, Sunny."

"I know. And I love him back."

"He and Marcus walked down to the beach, or I should say the bluff. The area is roped off, at the top as well as the whole cove, but they hoped they could see something of what was going on. They've been gone for a while."

His head turned as they heard noise at the front door. "There they are now." He leaned in, lightly touched his lips to hers, then rose and left.

She labored her way to her feet and reached for the towel.

Not wanting to show off her bruises, she dressed in an old set of gray sweats and then made her way downstairs. Barefoot. It'd take too much bending to get footwear on. As she descended the stairs, she overheard Marcus talking about signs of target shooting they'd discovered among the cypress trees, but he became silent when she came into sight. The parlor's soft, over-stuffed chair had been left empty for her and carefully she sank into it.

Ryan stared at her, and she stared back. She said, "You told me once we can never go back and undo anything. We accept what is and go on from there. Right?"

"Generally speaking, I feel successful when someone starts repeating my words back to me. But in your case—"

"Oh, shut up. I'm sorry. Okay? The gunshot wound was an accident. I still think so, and I saw no need to advertise it. But, rethinking it, I admit I was wrong not to mention it, and you're right."

He said nothing, apparently unable to come up with a good argument to that.

That's a good line, Sunny. Worked every time you've used it.

It was difficult finding a comfortable position and she tried not to squirm. She wanted to cross her legs, wondered how much effort it would cost, and then remained still. Ryan was easing up, and she didn't want to draw attention to her injuries.

"What does it look like down at the beach?" She directed the question to Marcus. He was in the other corner chair with Cat on his lap. When he was around, Cat seemed to forget all about Sunny.

"You're getting a new trail down the cliff as soon as they can get a bulldozer out there. One guy already took a fall but didn't hurt himself. I managed to keep a straight face, but watching those people negotiate that last run was a riot. They're working from the beach floor and the cliff. I hope you weren't too attached to your berry bushes because you're losing them. I also heard talk about the Coast Guard being called in, just in case it was a drowning, but I didn't see them out there."

"I wish it were a simple drowning," Sunny murmured. "But it wasn't. The tide doesn't reach inside the cove."

"Agreed. That'd be one more iffy element, and you've got enough already. There's a limit, even to coincidence. At any rate, the skeleton is going to have overnight company. They were setting up a tent to shelter it and its guard. If I were the guard, I think I'd want to sleep outside the tent."

Ryan rested his legs on the coffee table, crossing one foot over the other. His gaze moved to her bare feet. "You've got a perfect circle around one ankle. How'd that happen?"

She felt the thorny vines again and saw the sand rushing to meet her. She gave herself a moment to make certain her voice would be steady. "A vine caught and held me. It was only for an instant."

But it felt like eternity.

"That's exactly what it looks like." With a no-nonsense look that was vintage Ryan, he raised his gaze and met hers. "I want you to come home with me. Jonathan can handle things up

123

here, and the sheriff—deputy sheriff, whoever he is—has no objection to your leaving."

"Oh? You've all been talking, have you?"

"Don't look at me like that, and don't try to pick a fight with me. I'll damn well give you one. Somebody has got it in for you. It doesn't matter who, or even why right now. What matters is that you get yourself out of harm's way."

Sunny matched his stare for a long moment, and then blew her breath out in a loud whoosh and looked at the empty doorway. He was the only person she'd never been able to win an argument with. But she wasn't about to tell him that, and she hadn't yet given up on winning this one anyway.

She looked back. "Okay, listen. Really listen. That bullet may have been exactly what we thought, a stray, and had nothing to do with what happened today. Even if it was deliberate, it could've been meant for Jonathan instead of me."

She held up her hand to shush her audience. Marcus was the only one who didn't have his mouth open. "It's difficult sorting impressions after a fall like that and I could be way off. Maybe it was a dog, as Tom suggested. If it'd been one of the boys who pushed me, he might have hidden in the reeds when he saw me coming, panicked and then shoved me so he could get away undetected. All kinds of scenarios here. The mere thought that someone might be trying to kill me boggles my mind. There's no reason. Jonathan is the only person who would gain by my death, and that bullet could've hit him as easily as me."

Lowering her hand, she said, "Okay. Your turn."

No one appeared convinced, but neither did anyone jump in with a ready argument.

Taking advantage of the silence, she added, "And I can't go home yet anyway. Not without knowing who that skeleton is— was. If it was my father or not. I have to know, Ryan. You should understand that. And once it's identified, one way or the other, I'll tell my mother. I refuse to let anyone else do it."

CHAPTER FOURTEEN

The phone rang. Since Ryan was closest to it, he gave Sunny and Jonathan a questioning look, and when he got two shrugs, he answered it. Quickly his gaze went to Sunny. "Hi, Roberta. Yes, she's right here."

Sunny steeled herself. It was doubtful the call from her mother was a coincidence. Because of the short phone cord, she and Ryan had to trade places. She moved slowly and tried not to wince.

"Hi, Mom."

"And hello to you, too. Would you mind telling me what's going on up there? A reporter called to get my reaction to the lurid discovery at Corday Cove. *And* the attempted murder of my daughter. It was that last one that got me."

Sunny swore under her breath then glanced guiltily at Jonathan. "I'd hoped we'd have some time before the news got out."

"Well, the news is out. I was told a skeleton had been found in the cove, and that you'd been admitted into the hospital with extensive injuries."

"That second one is an exaggeration. I fell off the cliff." She turned away from Ryan's look of disapproval. Telephone privacy was in pretty short supply around here. "I've got bruises to show for it, but that's about it."

"Bruises, huh."

"Yeah."

Sunny let the silence ride. No sense volunteering information

126

that might have her mother hopping into her car and adding to the confusion up here. Wait until she knew something, then she'd lay it all out for her.

"I'm working on it," Roberta said slowly, "but I can't quite figure out how you managed to take a fall like that."

"Well . . ."

"All right," Roberta said. Sunny heard the weary sigh and could almost see her mother's long look at the ceiling. "If you're okay, I'm okay." Then she went on. "They'll try to identify the skeleton through dental records, and it may be your father's. This is a high-profile case and it may become difficult for you up there. Perhaps you should come back home."

"No. I can handle it. I want to stick it out until we get answers. And I've got a lot done. We're almost through with the attic." That reminded her of the bloody baseball bat, and she tried to turn her face even further away from Ryan. "And we found a Victrola. It's a beauty, Mom, a real antique. Ryan and Marcus will be helping Jonathan to get it down from up there."

"Jonathan?"

"Uh, yeah." She glanced quickly at him. "I met the other owner of Corday Cove. We, er, surprised each other." *Now that's an understatement if I ever heard one.*

"Good. I'd like to meet him, too. You haven't been bothered by the press yet?"

"This is a newly connected phone line, and I guess they haven't discovered it. For now it's just police presence, but I'm sure we'll be getting other visitors. Hope they take their time getting out here."

"The reporter who called isn't one of the ghouls. I've dealt with him before. And that rock star who shot himself last month will be the focus of the tabloids for a while. I dislike being callous, but that might give us a reprieve. Call me, Sunny, as soon as you know anything. I'd rather hear it from you first."

"I know. Take care, okay? Love you, Mom."

Slowly, Sunny placed the phone receiver in its cradle, and then stared at it instead of looking up at anyone. She wasn't above omitting details when it suited her, or even stretching the truth if it came to that, but she didn't like doing either with an audience.

"So you fell," Ryan said mildly, after the count of perhaps five long seconds. "You weren't pushed. And I noticed you didn't mention that new crease in your forehead or a certain baseball bat that was used as a weapon on somebody. Possibly on the very same skeleton that had rested peacefully in the berry bushes until you fell on top of it." His tone carried a deceptively casual note. "You and Roberta try so hard to protect the other, yet each of you know the other so well that neither of you is getting away with anything. I wonder if either of you knows that?"

Sunny allowed a smile but still didn't look up. "Games people play." As usual, Ryan had found a neat little nutshell that the situation fitted perfectly into. She studied her hand that rested on the phone receiver. Angry, red scratches marred it.

Then, as she recalled a comment Jonathan had made on the beach earlier, she looked over at him. "You said someone called this morning and that's why you went looking for me. Who was it?"

"I don't know. I didn't ask." He stared into space as he jogged his memory. "It was a male voice. I left the phone off the hook, if I remember right."

"You did," Marcus said. "But the person had hung up before I got back."

"Whoever it was, I'm grateful," Sunny said. "Whoever pushed me came down the trail after me, but then kept on going when he heard your voices."

She gave Marcus a questioning look. "When I came down

the stairs you were talking about checking out the cypress grove?"

He nodded. "Are you aware there's a road leading into there?" Cat was purring so loudly on his lap that she sounded like a small motor. Absently he stroked her back.

"I never go in there," Sunny said, and then she glanced at Jonathan, who shook his head, conveying that he hadn't come across it during his explorations either. "It must branch off from the main highway," she added. "I don't think there are any spurs off the road that lead to the house and the cove."

"Then there's another way in," Jonathan mused. "Other than the beach. We're not as isolated as I'd thought. We wouldn't see a vehicle in there, might not even hear it, and it's a short walk from the trees to here."

"That explains how easily the boys get in for their target shooting, and possibly why they chose that place," Marcus said. "I wonder if we'd be stepping on the sheriff's toes if we went to visit those kids tomorrow."

"We would," Jonathan said. "For the time being, we need to leave this investigation to the powers that be. We'd only end up muddying the waters more than they already are."

Sunny spent a bad night and was up at dawn for more Advil. She wanted another hot bath but didn't want to start it this early; the noisy pipes would wake everybody up. She started coffee instead and made muffins. The activity was good therapy and helped work out kinks in muscles and joints. She was taking the cupcake tin out of the oven when the hall floor creaked.

"Well, good morning, Jonathan. I've never seen you up this early."

"I missed you. What is that? If it tastes as good as it smells you could probably talk me into trying one."

"Get a plate. Coffee's ready, too."

As he poured a cup he eyed the ancient, scratched-up thermos next to the coffeepot. "What's that for?"

"Making friends. It's a kitchen holdover I hadn't thrown away, just in case. I scrubbed it, scalded the inside, and I'm gonna take coffee and muffins down to the beach. If I'm armed with food maybe I won't get chased away as soon as I get there."

"Good idea." He shoved the rest of his muffin into his mouth. "Let's go. And pack a couple extra of those. I'm not through."

Even inside their sweats, they shivered. Though it was light outside, the sun hadn't yet overpowered the morning clouds. Halfway to the cliff, Jonathan stopped and jogged in place. Sunny evidently wasn't walking fast enough for him so she broke into a run and sprinted past him. She wasn't the fastest she'd ever been, but at least her muscles cooperated. She heard his laugh. Then he caught up and matched his pace to hers until they reached the barrier of orange tape.

Two pup tents rested inside the cove, one at the top of the small hill where the skeleton lay, and another in front of it at the base of the incline to guard it. A man in a heavy jacket, police issue, sat on the sand outside the foremost one, on the trail's side. He looked curiously up at them. He didn't appear unfriendly.

"Hi," Sunny said, holding up the thermos and bag of muffins. "I'm Laurel Corday, but call me Sunny. And this is my cousin—very distant, family wise—Jonathan Corday. We'll exchange food for conversation."

"You've got a deal." The policeman got to his feet in a smooth, unbroken motion. "But I'll come up there. I could get in big trouble if I let you come down here." Tall and bony, but not awkward, he climbed the trail faster than Sunny could have.

"Thanks," he said, accepting the coffee. "My name's Joyce."

Jonathan squinted. "Uh . . ."

"Gotcha." He grinned. "Deputy Timothy Joyce. Call me

Tim." He opened the bag of muffins. "Still warm." He bit into one, then held it away and gave it an approving look. "That's real jam in there."

"No big feat. A combination of Bisquick and Mary Ellen." Sunny looked down the slope. "What were you able to get accomplished yesterday?"

"We got it partially uncovered, but still a lot of work left before it can be hauled away. Forensic people are fussy. Cameras were snapping shots from every angle. I was never so glad when everybody left last night and I could finally just sit and enjoy the ocean. It's pretty out here."

Joyce chose another muffin, then offered the bag back to them. "Too many in here for me. I'll share."

Sunny shook her head, but Jonathan took one. "Thanks," he said. "Is the Coast Guard coming in? We heard that—"

"That's no drowning victim. I'm no forensics expert, but it's lying on its front and there's a big dent in the back of the skull."

His audience said nothing. He paused in the act of lifting the thermos to his lips. "Hey, I'm sorry. Me and my big mouth."

"No," Sunny said. "That's why I came down here. I want to know."

He gave her a long look. "Those scratches on your face tell me you're the one who took that header from up here. But you didn't land on the skeleton, did you? It doesn't appear to have been disturbed for a long time."

"No. But it . . . its hiding place was uncovered as a result of my fall."

He drained the thermos and started on the last muffin. "You better not take another tumble. Those berry bushes are gone and won't save you again." He looked down the incline as he chewed. "When you fell, where did you settle? Farther down the slope, I'll bet."

She nodded.

131

"Good hiding place down there. Made to order. Pull that body back a little ways, throw some driftwood or anything else on top of it, make the spot look really natural, cover it up with sand and spread the vines over it. Not too much work. And it remained hidden for what looks like a mighty long time."

"Could a woman have managed to do all that?" Sunny asked. She frowned against the sick feeling building in her stomach.

"He'd been hit from behind, most likely was surprised, so he wasn't fighting back. Doesn't preclude a female perp." Joyce shrugged. "As for the rest of it, it depends on how much time she had, how much the body weighed. My guess is a woman could've done it with enough time. Pretty much isolated out here. She, he, anyone, would've had plenty of time."

Joyce dusted his hands free of crumbs. "Excellent muffins. By the way, I don't know if it's going to be good news or not, but you're going to get a new pathway down to there. Hendricks took a fall yesterday and ordered it ASAP."

"Who's Hendricks?" Jonathan asked. "He must be high up on the authority list if he can make that kind of order."

"Yeah, he's one of the big guns. I don't know which we had more of yesterday, generals or soldiers. Tom Fairly, you know him?"

His listeners nodded.

"He's a good guy. But Hendricks is just full of himself and when he took that fall, I thought Tom was gonna bust a gullet holding in the guffaws. And he wasn't the only one. You never saw so many strained faces around here. Hendricks ended up with his head stuck in the sand and his butt in the air. Made a memorable picture."

His gaze moved beyond them. "Well, here we go. My last chance to negotiate that cool trail you've got there."

They turned and saw a bulldozer approaching, led by one official four-wheel-drive vehicle and followed by another. "They're

132

getting an early start," Jonathan said.

"Yeah, and I better get back down there," the lawman said. "I was told not to talk to or even look at anybody who came from around here, even if their name was Corday." He tipped an imaginary hat to Sunny. "Thanks for the treat. Worth the lecture I'll get."

She accepted the empty thermos and bag, and Deputy Tim Joyce negotiated the trail on his way down as if he were part mountain goat.

The sun finally made its appearance while she and Jonathan walked toward the oncoming vehicles. Trying to get her mind away from the skeleton, Sunny wondered which she enjoyed most at the beach, sunrise or sunset. And how long it would be before she'd truly be able to enjoy either one again.

The lead vehicle gained speed and pulled away from the procession, then came to a stop next to Jonathan and Sunny. The passenger's window rolled down. "Your name Corday?" asked a gruff voice.

They nodded.

"I understand you may think you have a personal stake here, but you still don't belong down there at the beach. Consider it off limits until we pull out of here. Is that understood?"

He got two distinct frowns in response.

The window rolled up, and the black and white four-wheeler continued on its way.

"That must be one of Deputy Joyce's chiefs," Sunny said. "That was no peon."

"Hope it was Hendricks," Jonathan said. "He deserves to have his head stuck in the sand and his butt in the air."

She gave him a quick look. "Dr. Corday, I do believe I'm seeing a side of you I never saw before. You've got a touch of spite in you."

★ ★ ★ ★ ★

Sunny and Cat sat at the top of the stairs and listened to the voices in the attic. It was cramped quarters up there and another body, especially one who wasn't going to be lifting anything heavy and who was too sore to climb the ladder in the first place, wasn't needed.

"Yeah," Ryan said. "That's a beautiful piece of furniture."

"I've dusted it," Jonathan said. "And once we get it downstairs I want to apply some lemon oil. It's not scratched up, not that I can tell in this light, and I think I can rub a nice shine into it."

"Labor of love. I don't know if I'd have the patience."

"Look at that dressmaker's dummy," Marcus said. "Halloween's coming up. Think of the fun one could have with that thing."

There was a short silence. "To each his own," Ryan said.

Cat struggled to get out of Sunny's arms, but she wasn't needed in the attic either. Sunny got to her feet, put the pet inside her old bedroom and closed the door. Returning to the same space she'd just vacated, she situated herself with her back against the wall and drew her knees up in front of her. If she moved carefully, it wasn't too bad.

"Ow!" The word seemed to explode out of the attic, and Sunny grinned. That was Ryan. She wondered who was next. Marcus was smart enough to watch where he was going, and Jonathan had had practice dodging the rafters.

"Dammit!"

Her grin grew. Yep, Ryan might know the inside of his mind, but he didn't know how to protect the outside of it.

She worked her way to her feet and went to the ladder. She put one foot on the bottom step, waited for her body to protest, then went up one more stair. No bones creaked, so she kept going and poked her head into the attic.

"Hi, Sunny," Marcus said. "Took you longer to get up here

than I thought it would."

"You can have the dummy," she said. She grinned, then giggled. "Both of them."

Jonathan broke into a laugh.

"Sunny?" Ryan wasn't amused. "You looking for some more bruises?"

"Sorry," she said, figuring she looked anything but contrite. "Couldn't resist."

Then she asked, "How long are you guys going to wander around up here? Isn't it time you got to work?"

Marcus was closest to the ladder. "If you'll get back down there and give me some room, they can start handing stuff down to me."

The Victrola found a nice home in the front downstairs bedroom on top of several newspapers. That room had the largest windows and the best light. Jonathan already had his favorite brand of lemon oil on hand and looked like he couldn't wait to get started. But he surprised everyone by grabbing a broom, the dustpan and a plastic garbage bag, and then climbing back up into the empty attic.

Sunny smiled at the looks on her friends' faces. "What can I say? He's got a thing about clean."

There was a short silence. "To each his own," Ryan said.

Chapter Fifteen

"I never liked it in here," Sunny said with a frown. "It's spooky."

She stood next to Jonathan inside the shadowy interior of the cypress grove. Ryan and Marcus, who were slightly ahead of them, looked around with interest. Sunny shivered, lending credence to her words. Little sunlight got past the canopy of trees and it was chilly. She wondered if the ground in here ever completely dried out. The trees appeared ancient and their exposed root systems lent a skeletal effect to the scene. One tree had split, and its fallen half offered a perfect backless bench. Nature's furniture. She stared at it but wasn't inclined to sit on it.

The men were discussing the numerous shell casings that littered the ground along with a heavy layer of dried cypress branches and cones. As they speculated about the guns the spent shells had come out of, she wondered if any one of them really knew what he was talking about. She was surprised at the small number of cans and bottles. Within the grove itself the shooters had apparently been satisfied with stationary targets.

Jonathan wandered away, and then he laughed and motioned for her to join him. He was admiring what must have been, judging by the pockmarks in it, a favorite target. Nailed to a tree was a campaign poster featuring the unlikable likeness of Hendricks. They shared a smile.

Apparently becoming bored with the shells, Ryan looked up. He breathed deeply, as if testing the air. "Surrounded by nature in here. You may not appreciate it, Sunny, but I could learn to like this place."

The four of them wandered the grove, skirting puddles and roots, and eventually they came to the road, which was nothing more than well-worn tire tracks. It appeared to lead to the highway, as she'd suspected. Farther inland, eucalyptus trees were interspersed among the cypresses. As they walked that way, the terrain became prettier and was easier to traverse. They stopped in a clearing.

"This is even better," Ryan said. "Sunshine, wild flowers. Soil must be more fertile in here." He turned in a slow circle, nodding. "Yeah, this is nice. The beach is fine, but it's wide open, no shelter. Here you can hear the ocean, you've got both shade and sun if you want it, and even flowers. Orange and yellow poppies and whatever that purple bloom is." He paused, looking at the rectangular section of growth and color. "Looks like a cross between an ice plant and a wild daisy. It's pretty, whatever it is." He looked around again. "All you need is a picnic table."

"Yeah, maybe," Sunny said. At least it was warmer in the clearing. When she turned to go back, the men fell in step without comment. As they left the grove, a pickup appeared on the road. Sunny watched, wondering if it was going to stop at the house or continue on to the beach. She got her answer when it parked next to the Reviler. A figure emerged from the driver's side, then reached back inside for something.

"Bev Wilkes," Sunny murmured.

"That's what's nice about a small community," Ryan said as the figure straightened, holding a casserole, and then she nudged the pickup's door closed with her elbow. "Neighborly."

Bev mounted the steps to the porch, then wedged the dish between arm and stomach in order to knock on the door. Sunny called, hoping her voice would carry.

The woman turned, shielded her eyes, saw them and waved.

She smiled as they approached, and then she held up her offering with a hesitant lift of her shoulders. "I wanted to bring some food to help you out. Thought it might make it easier for you after you got hurt. I hope you like macaroni and cheese."

"Love it." Jonathan smiled, supposedly attempting to put her at ease. After opening the house door, he relieved her of the casserole.

Ryan said nothing, and Sunny grinned. Mac and cheese was way down on the list of his favorites. He'd probably boil a hot dog for dinner.

"Thanks, Bev," she said. "That's nice of you. Would you like some coffee?"

"Never drink it. But I wouldn't say no to a cola."

Sunny and Bev sat in lawn chairs on the back porch and the men carried out kitchen chairs for themselves. "We need more outdoor furniture," Sunny said.

"What you need is a picnic table, right there." Ryan pointed.

"What is this with you and picnic tables?" Marcus asked.

"Bev, have you met—"

"Yes, when they came in yesterday and cleaned me out of chicken and ribs. They told me what had happened." She gave Sunny an appraising glance. "I'm glad to see you up and about, even strong enough to hike to the trees. Is there activity going on over there, too?"

"No. Not all of us had seen the area over there, so we went exploring."

Bev sipped from her drink and sat back. "What's happening down on the beach?"

"We're not allowed down there," Jonathan said. "Your guess is as good as ours."

"Was it a drowning victim?"

"The consensus seems to be that it's not," Sunny said carefully.

"It might be Franklin." Bev stared at the floor. "Which could make it tough for you, Sunny. Are you doing okay?"

"So far."

Bev, I want to talk to you, but it's gotta be in private.

"Tom was over to talk with Matthew again." Bev was still staring at the floor. "About your . . . fall. He asked him outright if he'd pushed you."

"Tom's investigating. He has to do that. Matthew isn't the only person he's talked to."

"Matthew wasn't out here yesterday. He and I worked the store together. I don't know if Tom believed me, but that's the truth."

Sunny nodded, hoping to soothe the woman's worry. "Okay. But Tom isn't accusing anyone of anything, and neither am I. Someone was in the grove firing yesterday at the same time I was pushed. It could be that whoever was there saw something."

Bev looked up sharply. "Matthew wasn't anywhere around here."

"Okay." Sunny felt like she was on the defensive, as if Bev was accusing her of causing trouble. "I believe you. I don't think Matthew has it in him to willfully hurt somebody. It's okay, Bev. Tom will talk with the Bowers boys, and they'll back up your story. Right?"

"They already have." Bev's tension suddenly ebbed. She let her breath out in a rush. "I'm sorry. I'm giving you a bad time, and you were the one who got hurt."

She stood abruptly. "I really should be getting back. It's not fair leaving Matthew in sole charge of the store for very long. I hope you like the casserole."

Sunny walked outside with her, leaving the men on the porch. Standing next to the pickup, the two women looked toward the beach and its bustling activity.

Bev's eyes dulled. She appeared to be retreating within

herself. "What will they discover? So many years, so much time, so many people, so many secrets. What all will they uncover?"

At the sound of a vehicle, they turned to look at the road leading in from the highway.

"Oh, no," Sunny murmured.

"You've got company," Bev said. She walked around the front of the pickup and got in, moving fast. She wanted no part of the approaching TV news van. Sunny wanted no part of it either, but she didn't have the luxury of choice.

Bev and the van passed each other, and Sunny steeled herself. She hoped the men would stay out of sight. The inevitable questions of relationships might evoke the news people's interest. The men on the porch would've seen the approaching vehicle, but the mesh screen should've shielded them from being observed. She recognized the van's identification letters, which belonged to a fairly reputable news station, and she was grateful it wasn't the tabloids.

The news van braked, and a woman looked at her from the passenger's side. Her eyes were dark-brown and hard, and the red highlights in her hair appeared natural, as did the gray mixed in with it. If her eyes and features would soften, just a little, she might be pretty.

"Laurel Corday?"

Sunny nodded, hoping everybody would stay inside the vehicle.

"Would you consent to a filmed interview?"

She smiled politely. "No, thank you. I don't know anything, anyway. The action's down there." She looked toward the beach and a flash bulb went off.

You guys are fast. I didn't even see a camera.

She looked back at the van. The photographer was sitting behind the passenger's seat. The camera lowered, and he stared impersonally back at her. Wryly, she remembered Tom's advice about not posing for pictures. At least she was in jeans and long sleeves and not showing off her colorful limbs.

"Was it your father's skeleton that was found?" the woman asked.

"We don't know whose it is yet."

"Did you see it?"

I almost fell on top of it. "It was only partially uncovered."

"What part?"

Sunny hesitated, then told herself not to hesitate. "The hand."

"Did it look like your father's hand?"

Don't laugh, Sunny, and don't get mad. She's fishing for a reaction, any reaction. Don't give her one. "No."

"What did it feel like, being that close to a skeleton that might be your father?"

"I don't have an answer to that question. Excuse me. I'm going back inside."

She mounted the porch stairs at an unhurried pace.

"Who was that leaving as we were arriving?"

"Just a friend," she answered without looking back. She entered the house. Jonathan stood in the parlor's doorway, out of their visitors' sight. She closed the door behind her and looked at him, waiting to hear the van's departure. After a short moment, she heard it driving away.

"I'm glad you didn't show yourself," she said. "You would've fueled their interest."

"That's what Ryan said. We could hear you from the porch. You seemed to be handling yourself well."

I've had practice.

Jonathan added, "But weren't her questions, uh . . ."

"Unintelligent and meant to provoke? Yes. The trick is not to react. Be firm and polite and give them nothing."

"Bore them to death."

She grinned. "That's a good way of putting it. You'll do well."

He opened the front door, and they stepped outside but stayed within the shelter of the porch where they wouldn't be readily seen. The van's occupants had disembarked and were wandering the beach cliff. Two members started down the newly carved path that the Corday house occupants hadn't yet been allowed on. It appeared to be an easy descent. One of them was aiming a video camera as he descended.

"Hendricks seems to have no problem with their company," Jonathan remarked.

Good. Maybe we'll see him on TV tonight instead of me.

"Why doesn't that surprise me?" he added.

His question was rhetorical, but she answered it anyway. "Because you met him once and that's all it took. He's an easy read."

He turned her way and grinned. Then his eyes moved beyond her and his smile died.

Catching his change in expression, she turned to look at the road heading in from the highway. A big blue sanitary cubicle sat atop the back of a wide-bed truck. The vehicle traveled slowly along the unpaved road, its cargo gently rocking within its restraining bonds.

"There goes the neighborhood," Jonathan said under his breath.

Sunny looked pained. "Do they have to?"

Though her question was also rhetorical, he answered it. His head bobbed once in a resigned nod. "Yes, they have to. I don't like it either, but there are some needs one can't ignore."

CHAPTER SIXTEEN

Marcus sat behind the wheel of the shiny black coupe on Tuesday morning with its engine running. He'd been there long enough that he was staring into space. Ryan still stood on the porch.

"One more time," Ryan said to Sunny. "Come home with me. I'll even let you have the front seat." Since direct orders hadn't worked, he was now asking nicely. And repeatedly.

"No," Sunny answered again. "For the last time. And don't forget to pick up my car. If it stays there any longer, they might sell it again."

"You can pick it up yourself and then drive it back. If you're still needed up here, that is."

"And argue with you again? No thanks. Marcus, will you get this guy out of here? He's driving me nuts."

"I understand your wanting to stick around. I wish I could, too. I'm glad Jonathan's got the time, but he can't stay forever either. At least promise me you'll come home when he has to leave."

"We'll talk about it then. Get in the car, Ryan."

"Sunny, you're being evasive. I don't—"

"Yes, I am. Because you're being—"

"Get in the car, Ryan," Marcus said. "You keep stalling, we're going to hit traffic. It's as bad getting into the city as it is getting out of it."

"Yeah, in a minute. Sunny, sweetheart—"

"Ryan," Jonathan said, "get in the car. Go home. You're driving me nuts, too."

Sunny got the giggles. He really said that? And she'd once thought him conventional to a fault?

Ryan looked at each person in turn, at the ocean, gave a one-syllable expletive an extra syllable, then got inside the car. Marcus accelerated and they were gone.

Jonathan gave Sunny a long look. "Do you realize how many people are concerned with that pretty little neck of yours?"

Caught off guard, she dropped her gaze, and then she opened the house door and went inside. "More than I think I deserve."

"That's one person's opinion. And she's in the minority." Staying on the porch, he called after her. "If you don't have anything pressing right now, how about walking down to the beach with me and getting told off by Hendricks again?"

She stopped, grinned, and turned around. "Okay."

But it wasn't Hendricks in charge today. It was Tom. And he already had company. Mavis had been sitting on the ground atop the bluff, inside the rounded part of the horseshoe near a clump of reeds, and they didn't see her until she stood. Evidently this wasn't a working day because she wore baggy denims and a sweatshirt, but she still carried the familiar oversized purse on a strap across her shoulder.

"Hi, Sunny. Jonathan." Mavis seemed unsure of herself, and she seemed to have difficulty meeting Sunny's eyes. "One of your friends was loading suitcases in his car when I drove by, and I didn't want to disturb you."

Mavis had been a friend for as long as Sunny could remember, and she was uncomfortably aware of the distance between them. The chasm would continue to widen until it was bridged, and Sunny suddenly felt angry. She'd be damned if she'd let her miserable excuse for a father take anything more from her. Or from Mavis Fairly, if Sunny could prevent it.

With a jerk of her head she motioned toward the south side of the bluff, full of cars but empty of people. "Walk with me? We need to talk."

Not waiting for a response, she walked away, passing the ugly potty sitting conspicuously on the edge. Some of the numerous vehicles were official, some not. It looked like a disorganized parking lot. The new path of raw earth leading down to the beach was as wide as a one-car driveway. Down in the cove the tents had been set aside, but not broken down and packed up. The whole scene was an abomination, and Sunny hated it.

Though Mavis had hesitated, she now caught up and fell in step. She had her hand inside her shoulder bag, probably searching for cigarettes.

Sunny spoke without looking at her. "This one-night stand of yours happened a long time ago," she said mildly. "Don't you think you've punished yourself enough by now?"

No answer. Mavis was still fumbling in her bag. Then she came to an abrupt halt. "I did it again. I forgot that I quit." She looked desperate enough to cry.

Sunny stopped and faced her, but the older woman wouldn't meet her eyes. It was Mavis's guilt, so therefore her problem to deal with, but Sunny refused to give up.

"From what I've heard about Franklin, that was not unusual behavior for him. It takes two, of course, but Roberta wasn't hurt—at least not that I know of. If you need absolution from her, you'll have to talk to her about it. Tom has forgiven you, and if you need my forgiveness, you've got it. Now can you forgive yourself, and maybe we can get rid of this strained silence between us and get on with being friends again?"

Sunny waited, and when she still got no response she turned to walk back. She could say or do no more. But after a few steps, the older woman joined her. They glanced sideways at each other. Although Mavis still said nothing, the tension in the air wasn't quite as heavy.

Tom stood at the top of the path next to Jonathan when the two women returned. "I saw you reach for cigarettes," he said to his wife. She mumbled something unintelligible. He put his arm around her shoulders and pulled her to him. "Hang in there. You can do it, babe."

Sunny caught his eye and motioned toward the sanitary cubicle. "You do understand that when you go, that goes."

He laughed, releasing Mavis. He rolled his shoulders and stretched, getting the kinks out. "That is a beauty, isn't it? We had no problem in the beginning, you know, but once our work force turned coeducational . . ."

Looking down into the cove, Sunny's gaze fell on the back of a slender figure wearing a ponytail, loop earrings, khakis and a navy blue t-shirt. The person knelt next to the skeleton, obscuring it from view.

Tom followed her gaze and laughed. "Nope. Wrong. That's a him. That's Danielle behind you."

Sunny turned. As Danielle exited the tall, boxlike structure, she was still straightening her clothes. She glanced at Sunny and gave her a friendly smile. "Cramped quarters in there." She headed for the driveway that led down to the beach. "And it sure is a long way from the potty to the wash basin." She sprinted down the trail and trudged across the sand to wash her hands in the surf. She also wore khakis and a suitable-for-either-sex t-shirt, hers in bright-plum.

Tom lifted his non-police issue Stetson, scratched his scalp, then replaced the hat. He looked at Sunny, Jonathan, then down at the cove. "I'm glad you showed up, both of you. I was going to come up and talk to you in another couple minutes. We've got it uncovered and are close to carrying it out of here. I thought you should know."

Sunny swallowed. She was glad the ponytailed worker hid

most of the skeleton from view. Then Danielle joined the worker, and he got to his feet and stepped back, and the whole skeleton was in full view. The worker looked up the incline. "Yo, Tom."

"Right there."

Tom went down the slope at a slower pace than Danielle, but Sunny was barely aware of him. Her eyes were riveted on the bones exposed atop the sand. It was all there, partially draped in frayed, drab cloth. One leg was bent at an impossible angle and one arm stretched above the skull, as if reaching. That was the hand that had finally caught someone's attention.

Jonathan's arm encircled her shoulders.

"Tom decided not to call you until he knew for certain," Mavis said tonelessly, her attention also on the scene below. "But I think you should be aware, just in case. The only thing positive is that it is . . . was . . . a male, a slightly built male."

Sunny was aware of Jonathan's glance, though he remained silent.

"Franklin was five-seven and small-boned," she explained, answering his unasked question. "As is a significant percentage of the male population." She gave him a direct look. "I got my stature, physical stature, from him. My mother is also five-seven, and almost matched him in weight as well. And I got my blond hair from him, too." She paused. "But that's all I ever got from my father."

She turned abruptly and started back up the road to the house. She was angry, fed up, burned out. If she could get the world to stop she'd get off for a good, long breather. Jonathan fell in step with her, and she was aware when he then came to a stop, but she continued.

"Uh, Sunny."

Her eyes were downcast, and she was walking fast. Impatient, she looked up and saw what had caught his attention. The news van was back.

Watch it, Sunny. You need mellow, and you're a far cry from that mood right about now.

Jonathan arrived at her side. Then she was grasping his hand without realizing that she'd reached for it.

It was the same van carrying the same people, and when it stopped, the same woman stared hard at Sunny out the passenger's window. The reporter seemed hungry, like a shark, and Sunny cautioned herself again to be careful. The woman was sharp—she'd clearly sensed Sunny's mood—and her gaze dropped to the pair's clasped hands.

"Hi," Jonathan said, drawing her attention. He looked back toward the beach. "You're just in time. They've uncovered the skeleton and are ready to cart it out of there."

The van inched forward, but the woman jerked her left arm out, fingers splayed wide, to halt the driver. She kept her eyes on Jonathan. "Are you Jonathan Corday?"

He nodded.

Her gaze fell again to their clasped hands. "Cousins, right?"

His grip didn't tighten or loosen, but Sunny felt the shift in his mood.

"Yes, but I've lost count of how many times removed we are," he said mildly. "Being a news person, you've probably already researched it and must know the exact relationship, so you'll have to tell me."

Sunny had never seen a smile as disarming and as insincere as the one he gave the newswoman. The reporter must've realized she'd run into a blank wall; she switched gears back to Sunny. "You saw the skeleton? It's uncovered?"

She nodded.

"Was it your father?"

Sunny felt a stony mien come over her, and sensed that the reporter caught it because her eyes sharpened. "It didn't look a bit like him," Sunny said in a flat voice.

Jonathan squeezed her hand, and then with his free arm he motioned toward the beach. "They're preparing it for removal. You might miss something if you don't hurry."

He resumed walking, leading Sunny away. The van would have to travel in reverse if its occupants wanted to stay with them, but after a brief moment it continued toward the beach.

"Thanks," she said, keeping her eyes downcast. Then when Jonathan came to another halt, she had to stop because he still had her hand. She looked up, and again he squeezed her fingers as the neutral-colored minivan passed them, the one word in small black letters on its side identifying it: *Coroner.*

CHAPTER SEVENTEEN

Within a week, Sunny was feeling almost normal again.

On a lazy morning, Jonathan rolled onto his back, reached for her hand and squeezed it. There was little energy in his clasp—he'd just spent most of it—but the message was clear. She was special. She was important. She was loved.

And so are you. Her breath caught and for an instant her gaze froze on the ceiling, then mentally she shrugged it off. *Nope. Not going anywhere with that right now.*

He pulled her into the circle of his arm. As she settled her head on his shoulder, her fingers played with the curled hair on his chest. Not too much hair, just enough. There was also little strength in her fingers. Her hand stilled and her eyes closed.

"Gorgeous view," he said.

"Umm." She lifted her head to look through the old-fashioned paned windows then realized that he meant her, not the ocean. The scratches were healing, and the bruising was less prominent, but she still had a ways to go before she'd look normal again. Apparently Technicolor didn't turn him off.

"Oh, stop it." She reached for the sheet, feeling both complimented and flustered.

With only the sheet to look at now, he directed his eyes to the window.

"There's something I've been curious about," he said lazily. "This is the best bedroom in the house and you had your choice of any one of them when you moved in here. Why did you choose that dinky little room in the back corner?"

"It's closest to the bathroom."

"Very funny." Her hand got squeezed again. Then he chuckled. "On second thought, considering that uncomplicated side of yours, that could be the truth."

She rose onto her elbow, taking the sheet with her, and looked around the room, studying it. "Yes, this is the best one. The master bedroom. It was my parents'." Quietly, she added, "I might have been conceived in this room."

At the look on his face, she smiled. "No, I haven't done any conceiving. We can both guarantee that."

"That's not what I was thinking. I was thinking about your ties to this place, the people, the history. I still don't think of you as a Corday. I guess because you didn't introduce yourself as such in the beginning. I can't imagine the mixed feelings you must have."

Mixed feelings? That's what you call it?

"I guess you could say that." Propping her back against the headboard, she stared straight ahead. "Feelings and memories. But the memories I'd prefer to forget aren't of this place and Franklin. What I wish I could forget is much later than that. I was the most mixed-up person I ever want to meet. I fought— not just rebelled, but actually fought—everything and everybody. Roberta, school, society, you name it. Franklin was never in my life, so I couldn't fight him, which might have been the problem. If I could've just once lit into him, beat up on him, told him what I thought of him, maybe I wouldn't have abused myself and everybody else so much."

Bringing her knees up to her chest, she leaned forward and clasped her arms around them, unmindful now of the view she allowed. Her mind was full instead of past pain. She'd come a long way, but there was still much in her that hurt. She looked down to meet his eyes. She'd gone from serene to disquiet in record time, and she wondered if it showed.

Apparently, it did.

"I must have hit a nerve," he said, and touched her face with his fingers as if to smooth the lines from it. "I'm sorry."

"No need to be." She took his hand and kissed it. "I've got a lot of history, as you know. Sometimes it sneaks up on me."

"Do you need to air it?" His gaze held hers. Gently his fingers moved to the back of her neck and massaged.

You don't know what you're asking for, Jonathan.

And you don't even want to think about it, Sunny. He's the best thing that ever happened to you. Don't scare him away.

But she said, not allowing herself to talk herself out of it, "Yeah, maybe I do." And then her gaze left his. It was easier talking if she concentrated on the distant blue of the ocean.

"I got into drugs early." She spoke slowly, her voice even. "But somehow I managed to stay away from the hard stuff. No coke or acid, and I never stuck a needle in my arm. Booze didn't turn me on, either. It was pills, uppers, downers, every combination, any combination. I still don't know how I didn't kill myself. I took anything I could get my hands on, but I had favorite combinations that turned me so mellow and warm that I just wanted to stay that way forever. But then when the high wore off, I turned so jittery and jumpy that it scared me, and I didn't want to ever do it again, but then I did anyway . . . and . . ."

If you want to break it off with him, Sunny, there are easier ways to do it than this.

But she went on, her voice quiet yet surprisingly clear. "I don't remember what I was on the day I married Alec. We were both so high we were floating. As young as I still look, I don't know how we pulled it off. We'd crossed the state line into Nevada. He was old enough, and we just kept going until we found someone who just looked at us, said okay, and then said the words. And that was that." She paused. "Then Roberta had it annulled three days later."

She breathed in, out. *Okay, enough.* But still she didn't listen to herself. "She watched me like a hawk after that, and I was forced to back off from the pills. So I got back into school again, and that's when I met Ryan. We were both seniors, and we hit it off right away. Maybe because both of us were misfits, trying to find ourselves and fit in, and I guess we leaned on each other, supported each other. But then he grew up. And I didn't."

Again she breathed deeply, aware of, but not caring about, the tears building and burning in her eyes. If she blinked, they'd break through. Jonathan remained silent, and she didn't look at him.

"I got back on the pills again, heavier than before." Her voice was a mere whisper now, barely audible within the quiet room. "Ryan had also hit it off with Roberta. She'd sensed right away that he had his head on. They both saw what was happening, and they ganged up on me. It was the day after graduation. He'd brought me home from grad night. I don't remember exactly—I was really out of it—but I think he had to use force. They'd already talked it out between them, had a rehab place in mind, all the plans made. Roberta had to get a second mortgage on her house to get me into it, but it was a good place. Out in the country, healthy food, exercise, full-time therapy, physical and emotional, professional company. They cleaned me up."

She looked at Jonathan then, noted that his gaze was level and patient, and remembered he already knew much of her past.

He'd known the facts, but not the feelings. Is that what you needed to tell him?

Why, Sunny? Why do you want him to know?

Fast on the heels of the question, its answer struck her, and then the tears broke through. Not only had Jonathan grown to be very important to her, but in many ways he'd shown her the feeling was mutual, and for the first time in her life it seemed something solid was within her reach. It was wonderful, and it was scary, and honesty was as painful as it was essential. Rarely had Sunny looked so deeply inside herself, nor had she ever even wanted to.

Since no tissue box was at hand, she dried her eyes with the heels of her hands. Feeling shaky but determined, she looked back at the window and resumed her story. "Both Ryan and Roberta wanted me to go to cooking school and then to business school, so I could open my own restaurant. But I didn't think I could deal with fussy people." Because she'd already proved to both herself and Jonathan that she didn't deal well with fussy eaters, she gave him what had to be a weak smile. He smiled back, but made no other response.

Then again she directed her eyes to the ocean that looked so calm in the distance, yet was constantly in motion. "I talked to Mavis instead. She tutored me and I got my license, and then I got in with a successful agency. I was no whiz, but I made enough to support myself. It seemed I was finally on the right track, and I should've been happy . . . but . . . I don't know how to explain it. There was something missing. I wasn't just unsatisfied. Sometimes I was angry, too, but I didn't know at what, and sometimes I got the feeling that I just had to break out. Then I met this guy."

She leaned her head all the way back against the headboard. The tears were coming in earnest now, and she wiped at them again, the action angry and impatient.

"He was bad news. I knew that right away, but I didn't care. I was in self-destruct mode, stronger than ever before. I turned my back on Roberta, Ryan, my job, and was back on the pill scene before I knew what hit me. I even married the bastard, and it was legal this time. No one could annul it."

When her hand slid down to the mattress between them, his hand moved to cover hers. Her breathing, which had grown agitated, soothed at his touch. "My first marriage had lasted three days. The second one lasted two months. And he put me in the hospital three times during those two months."

Her throat had grown so tight and dry that it was difficult swallowing. She concentrated on taking even, calming breaths, and then she went on. "The last time, he came after me with his belt. I tried to run, even though there was no place to run to, and I knocked over a chair—we had one of those really cheap, lightweight dinette sets—and he was so close behind me that he tripped over it. I saw what had happened, and I picked up another chair and hit him with it, and then hit him again and again, until the chair broke. Then I realized he wasn't moving. And he was bleeding. I'd never seen so much blood, and I thought I'd killed him. The phone was on the wall in the kitchen. I tried to call for help, but I couldn't remember nine-one-one. It just wouldn't come to me. I had to look at each number in turn, and I finally got to nine, and then I remembered it. But when the woman came on the line I couldn't talk. He'd broken my jaw, and all I could do was cry and make this funny sound deep in my throat. But she figured out that I needed help. When I heard the sirens, I collapsed. They had to pick me up off the kitchen floor and pry the phone from my fist."

Jonathan's hand was still on hers. She looked down at it, but not at him. "I never saw him again. As it turned out, I hadn't killed him. I'm glad now that I didn't, but then I didn't care."

She paused again, her gaze remaining on his hand. "As much as I hated my father, after the divorce I legally changed my name back again. I couldn't stand to wear the same name as the brute I'd married. So I chose Corday. It was still my mother's name."

She curled her fingers under his and squeezed. He squeezed

back, and she resumed her story. The telling was getting easier.

"When I got out of the hospital, I moved in with Ryan. I got clean again, but I did it on my own this time—with his help and my mother's. No clinic. But I wanted it. I wanted to be clean more than anything I'd ever wanted in my life. That's why I was able to do it, and that's why I've been able to stay clean."

She shifted, burrowing into the bed and resting on her hip, facing him. He didn't look shocked, appalled, disgusted. He just waited, still listening, giving her time. "You were right when you said I was using Ryan. I swore off men and relationships, any relationship. With a track record like mine, that was the only safe thing to do."

She lifted her hand, traced his cheekbone with her fingertips, and held his gaze.

"Until you," she whispered. "But you're not just the first man I've made love to since then. You're the first man that I've ever really made love to. I'm not saying I never climaxed before, but . . . but it's different with you."

Sunny was drained, but this was important and she searched for the right words. Then she finished, voice choking. "With you, I feel loved. I don't feel used." Her forefinger trembled as it traced the line of his lips. "I don't feel used, Jonathan," she whispered. "I don't feel used."

He drew her face down to his and kissed her, long and deep, and then they made love again. Slowly, sensually, thoroughly. When he entered her this time it was more than a physical union. They truly became one, in every possible way.

At climax, she cried again. With his breath still coming in uneven gasps, he leaned down and kissed her tears away. He said nothing. He didn't need to.

Two days later, Sunny watched Jonathan as he spoke on the phone. He'd been on for a long time and clearly didn't like what he was hearing. When he finally replaced the receiver in its cradle, he gave her a worried, frowning look.

"It's no big deal," she said, and then forced a smile, but figured her annoyance still showed. "I've told you that ten times already. Don't turn into another Ryan. Please."

"I can get another week but that's it. Then I've got to go back, at least long enough for them to go through the interview process and hire someone to cover for me."

She merely shrugged. He had enough mother-hen protectiveness in him for a whole brood of baby chicks. But since he only had one—her—she got it all. "It may be settled in a week," she said as patiently as she could. "I may be home in San Francisco in a week. I don't know what a week holds any more than you do."

"But if it isn't settled by then, will you—"

"We'll talk about it then. Now please shut up." She smiled to soften the words. "Please. If you keep after me about it I'll be forced into giving you an outright no. Then I'll be stuck with that, no matter what, and that wouldn't be good for either one of us. Right?"

His expression was both critical and irritated. "I've never before met anyone with a sense of logic quite like yours." Then, exhaling loudly, he looked at the parlor's doorway. "Maybe it will be settled by then. It should be. I'm surprised it's taken this long."

"They must be double-checking. They want to be sure." She paused. "You know, it's funny, but . . ."

When she didn't finish, he looked at her curiously. "What? What are you thinking?"

"Well, the longer it takes for them to identify the skeleton seems to lessen the odds of it being Franklin. And I don't know how I feel about that. On one hand, it'd be closure for Roberta and for me. But at the same time, I don't want . . . well, it doesn't feel good thinking that . . ." She shook her head, giving up on clarifying the thought.

But he said, "I think I understand. You don't want him to have been murdered, but you do want his body found."

"Yeah . . . well." She stood abruptly. "Time for dinner. And it's a simple one. I hope you like hamburgers and potato salad." She figured he'd at least eat the hamburgers.

"What kind of potato salad?"

She gave him a quizzical look. "How many kinds are there?"

"Homemade? Or did you buy it at the deli?"

"I made it."

His face perked. "I think I'll like it."

For a short moment she watched him, thinking about the pickles and onion and celery and eggs she'd chopped up and mixed with the potatoes, and recalled that he hadn't liked anything mixed with his breakfast potatoes, but she made no comment.

Jonathan liked the salad; none was left for tomorrow. Though Sunny didn't exactly understand his food preferences, she was learning them. She was finishing the dishes when she heard him calling from the parlor.

"Sunny? Where's the remote?"

Good question. She squinted at the wall. "I was sitting in the big chair in the corner. Check the cushions. Maybe . . ."

"Is it too much to ask for you to just put it back on—"

The phone rang.

Saved by the bell.

She heard his voice as he spoke on the phone, but she couldn't discern what the conversation was about. When he came to the kitchen, she looked up. "Who was it?"

"Tom Fairly. He'll be here in ten minutes."

She literally didn't breathe for the space of several seconds.

As she remained motionless, he took the towel from her and finished drying the cutlery. She stepped back to give him room.

"Well," she said. "We wanted to know, and I guess we're about to find out."

Tom took longer than ten minutes, and the longer Sunny waited, the more nervous she got. She got the broom and was sweeping the hall, even though Jonathan had already done it once today, when Tom finally arrived. His knock on the door made her jump, and the broom clattered to the floor. Jonathan picked it up, stood it upright in the corner and opened the door.

Sunny and the deputy sheriff stared at each other.

"It's not good news," she said. "No matter what it is, there's no way it can be good. So you might as well just spit it out."

When he stepped forward to put his hands on her shoulders, she guessed that her dread showed in her eyes. "We found him, Sunny," he said gently. "Without a doubt, that was Franklin in the cove."

She was aware that the attention of both men rested on her. She nodded once then looked at the stair rail just past Tom's right shoulder. *He was murdered. Someone killed him.*

"What took so long?" Jonathan asked. "His dental record must have been the first thing you looked at."

Tom nodded, and dropped his hands to his sides. "You're right. But the powers that be—I didn't like it, but had no say in it—said to keep a lid on it until the cause of death was also determined. Beyond doubt."

Jonathan's brows drew together. "But that dent in the skull . . ." He must have realized the fruitlessness of questioning the powers that be because dispassionately he finished. "And the cause of death is, beyond doubt . . ."

"A heavy blow to the back of the head with a blunt instrument."

"Like a baseball bat."

Tom's head bobbed once in a decisive nod.

"And the one we found . . ."

"By all odds had killed somebody, but not Franklin. We've got a body with a missing murder weapon, and we've got a murder weapon with a missing body. But my guess is that we've only got one murderer."

CHAPTER EIGHTEEN

Tom wanted beer, but he settled for coffee. "Officially, I'm still on duty until I walk out your door tonight. But thanks anyway."

Jonathan was a better host than Sunny was a hostess. The identity of the skeleton wasn't a surprise, yet it hit hard, and part of her wanted to scamper away and hide. And medicate herself with an arsenal of pills as had once been her custom?

As he settled in the corner armchair—Cat had the bigger, overstuffed one—Tom looked at his mug of coffee. "I have to ask you this, Sunny," he said, but went no further.

Because she was slow putting things together, she just looked at him, wondering what she was missing and why he didn't just go ahead with it, and then she got it. "Oh." She looked down at her lap. "Where was I seven years ago? What was going on with me?"

She laughed without humor, brought her hands up and buried her face in her palms. "Oh, boy. Here we go." Her voice was muffled.

And Mom. Where was she seven years ago? Does anyone know where he or she was seven years ago and what was happening in their lives?

"I don't envy you this, Tom," Jonathan said. "This is not going to be an easy job."

"No, it's not. Local, personal, and high profile. But I'll have help." He paused, and his eyes grew distant. "And I expect to be relieved of the responsibility anyway."

161

Jonathan's eyes narrowed, as if the other man's statement had puzzled him, but he didn't comment on it. "What about me?" he asked after a short moment. "I also stood to gain at Franklin's death, though I didn't know it at the time. Should I try to figure out where I was and what I was doing?"

Tom shook his head. "That's a long shot if I ever saw one. The contents of the will weren't disclosed. Your name didn't even come up until this year."

"Are you looking at profit as a motive? It doesn't make sense if whoever killed him stood to gain by his death, and then left him under the sand and berry bushes for seven years."

"Exactly. That's the part I don't like."

His attention returned to Sunny. "Okay, we've gotta start somewhere. What can you tell me about your time and circumstances when your father disappeared?"

"Okay." She blew her breath out and stared at the area rug in a faded pattern of purple and blue. The colors fit her mood. "I was just out of rehab. Someone said he was up here, and then no one knew where he was. There was some speculation about that, but no real alarm. I didn't pay much attention. I . . . didn't care."

"Who said he was up here?"

"I don't know. A conversation between Roberta and someone?" She frowned as she concentrated on memories, impressions, feelings. She couldn't recall who'd borne the news, whether it was Mavis or not, but Sunny remembered speaking to her about the real estate profession around that time. Had she been edgy? Distant? Nervous? That would've been close to the time of her and Franklin's encounter.

"Where were you, Tom?" she asked.

He gave her a sharp look and so did Jonathan. Then, gaze steady, Tom relaxed. "Mavis told me she'd talked to you. That's another thing I like about you, Sunny. You don't pull your punches."

Jonathan's gaze remained fixed on Sunny. He now appeared annoyed as well as puzzled.

"That's why I expect to be relieved," Tom continued. "Mavis and I will be joining you and Roberta on the list of suspects. Ol' Franklin is affecting people's lives as much in death as he did when alive. Is there no limit to the man's . . ." He rubbed his hand down his face without completing the sentence.

Jonathan directed his attention from Sunny to Tom. "You must have compared our prints to those on the bloody bat. Have you checked any other prints?"

"Not yet." He hesitated. "It's sticky. I agree with you that the bloody bat ties in. I just don't know how it ties in. But nothing ties it to Franklin, other than that it was found in his attic. I don't want to force it, but I will be asking Roberta for her prints. And then she can at least clear herself of the bat, same as Sunny did."

Sunny asked, "May I talk to her first? I don't want the news about Franklin coming from anyone else."

Fatigue lined the deputy sheriff's face as he looked at her. "Go see her tomorrow. I can wait that long, but no longer. Now that I've finally been given the go-ahead, they're gonna want me to move on it."

He stood but didn't seem in a hurry to leave. He smiled wryly. "I give you fair warning. Next time I'm out here, I'll want that beer. And I'll want to sit on the back porch and stare at the ocean. And I'll want to talk about something else besides Franklin Corday and bloody bats and skeletons on the beach."

After seeing Tom out, Jonathan returned to stand in the doorway to glare at Sunny. "Why are you so damned stingy with information?"

She jerked her head up. *Did he just swear at you?*

163

"Now I know how Ryan felt," he said, words clipped. "If I don't know what's going on—"

"Hey, wait a minute here. I've been taking care of myself for a long time and I don't need—"

A sharp wave of his hand cut off her speech. "It's not just you that is dealing with this house and the people around here. If you're withholding information, I could get blind-sided, and that wouldn't be good for either of us."

Again she opened her mouth, and he held up the same hand to silence her. "You bared your soul to me the other day regarding your past, but evidently there's a lot going on right now you're holding back from me. What did you mean when you asked Tom where he was when Franklin was killed? And why is he being relieved from duty? And is there anything else I should know that I don't even know I don't know?"

Cool it, Sunny. He's got a point.

She settled back, looked at the small kitten sleeping peacefully in the huge chair, and felt her brow furrow as she gathered her thoughts. Then she clasped her hands in her lap, gave Jonathan a direct look, drew in a breath and started talking. She took her time, careful to leave nothing out as she reiterated Mavis's confession, Bev's alleged involvement with Franklin, Matthew's visit, and her conversation with Langley Bowers. As she brought up each point, surprise mounted at how much there was. No wonder Jonathan was on the pissed side. Although that wouldn't be the word he'd use. Or maybe, considering the look on his face, that was exactly the way he'd put it.

Halfway through her narration, appearing both spellbound and irritated, he entered the room and sat down. When she finished, he looked more displeased than he had when she'd started. He said dryly, "I guess I should be grateful I was in the same room with you when you found the bat, or I wouldn't have known about that either."

She frowned, wondering how valid that comment was.

He asked, "Are you always this . . ."

"Damned stingy? I didn't think I was. I never thought about it."

"You're just used to taking care of yourself."

"I guess so."

Without breaking eye contact, he sat back. His expression held exasperation that bordered on anger, but he wasn't exactly challenging her. She stared back, not backing down, but not challenging him either.

"Promise me one thing," he said, voice sounding measured. "If that drunk ever shows up again and you're on your own, instead of relying upon an empty soda can to defend yourself with, will you please very quickly put a locked door between yourself and him?"

That was too sensible for her to argue with. "Okay," she said guardedly.

"And if something else comes up, will you tell me about it *when* it comes up?"

"Uh, all right."

"And one more thing. If you want to go see your mother tomorrow, may I go with you? I'd like to meet her."

Because he'd dropped the subject of her secretiveness—which hadn't been deliberate, but that was what it was—without allowing it to become a contentious issue, Sunny felt disconcerted. He'd again proven he was by far easier to get along with than she was.

"Sure," she said a little sheepishly. "She wants to meet you, too."

"There," Sunny said, pointing, and Jonathan slowed the SUV to turn into the driveway of the gated community.

"Corday for Corday," he told the security guard. The man

checked his list then waved them through. Conventional town-houses, close to identical, lined the streets that the SUV coasted along at five miles per hour.

"She likes it here," Sunny said, "but I couldn't stand it. Everything the same color, size, shape. Originality isn't allowed."

"It's the speed bumps that get to me. We could walk faster. My folks live in a community like this one. They like it, too. Security, little maintenance. To each his own, as Ryan says."

Roberta opened her front door before they got to it. Her hair and attire were, as usual, immaculate. Rather than making her appear older, the gray in her hair enhanced her natural light-brown color, and she'd smoothed it back into a French roll. She wore a pants suit, in camel and gold, and open-toed shoes with the high, blocked heel that Sunny hated, but on her mother they looked good.

Sunny hugged her mom and got the wind squeezed out of her in return. Roberta always made her feel like a little girl coming back home again. Then her mother held her at arms' length. "Something's different about you," the older woman said with a small frown. "What is it?"

Sunny met her eyes straight on. *You cannot tell, simply by looking at me, that I'm engaged in a sexual affair. That . . . is . . . not . . . possible.*

Roberta wrapped her left arm around her daughter's shoulders and then extended her right hand to Jonathan. "And you're Jonathan Corday. Half owner of Corday Cove, and the man who must be responsible for that healthy glow in my daughter's cheeks."

Oh, gee whiz.

Jonathan didn't seem to know if he wanted to laugh, be uncomfortable, or pretend to misunderstand. He settled for returning her smile. "Hello, Mrs. Corday. I'm glad to meet you."

"Roberta," she corrected, then tilted her head. "Tell me, Jonathan, have you ever wondered why the little short ones like her like flats, and the tall ones like me prefer heels?" Her eyes were almost on a level with his. Sunny now felt even more like a little kid.

"No, I can't say I've ever given that much thought."

"Well, come on in. We can talk about that and other things as they come up."

She motioned them toward the sofa. "I don't know if Sunny told you, but I'm not a drinker and neither do I like carbonated soda. But I have nothing against caffeine. You've got your choice of hot coffee, iced tea, or any kind of fruit juice I've got, and I've got quite a variety."

"Iced tea with sugar would be good."

"Sugar?"

"Mom, give him iced tea with sugar and be quiet, please?"

Roberta grinned. "Someone sounds out of sorts." She glanced back at Jonathan. "I'll dump a packet of artificial sweetener in your glass. Will that do?"

"Yes, ma'am."

She exited the room in a brisk stride.

"Sometimes she comes on kind of strong," Sunny murmured. "Just humor her."

Evidently there was nothing wrong with Roberta's hearing. Her voice rang out from the kitchen. "Somebody is definitely out of sorts. I must've been right on target with that crack about a healthy glow."

Out of deference to Jonathan, Sunny clamped her mouth closed to keep the swear word from getting out. She put her elbow on the arm of the couch, rested her chin on her fist and glared at the wall. Out of consideration for herself, she refused to look at Jonathan because she suspected that he and her mother already liked each other. But somehow that circumstance seemed to come at her expense.

Roberta reappeared bearing a tray with the iced tea and what looked like glasses of cranberry juice for herself and Sunny. She served her guests, then sat in the armchair placed diagonally next to the sofa. She was close enough to her daughter to touch her, and she did, briefly covering her hand with hers.

Then she sat back, picked up her glass and sipped from it. "The skeleton was Franklin's, wasn't it." There was no question mark in her voice. "That's what you came to tell me."

Instantly, Sunny's pique disappeared. "Yes."

"Well, it's best to have an end to it." Her expression and voice were level. "It might have been worse if it hadn't been his." She waited a beat, then asked, "How did he die?"

There was no easy way to say it. "There was a dent in the back of the skull."

"Accidental?" The word, and her mother's voice, had a hopeful edge to it.

But there was still no subtle way to put it. "No. Blunt instrument. Hard enough to kill."

Without looking at Jonathan, Sunny was aware of the pointed look he gave her. But she'd already decided Roberta should be told the truth. All of it. "And there's more. When we were cleaning out the attic, we found a bloody bat—"

At the look on her mother's face, she stopped. "No, Mom, no. It wasn't his blood type, and neither were his fingerprints on it. But that's all anyone knows."

Roberta gave her a quick nod. "Okay. Go on."

"One day when Jonathan and I were on the beach, we—I, I mean—I was hit by a stray bullet. It creased my forehead."

"Well." Roberta's eyes didn't stray. "Really. Okay. Anything else?"

"Yes. I didn't fall off the cliff. I was pushed."

Roberta held her gaze for a long moment. Then she looked at

the arrangement of artificial roses on the stand near the front door. Her throat worked as she swallowed. "It's times like this that make me wish I hadn't quit smoking." Then her eyes, again calm and steady, returned to her daughter. "But there's yet more, I can tell."

Sunny drew in a breath, blew it out. "Apparently, Franklin, was, uh . . ."

"A womanizer?"

"You knew?"

"Oh, yes. I knew. That was how he and I met. He and Bev Wilkes, who was Bev Hayes at the time, were going together. And probably would've been married if he hadn't cheated on her with me."

Then she looked away from what she saw on her daughter's face. "I'm sorry, Sunny. I'm not proud of that and I wish I didn't have to tell you. But it appears you'll hear it eventually, and I prefer you hear it from me."

That's what Mavis said.

Roberta studied her glass of juice. "Your father was very charming, very glib, and he zeroed in on a person's vulner-abilities, weaknesses, wants, with . . . with such precision it was almost uncanny. It was a special skill he had, and he used it without conscience. He exploited everybody he met. I loved him once, truly I did, but by the time we were divorced there was no love left."

Sunny winced with memory and guilt. "I was always so . . . full of myself, my own hurt and anger that I never thought much about you. You had to have been carrying quite a load back then."

The look of reminiscence that spread across Roberta's face didn't indicate pleasant memories. "It was tough at times, but I got through it." She drained her glass as if it had something more bracing in it than cranberry juice. "All the relationships will come out in a murder investigation anyway. Now that I've started, perhaps I should just give it all to you."

Sunny studied the scalloped gold carpet. She wasn't comfortable hearing about the misconduct of the previous generation, and she felt even more awkward with her mother's candor than she had with Mavis's. But both women were probably correct that eventually it all would be aired and that it might be easier coming from them.

Roberta folded her hands in her lap and looked down at them instead of at her guests. She spoke in a level, unemotional voice. "I fell in love with Franklin, blindly, fully, and fast. And I continued to love him even when I realized I was no more than a romantic interlude to him. He married me on the rebound from Bev, who had of course married Howard Wilkes on the rebound from Franklin. What an intricate and unhappy mess we made of our lives, all four of us. Their marriage was no happier than ours."

She looked at her daughter, and her expression hardened. "But whatever we adults did with our lives, nothing excuses what he did to you. That was unconscionable."

Sunny looked at her hands. She'd never had the courage to give voice to the question that sprang to mind, and because she'd never asked, the disquiet had remained through all the years. "Why did he do that, try to disown me?" She sounded like the child she once had been. "Did he really not trust you, or was it because . . . because of me, something about me?"

"No, Sunny." Roberta's voice sharpened, and it seemed her daughter's pain crossed her own face. "It was not because of you. Get that thought right out of your mind. In fact, it was he who gave you your nickname, honey. He said the color of your hair reminded him of a ray of sunshine and that your smile was as warm as the sun itself. And you should also know this. I'm not attempting to defend him, understand, but he'd suffered

170

mumps in his teens and he truly thought he was sterile. He'd told me before we married that he'd not be able to give me a child. But he'd accepted the pregnancy, and didn't even contest child support, not at first, and then a year after the divorce he dropped that bombshell. I doubt if we'll ever know why."

"Who suggested the divorce?" Jonathan asked, voice as straightforward as Roberta's.

"He did," she answered, "but I agreed immediately. In truth, I was relieved. I'd fallen out of love by then and wanted more out of life. There had to be more than what I shared with him."

Her eyes again found Sunny. "When he petitioned to cease child support on those grounds I was floored. But then I got mad, fighting mad, and I petitioned right back. But proving paternity wasn't enough, so I went all the way and got the injunction regarding Corday Cove. You deserved that much, but at the time I admit that it was spite guiding me. Then, as you grew up and I saw your pain, I realized I had to give up my hate, just as I'd given up my love. It was eating me up and do-ing the same thing to you. So I let go. I finally let it all go."

Age Sunny hadn't seen before now lined her mother's face. Then Roberta went on. "And you beat it, too. You turned yourself around. I'm proud of you, Sunny. You've got guts and strength, more than I think you're aware of."

Her mother's quiet and simple delivery lent weight to her words.

Roberta said, "You're his closest kin. Will you claim his remains?"

Oh. Well, who else was going to do it? Sunny nodded.

"And I'll help," Roberta added. "Financially, and with mak-ing arrangements. You shouldn't have to do that by yourself."

Again Sunny nodded. But she wasn't yet done with the past, and if she didn't bring it up now, she feared she never would and then it'd pop up and bite them.

"Uh, Mom . . ."

"More transgressions? Okay, we need to bare it all before we can be done with it."

"Langley and Louise Bowers." Sunny went for the easiest one first. "Do you know them?"

"Not well, but I knew of them and guessed that she was involved with Franklin. In that case, however, he may have unintentionally done a good deed. Louise needed courage to break away from Langley, and Franklin may have supplied her with that. I don't condone infidelity, but marriage does *not* give one a license for abuse." Her expression grew hard; clearly she was recalling her daughter's second marriage in which physical abuse had also existed.

Then, as she watched Sunny, her face slowly cleared. "Why are you hesitating? You especially don't like this next one. Is it Mavis?"

Sunny felt her eyes grow wide. "You knew?"

Roberta closed her eyes. "I do now."

The older woman shook her head, appearing more impatient than hurt. "Oh, Mavis, you stupid, stupid fool." She blew her breath out in a soft sigh. "I even know when it happened. When you were in the clinic, Sunny, Tom and Mavis were having a rough time. Tom's parents were splitting and it was tearing him apart. He was bound and determined to save that marriage, and his own marriage was taking a hit because of it. And somewhere around that time I noticed that Mavis wasn't able to look me straight in the eye. She would look everywhere but at me, and I, well, I worried about her."

Sunny felt guilty again, remembering how self-absorbed she'd been at that time. She'd been so full of her own despair that she'd not had a thought for anyone else.

Roberta looked tired, lines becoming more prominent in her face. "I hoped I was misreading the signs, but for her sake, not mine. I felt no sense of betrayal. In fact, that was when I realized that I really had let it go."

Her gaze settled on Sunny. "So she talked to you. How about Tom? What . . ."

"They're okay. She'd told him, and they've dealt with it."

"The only reason she talked to you was because her name, and Tom's, might be coming up now. If Franklin was murdered, they each have an excellent motive, don't they?" She shook her head again. "What a mess. What a hellish mess."

Looking at the floor, she lifted her hand to briefly massage the back of her neck, then she looked back at her guests. "Okay, enough of the past. We've got plenty going on right now that needs our attention. Such as who pushed you off the cliff and fired at you, Sunny? That's two violent acts too many. Are you thinking, specifically, of any of the people we've talked about? Langley, Bev, Tom, Mavis . . ."

"Any of the above," Jonathan said.

Her gaze flicked to him. "A man with an open mind. It should serve you well." Her attention returned to her daughter. "And you, Sunny? What are you thinking?"

"The bullet was a stray, unrelated to anything else. And one of the Bowers boys pushed me off the cliff. But not to harm me, just to keep himself out of trouble."

Jonathan looked at the ceiling. "Save me from . . ."

Sunny sent a fast frown his way. "And what are you thinking? That whoever killed Franklin for whatever reason also wants to kill me for the same reason? And what reason is that? What could he and I possibly have in common other than the same name and bloodline? And in that case, you'd also be a target."

His gaze snapped to hers. "I don't profess to know the mind of a killer. But we have too many coincidences to continue to call them coincidences."

"Okay, then, let's look at it your way." Strain put a bite in her voice, and she also heard a hint of the sarcasm that she knew he didn't like. "Someone killed someone with a baseball bat and then killed Franklin with a different bat. Seven years later this person saw me on the beach, just happened to have a rifle handy so fired off a shot, then a couple days later found me standing conveniently on the cliff's edge and gave me a shove. Did this person plan all this, or does he kill on impulse and all of us— the missing victim, Franklin, me—just happen to be in the wrong place at the wrong time?"

Jonathan's manner was as stony as his voice was clipped. "The next time you're in the wrong place at the wrong time, where is it going to be? And who will it be who finds you there?"

Sunny held his stare. Of course there was no answer to that, which is exactly why he'd phrased it that way.

Roberta's attention had been darting from person to person as if she were watching a tennis match. Now she looked at her daughter. "Your turn."

Sunny's eyes flashed at her mother instead of at Jonathan. "That's *not* funny."

"You bet it's not. It's your life. Now that you're back down here, will you stay put? Jonathan can drop you off at home, and then he can go back to Chester and close up the house."

"No."

"Sunny—"

"Stop it, Jonathan. We already had this conversation."

"No sense arguing with her." Roberta appeared relaxed as she sat back and crossed her legs. "Hasn't worked since the day she was born. Just keep an eye on her. If we have to, we'll hire a bodyguard."

"No way. No bodyguard."

"You're right, Roberta," Jonathan said, sitting so straight his back didn't touch the sofa's fabric. "We'll do what we have to do."

Sunny glared at the ceiling.

Roberta's look turned thoughtful as she studied Jonathan. "I bet that drives her up the wall. When you get uptight, you have a tendency to become stuffy."

CHAPTER NINETEEN

"It's beautiful," Sunny said with feeling. She stood next to Jonathan as he rested on his knees in front of the Victrola that now shone like a mirror. When he leaned back on his haunches to regard his handiwork, his eyes gleamed along with the cabinet.

"Amazing what a little bit of lemon oil and an old t-shirt can do," he said.

"A whole lot of lemon oil," she corrected. "And umpteen t-shirts."

He chuckled. "Okay."

"And time, patience, and elbow grease. What did Ryan call it? A labor of love."

He looked up. "I'd prefer not to talk to an antique dealer about it. If you agree I'd like to make a gift of it to Roberta. That only seems right."

"You can offer, but I think she'll turn it down. It seems more right to me, and probably will to her, too, that you keep it. Like I said, it's been a labor of love."

She smiled, nudged his shoulder with her hip, then nudged harder until he stopped resisting and toppled over onto his side and then onto his back. She followed him down and covered his body with hers, as much of it as she could stretch to. He was long. She folded her arms across his chest and placed her chin atop her hands, her eyes scant inches from his.

"You don't take no for an answer," he observed.

"Are you telling me no?"

176

"No."

Their lips met. When she raised her head, he said, "But I can think of a softer surface than the one I'm lying on."

"Yeah, but that softer surface is pretty far away." Again she lowered her mouth to his.

"You've got a point," he said, when next given the opportunity to speak, and he made a move to change their positions.

"Well, wait a minute," Sunny said. "If it's going to be my back on the floor, maybe that softer surface isn't that far away after all."

He flashed a quick smile, showing off bright-white teeth any dentist would be proud of, and then jumped to his feet. He pulled her up, tossed her over his shoulder and carted her up the stairs. Now that they were becoming more familiar with each other, he was constantly surprising her with some very agreeable and very sexy moves.

That evening Sunny stood alone in the kitchen, staring into space while steaks sizzled under the broiler. Fat snapped and made her jump. She turned the steaks, checked the potatoes, drained them and got out the masher. It was a simple dinner, the kind Jonathan liked, for their last night together.

"Five minutes," she hollered.

How had he become so important to her so quickly?

Well, it didn't exactly sneak up and bite you on the butt, Sunny. You walked right into it.

It wasn't necessarily the end of their relationship, she reminded herself; he'd be back for the memorial service. But there'd be a lot of other people around then, too. So, yes, this was the end of something very, very special.

Realizing her eyes had again become unfocused, she gave her head a couple of quick shakes, washed and dried the masher, put it away and hollered for him again. She drained the green beans and put the lid back on the pot to keep them warm.

Where was he?

The outside hose turned on, answering that question. He was washing the SUV. Well, if she could hear the rush of water, couldn't he hear her voice?

Apparently not. She stared at the porch door. Her eyes burned.

"Okay. Enough." She splashed cold water on her face, dried off with a paper towel, and then walked outside to drag Jonathan inside.

The atmosphere at breakfast the next morning was strained. Jonathan seemed to eat in slow motion. He'd also packed slowly and had set a snail's pace traveling up and down the stairs.

Exhaling loudly, Sunny pushed away from the table and got to her feet.

Talk about a couple of lovelorn lovers. We'll just have to wait and see what the test of time and distance tells us.

Taking his empty plate and hers, she looked down at him. "Please don't take this wrong, but would you please hurry up and get out of here?" When he looked up she gave him a real smile, not forced, and then she crossed to the sink. "You're not making this any easier," she said, grateful for the mild tone she'd managed. "If you've got to go, then go."

She stooped to get the dishpan from the cabinet beneath the sink, put it in place and turned the water on. "Just don't take Cat with you. She stays."

At the sound of his quick, unforced laugh, she relaxed. His chair scraped back, and then she heard his steps in the hall. Clearly for her benefit, he made a clicking sound with his tongue and patted his leg to call Cat. Sunny acknowledged the act with an amused nod but didn't look after him.

An hour later he was still upstairs. She sat outside on the back porch stairs, hugging her knees and waiting. A slow man, meticulous, deliberate, reserved, not at all her type, and she'd fallen for him like a collapsed skyscraper. Cupid had a sense of humor.

He finally showed, passed her on the porch stairs, and deposited his suitcase in the rear of the SUV. He looked up, giving the road leading to the highway a long study. Coming back, he sat beside her, gave her a small smile and then checked the road again. His eyes sharpened. He leaned toward her, pecked her once on the lips, rose to his feet and was in the driver's seat of his truck before she got past her first blink.

"Huh?" She got to her feet, staring at him as he drove past. Then she noticed the dust storm on the road and the sporty black coupe that led it. Ryan's shiny little car. The vehicles' horns exchanged greetings.

Sunny leaned against the house wall, folded her arms, and watched the new arrival.

"Hi, doll." Ryan exited the car and walked around to the trunk. Then he stopped and gave her a longer look. He turned his head to follow the retreating SUV, then looked back at her. "Something tells me you weren't expecting me."

"Something tells me someone else was expecting you. What is this, the changing of the guard?"

"Hmm," he mused. "How about that. He didn't tell you."

"There are two people I could cheerfully strangle right about now," she said conversationally. "And you're one of them."

He opened the trunk and withdrew his suitcase. "Got any coffee on? I could use some. And if you've got the makings, I could go for lasagna tonight. And a tossed salad with lots of tomato in it."

She pushed away from the wall. "How did you get away from your practice? I know there are people you're concerned about."

He frowned, not looking at her. Clearly he didn't like this part. "They've got my cell phone number, and I gave them this number as well. And I want to sleep downstairs, in order to be closer to the phone. Just in case. But nobody is, er, in a danger zone right now."

"And if somebody does need you and you have to return quickly?"

When he didn't respond, she repeated the question, voice still mild and still insistent.

He met her eyes straight on. "Marcus said he could get a couple days off if he has to."

She swore softly.

"It's okay, Sunny. Don't—"

"No, it's not okay," she snapped. "I'm not a child who needs babysitting or rescuing. I made the decision to stay up here, and that's my right. And I resent you and Jonathan and anyone else rearranging their lives in order to interact with mine. That's the same thing as taking over my life and arranging it for me. Think about it, Ryan. Am I right?"

"I think I understand why Jonathan didn't tell you I was coming."

"Am . . . I . . . right?"

He gave her another straight on look. "Yes, Sunny, sweetheart, you're right. But I'm not going to back off, and neither is he. You're stuck with us. Now can I have that coffee?"

She held his eyes for a long moment. Marcus was in on it, and unless snowballs now thrived in hell, so was Roberta.

Dammit anyway, they did it. You got your bodyguard.

So . . . roll with it. What the hell else can you do?

She showed him her back and stomped up the porch stairs.

At the kitchen table, she worked on a grocery list while he drank his coffee and unwound from his time behind the wheel. He'd never liked long driving trips.

180

"Actually," she admitted once she'd also unwound, "your presence allows me some freedom. I was planning on sticking pretty close to the house. Because, uh . . . well . . . anyway."

He grinned, but said nothing.

She put the grocery list aside. "Why don't we take lunch down to the beach and go shopping later? Looks like a nice day. No need to spend it inside if we don't have to."

He agreed, got up to put his empty cup in the dishwasher, then must've remembered there wasn't one because he stood in the middle of the floor with an I-don't-know-what-to-do look.

"Oh, for Pete's sake. Put it in the sink."

While he unpacked, Sunny made tuna salad sandwiches, including one for Cat. The kitten also liked bread, pickles, and mayonnaise. Both Cat and Jonathan had unusual eating preferences. She added two oranges, four cookies, and two bottles of water to the tote bag.

Halfway to the beach, Ryan stopped. "Sunscreen. If I spend five minutes down there without it, I'll turn into an overdone hamburger."

He went back for suntan lotion while Sunny continued alone. Cat hadn't yet caught the aroma of tuna and was wandering around on her own somewhere. The naked bluff, lacking its berry bushes, was an eyesore. Sunny wondered if she'd ever get used to it. And the new trail was too tame. Half the fun of a walk to the beach had been negotiating the precarious trail down the cliff. Deputy Tim Joyce had also recognized that fact.

The sound of approaching voices surprised her. Other than the recent police presence, she'd never met anyone else on this section of shore. When she reached the bottom of the path the sand slowed her down. Whoever they were, they were male and were still on the firmer, wet sand at the tide line, not yet parallel with the cove. Once she emerged from the horseshoe, she saw them.

She recognized Matthew Wilkes, but he wasn't the first to notice her. His two companions were tall, possibly six feet or more. But they were no older than Matthew, perhaps sixteen or seventeen at the most. Their hair and features were as similar as their height.

Toby and Langley, Jr., I presume. You're certainly taller than your father. Do your social graces also surpass his?

The one on the inside was slightly ahead and saw Sunny first. When he stopped, his companions passed him then looked back, and then followed his gaze to her.

"Oh. Hi, Sunny," Matthew said. "We just wanted to see where the skeleton was found."

He seemed ill at ease, and she wondered why.

"Sunny," said the one who had seen her first, probably the oldest. He was the one most full of himself. "The famous Sunny Corday herself. Except your name's supposed to be Laurel, isn't it?"

She pursed her lips and narrowed her eyes, exaggerating her thought processes. "Toby is the oldest, and Langley, Jr., is the youngest. You're Toby, right?"

"Smart, too." He crossed behind his companions toward her, not just taking his time but actually swaggering as he moved across the sand. "Cute, built, and smart. Good combination."

"Uh, Toby," Matthew said.

"And you've got a mouth on you, too. You're not shy. What else is your mouth good for, Sunny?"

"Toby," Matthew said. His voice had tightened. He now appeared more commanding than tentative, but each of the others was several inches taller and several pounds heavier.

Toby was trouble. She wasn't sure about Junior yet, but his brother was a born bully, and if presented with a hard choice, the younger guy would probably side with his kin.

Ryan, I hope you're not having trouble finding your suntan lotion.

I might get in one good swing with this lunch bag, but that's about it.

Matthew walked faster across the sand than Toby had and caught his arm before he reached Sunny. "Come on, it's time to head back."

Toby's eyes moved down to Matthew's fingers on his arm, then up to his face. "You do what you want to do. I'm gonna stick around here for a while."

When Matthew didn't move, Toby raised his voice. "Junior, you come on over here and help this do-gooder get back to town with you."

If Sunny had been on her own, as Toby undoubtedly thought she was, she would've headed back up the trail a long time ago and trusted that Matthew would hold Toby Bowers at bay long enough for her to get out of sight. By not moving, she now realized she'd prolonged a difficult situation for Matthew.

"Well, hello, everybody," said Ryan's voice.

Trying not to be obvious about it, Sunny drew in a deep breath.

Toby frowned, losing much of his bravado, as he looked up at the cliff and the newcomer.

Ryan started an easy descent. He'd apparently gotten a handle on the situation and he wasn't trying to hide his contempt. "I recognize Matthew, and the role he's playing, and I can't miss the bully and his role, of course, but I'm wondering what your part is?" He looked pointedly at Junior.

"Hey, man," Toby said. Clearly he was working hard at being belligerent, but he wasn't quite able to pull it off. Junior, apparently not happy about being singled out for attention, explained his role by turning around and heading back toward Chester.

Ryan looked at Toby. "Yes? Did you want to talk to me?"

Toby glared at his brother's retreating back, then directed the scowl at Ryan, then wordlessly he turned and followed his brother. There was very little substance in any one of the

Langley men. Sunny thought fleetingly about Louise. Was this a result of her leaving, or was this the reason that she'd left?

The brothers tramped back to the wet sand where the walking was easier. Remaining where he was, Matthew looked after them.

"Thanks," Sunny said with feeling, her gaze on the young boy.

He looked at her, then Ryan. "You didn't need me."

She uttered an unladylike snort. "Think again."

He looked down at his feet, appearing embarrassed. "Yeah, well . . ." Then he looked back up. "I saw your cousin heading out of town. I'm glad you've got somebody else with you. You shouldn't be alone all the way out here." He turned to leave.

"Will you be okay?" Ryan called after him. He directed his gaze to the Bowers brothers farther up the beach, then back to Matthew.

"Oh, yeah," he said easily. "They just talk big, that's all."

They take after their father.

Matthew glanced at Sunny. "But then again, you don't want to take them lightly, either. Take care, Sunny. See you around."

"Seems like a good kid," Ryan said, as he watched Matthew trudge his way up the beach. His bare feet left deep gouges in the wet sand. The tide was rising. The other boys' prints had already been wiped clean.

She nodded absently, agreeing with Ryan, but her mind had lit upon an unsettling fact that she'd almost missed.

Ryan gave her a sideways glance, eyes narrowing. "What's the matter? Are you still worried about them?"

But she barely heard him. She continued to watch the receding figures. "It wasn't either one of them," she murmured. "It couldn't have been. There goes my whole scenario."

He looked at her, at the three boys in the distance, then back at her. "What are you talking about? You're not making much sense here, Sunny."

"Neither of them pushed me off the cliff. They're too tall."

Her eyes met his then, hers intent as she continued to work it out. "When anyone that tall stands next to me—I feel it with Jonathan sometimes—there's a sensation of height. It's like someone's looming over me. But I didn't get that feeling when I was pushed. Whoever came up behind me wasn't a whole lot taller than I am."

He looked thoughtful and dubious at the same time. "Are you thinking it was Matthew?"

She looked away. "It could've been, but I still don't think it was."

"Come to think of it, Tom's not a big guy, either."

"No, he's not. And Langley Bowers isn't as tall as his sons. But it wasn't he, either, unless he went on the wagon. I didn't smell booze." She laughed without humor and shook her head, as if to clear it. "And I guess that also lets Mavis out. Neither did I smell tobacco."

Then, for an instant, she froze.

She quit, Sunny. Remember?

CHAPTER TWENTY

Sunny had never been addicted to television, not in San Francisco nor at Corday Cove. Although she might sit in front of a television set to keep company with its viewer, generally she'd have something in her lap to read or work on.

Tonight, however, she refused to share her book with the TV. At the supermarket she'd found John Grisham's latest in paperback. She planned an early bath and then propping herself up in bed and reading the night away. The author was the best substitute she could find for Jonathan Corday.

Thinking of Jonathan made her glance yearningly down the hall toward his room. *But you come in a distinct second, Mr. Grisham.*

After her bath, she pulled the covers back on the bed in her old room, added extra pillows and then slipped between the sheets, wondering if she also wanted to indulge in a cup of hot chocolate. Then she paused, shook her head, and swore softly. She got out of bed, donned her robe, and descended the stairs.

Sounds issuing from the parlor told her Ryan had found a car chase on TV. When she appeared in the doorway, he put his hand up, unable to tear his attention away from the screen. She waited, listening to grating gear changes and accelerated speeds.

Stepping into the room, she faced the set. The front wheels of a car rocked on the edge of a gully, then settled. The camera cut away to where flames and smoke mushroomed. Then the scene flashed back to the stalled Mustang that was a safe distance from the exploding gas pumps, with a pained-looking but stoic Steve McQueen sitting behind the wheel.

You might not be able to drag him away from this one, Sunny. Can you do without?

I can if he can.

When the set switched off, she looked at Ryan in surprise.

He shrugged. "It's over. Or at least the car chase is. Did you want to talk to me?"

"Yes. I wanted to ask a favor. I, uh . . . ."

He grinned. "Forgot something at the grocery store and you're not exactly dressed for another shopping trip. Seems like old times." He lifted Cat off his lap and stood. He'd been in the animal's favorite chair, and she quickly jumped back up to claim it. "What do you need?"

"Coffee."

"Okay. Come to think of it, I saw you empty the can when you made that pot for me this morning. But I didn't remember it when we were at the store either." On his way out of the room he deposited the remote on top of the TV where it belonged, then reached in his pocket for keys. "Is Bev's still open?"

"If you hurry. She stays open until dark, usually."

It didn't seem right to go back to bed while her guest was out running errands, so Sunny brought her book downstairs and warmed milk for hot chocolate, making enough for Ryan if he wanted some when he returned. The evening was still, the air was cool but comfortable, so she took the book and her cup of hot cocoa to the porch and snapped the light on. Cat must've gotten bored without the TV on because she came to join her mistress. Sunny sat on one chair and propped her feet on the other.

I could get used to this. It's nice.

Then she felt her eyes turning empty. Several times today

she'd gotten the feeling that the house itself missed Jonathan. The kitten stood in front of the screen now as if looking for him. With a sharp shake of her head, Sunny opened her book. Grisham's first character gripped her immediately, and she was into the second chapter before her concentration was broken. Her head snapped up.

What was that?

Cat's head was also tilted, as if in listening mode. Sunny waited for the sound to repeat, but it didn't. Was someone out there? It had sounded like a footfall, a stealthy step that had dislodged pebbles in the graveled driveway that circled the house. Twilight had turned into dusk and she could see little of the yard through the wraparound screen. As she put the book down and then stood, her mind raced over the house, every window and door. She'd checked them all before getting into the bathtub and the house was locked up tight.

Except for the screen door right in front of her.

Ryan had gone out that way, and she hadn't secured it after him. Quickly she slid the locking mechanism into place. Her hand didn't tremble, but her heart was beating extra fast. In almost the same motion, she flicked the outside light on and the inside one off.

Only the porch stairs were illuminated, but at least she wasn't as brightly outlined as she had been. Cat stood poised in front of the screen door, as if waiting for it to open.

I'm not opening up for you or for any other reason.

She picked up Cat and entered the kitchen, locking that door behind her as well. The book and her cocoa remained on the porch. She wasn't going back after either one.

It was more than the solitary sound that had convinced her someone was out there. Her senses, especially that inexplicable sixth one, told her that someone was there who meant her harm. She couldn't explain it. She just knew it.

Her baseball bat was under her bed upstairs, but she wanted to be downstairs where she could hear and identify sounds. She and Cat sat on the bottom step of the staircase and kept each other company. Once Ryan returned, the car would scare away the intruder. The person might have already lit out once he'd realized Sunny was aware of him.

"What's taking our friend so long?" she whispered to Cat. "Did he get lost?"

In response, Cat turned her motor up a notch and settled more comfortably. She didn't have a care in the world. Apparently she'd wanted out to roam, not to take care of urgent bathroom needs.

Sunny stroked the kitten's back.

A stray hiker from the beach might've walked up here. Someone could've been in the cypress grove and seen Ryan's car leave. Perhaps a member of the Bowers family? She'd seemed to have rubbed every one of them the wrong way, and she hadn't even been trying.

Every sense remained alert. She was tense and tight, muscles rigid. When the phone rang, she jumped and squeezed Cat so tightly the kitten squealed and fought to get away.

That must be Ryan. Did he run out of gas?

But there was no response when she answered the phone. She listened, spoke again, then heard the receiver click in her ear. She hung it up and stared at it. What was that about?

She went back to sit on the bottom stair. Cat didn't trust her and stayed away. Bev must've already closed up, and Ryan had to go to Castleton for the coffee.

Too bad you remembered you'd forgotten it. Maybe you should give it up. Judging by tonight, coffee might prove to be hazardous to your health.

When she heard a car she tilted her head, listening intently, then recognized the coupe's doctored muffler. Breathing easier, she walked to the kitchen to let Ryan in. Cat was waiting at the door and went out as Ryan entered.

"Bev was closed?" Sunny asked.

"No, I lucked out. I was their last customer. They were locking the door when I was getting in the car." He hesitated. "I, er, had a little bit of a problem, however. But it wasn't your fault, and I don't want you to worry about it."

She felt wary. She understood a little bit of psychology herself. If he needed to clarify that it wasn't her fault, then in some way it probably was. "What happened?"

"As I was leaving, another car backed into me. I'd backed out first, then saw his car in motion so I gave him room and waited. But he pulled out at a bad angle and a little too fast and he broke my headlight."

"Oh, I'm sorry." But why was that her fault? He drank coffee, too.

"No big deal. Not much damage, and he accepted responsibility. I'll only drive in daylight until I get home and can get it fixed."

"Did you try to call me?"

"No." He frowned. "Sorry, I guess I should have. It took a while exchanging information with that guy. He was pretty nervous."

Impatiently she shook her head. "That's not what I meant. Someone called but was disconnected. I thought it might've been you."

He deposited the grocery bag on the table and reached inside it. "At least one thing worked out well. They had banana nut ice cream. I'll get the spoons if you'll get the bowls."

"Have they given you any indication as to when they'll release your father's remains?" the reporter asked.

"No." Sunny had stepped outside onto the front porch to talk to him. The man was gray-haired and had angular, lined features that lent character to his face. He was on his own and didn't have a camera. He was older than the redheaded female vulture, and he seemed seasoned. So far it appeared he was after facts, not emotional reactions.

"Do you have any idea as to why they're holding it so long?" he asked.

"No."

Despite her monosyllabic responses, his pencil remained poised above the notepad. "Will there be a formal service held for your father?"

"Private interment and a memorial service."

"Where and when?"

"That hasn't been determined yet." *What part of the word* private *did you not understand?*

"Do you foresee any difficulty in working with Deputy Tom Fairly's replacement?"

Her surprise must've showed because his eyes sharpened. "So you weren't told. Do you have any idea why he was replaced?"

"No."

Oh, boy, oh boy, wouldn't you like to know.

He consulted his notes. "Deputy Timothy Joyce, and he'll report to Sam Hendricks out of Cullen County's Sheriff's Department. Do you know them?"

"Yes."

That's not too bad. Joyce is okay, and Hendricks will only be in the picture when it's time to take credit. But Tom should've told us.

He closed his notebook and gave her a studying look. "Anything you care to add?"

"No," she said, and noted that he'd caught her involuntary smile, as slight as it must have been.

He smiled back. He was as sharp as any, but not as callous as

191

some. "You've got my card. You ever want to volunteer anything, you give me a call." He gave her a two-fingered salute in good-bye and walked down the stairs to his waiting sedan.

"Thanks, uh," she looked down at his card and then finished, "Dean Ray Trent." She looked back at him. "That's quite a handle."

He grinned on his way into the car. "Any one of the three will do."

She stepped back into the house. Ryan was lounging in Cat's chair with another cup of coffee. She should've told him to get two cans; he lived on the stuff. On the floor next to his feet were two plastic grocery bags filled with something that bulged at odd angles. She gave the bags a puzzled look, but he didn't comment on them.

"That's the second one today," he said. "And the phone's been ringing off the hook as well."

"Uh-huh. He's also the nicest one. The only one I ever smiled at, in fact."

"Should Jonathan worry?"

She smiled, then laughed. "No."

"He must like oranges."

She squinted. "Uh, what?"

"Jonathan must like oranges."

"Oh. Yes, he does. Why?"

"That's all you have left." He indicated the bags at his feet. "I packed the last banana for me—you get an orange—and a couple bottles of water. I made boloney and mustard sandwiches and added two boiled eggs. I even found that bag of potato chip crumbs you'd been hoarding. I put some journals I want to read in the other bag, along with your new paperback." He got to his feet. "You need a break from the press. Are you ready to go?"

"The beach again? I didn't think you were that fond of sitting in the sun."

"I'm not. You can carry the bags and I'll get the fold-up chairs. I want to picnic in that eucalyptus grove, and I want a decent chair to sit in."

They walked directly to the clearing with its pretty rectangle of wild flowers, and as long as the sun was shining on Sunny she was comfortable. While she enjoyed the sun, Ryan sat in the shade. The sandwiches were drowning in mustard, but she gave Ryan credit for trying. Cat didn't mind the mustard, however. The pet wasn't fussy; if it was people food, she liked it. The animal was acting more and more like she thought she was just another person.

Sunny finished her orange and poured bottled water on her hands to rinse off the stickiness. Then, replete and relaxed, she leaned back in her chair and let her senses take over. The scent of the orange lingered, mingling with the aromatic eucalyptus leaves. A particularly loud wave crashed in the distance. The sun was just right, not hot. A slight breeze caressed her skin. A nap would be nice, and she wished they'd brought a blanket because she'd never been able to sleep sitting up.

She stretched. "Ryan?"

"Yeah?"

"That's a crossword puzzle. It's not a journal."

He grinned, but didn't look up. "Shut up, Sunny. I'm happy."

Then, after a short moment, he looked up. "How about you? Are you happy?"

She knew he wasn't referring to the day. She smiled slowly, and self-consciously. "Yeah, I guess so. I like Jonathan. But I, well, I'm surprised. I really didn't think that, uh, I hadn't expected to ever, well . . ."

When she didn't finish, he did it for her. "Ever find someone you liked who was good to you, and for you, and who liked you back."

She nodded, agreeing but not elaborating.

"You always sold yourself short, Sunny. You're a very special person, and you're as good for Jonathan as he is for you."

With a slow wag of her head, she moved her gaze away. She wasn't as relaxed as she'd been a moment ago. The long patch of purple and yellow flowers blew gently in the breeze. Another wave crashed, a big one that sounded like thunder.

"Do you realize how far apart we are?" she said. "And not just in temperament. He has a good relationship with his parents, and—"

"Don't you?"

"Both parents. And he's never been married. I've been through two disastrous relationships, and have—had—a drug problem. You couldn't find two people less suitable for each other than Jonathan and me."

"Oh, yes, I can. You were punishing yourself with the other two men you were involved with, and they punished you as well. Those relationships were the unsuitable ones. Jonathan has nothing whatsoever in common with those two people, and much, very much, in common with you."

So that's the way you see it. But I'm scared, Ryan, and you're reminding me of just how scared I really am. I almost wish I'd never met him.

"Stop it, Sunny," Ryan said quietly, and she looked up, surprised.

He went on, eyes and voice level. "You're backing away from him, the relationship, everything. I can see you doing it. In this case, distance is giving you the opportunity to close doors. You're so afraid of getting hurt again that you're not giving him and the relationship a chance. Let it grow, doll. Let yourself grow."

She held her silence for a long while, looking into space, yet was uncomfortably aware that Ryan's attention remained on her. He was right, but acknowledging her memories of mistakes, and her fear of getting hurt all over again, didn't make her feel any better. She'd come a long way in four years, but how far had she actually come?

Despair was no longer a constant companion, but she was still too often more uncertain than assured, more scared than confident. She felt afraid to hope. Because she had no faith in herself? Or in Jonathan?

"You didn't mention," she said, her voice carrying a pleading note that she was ashamed of but couldn't quite quell, "that he's got the same opportunity right now that I do to close doors."

"Do you really think that's going to happen?"

She didn't respond. Instead more questions arose in her mind, making her even more uncertain. *Well, Sunny, what do you really want? Do you want to break it off? Do you want him to?*

"Like I said," Ryan went on when she remained silent. "You're selling yourself short. Give it a chance, Sunny. Give yourself a chance—and him."

CHAPTER TWENTY-ONE

"Hi, Sunny," Tom said when she answered the door that evening.

Noting that he seemed unsure of his welcome, she deliberately let him wait. Then she asked pointedly, "Is there something you forgot to tell me?"

He lost his tentative look, even seemed relieved. "You heard."

"Yep."

"Okay. Then you know that the beer I want is legal." He waited, watching her patiently. Then he said, "I know where the back porch is. If you'll get out of my way and let me in, I'll go on out there and you can bring me my beer."

"Sunny, get out of his way," Ryan called from the kitchen. "The man is thirsty."

Sunny stepped aside then followed Tom to the kitchen, and he followed Ryan and the two beers onto the porch. She grabbed a soda and joined them. A beer lover, she wasn't. They had the webbed chairs, so she pulled up a piece of floor to sit on.

"Oh," Tom said and started to rise.

"No," Ryan said. "Here, Sunny, take mine. I'll get another one."

He left and brought back a straight-backed kitchen chair, but she stayed where she was and popped open her can of soda. "Come on. If I'd gotten that cushiony chair before you did, would you have expected me to give it to you and go get a less comfortable one to sit on? I'm fine where I am."

He gave her a long-suffering look. "Sunny, I'm just trying to be nice. Will you please get up off your stubborn rear, take the stupid chair, and behave yourself?"

She shook her head. "That's not nice. It's sexist. And you're supposed to be a psychologist?"

"You two get along well," Tom observed.

Ryan had lost this round, wasn't used to that circumstance, and clearly didn't like it. Sunny grinned at the wall. He finally sat on the hard chair, his spine straighter than the wooden back, and the comfortable lawn chair with its foam cushion was left unoccupied.

"So, Tom," Sunny prompted. "Was there something you wanted to tell us?"

"Two things. One you already know, so I won't waste my breath or your time. The second is that Joyce called today. They're releasing the hold on Franklin's remains."

She sobered quickly. "Okay. I'll call Roberta. She has everything set up. All we need to do is choose a date." As Sunny sipped from her can of soda, Cat sidled up, appearing interested in the colorful can. Sunny smiled, stroked her back, and directed her toward her water dish.

"I assume your removal from the case was voluntary," Ryan said point-blank to Tom, telling him he knew the circumstances and that he believed straight talk was the best policy.

Tom shrugged, conveying that the fact was history. "My disclosure of information was voluntary, but once I opened my mouth, my removal was imminent." He looked into his can of beer. "But I have to admit I'm relieved to be relieved. I'm too close to it, to the people, to everything. The truth is that I wanted out. And Joyce is both good and fair. He's not showing me his back. Hence, my visit tonight. He gave me the choice of coming out here if I wanted to, with him or without him."

He looked at Sunny sitting on the floor facing the two men

with her jeans-clad knees drawn up. "Can I ask you something?"

She glanced up questioningly. "Sure."

"What are you still doing here?"

Good question.

She noticed that she also had Ryan's attention, though he said nothing. Hugging her knees to her chest, she rested her chin on them. "Okay, I'll try to be as candid as you were. Franklin doesn't deserve my loyalty or consideration, so it's not because of him. Neither am I sticking around for my mother's sake. She's competent enough to make her own decisions and follow through. So I guess it's for me. I don't feel right, just . . . leaving."

She grew quiet, thinking, then continued. "He was murdered, and he was my father, and I can't just take off and forget all about that. I want to stick around until he's decently buried. I'd prefer for the whole thing to be resolved before I clear out of here, but I don't think that's going to happen. It's too muddled, too long ago. But I'll stick around until he's in the ground and the words have been said. Then I'll go home."

Her chin remained on her knees as she stared at the floor. Ryan's loafers, black and polished, contrasted with Tom's scuffed oxfords.

"Well said." Ryan gave her a thoughtful look with both pride and admiration in it. "You're growing up, Sunny."

"Thanks for bringing this back," Bev said as she accepted the Pyrex dish from Sunny the next day. She'd been straightening shelves near the back of the store when Sunny found her. "I wanted to make something for Friday, for the reception following the service, and it's the only casserole dish I've got."

"I'm the one who should be thanking you." Sunny wondered what to do with her hands now that they were empty. She stuck them in her jeans pockets. "You were thoughtful to bring that over and I appreciate it. And as far as the reception goes, I'd wanted to just serve cold cuts and breads and such, but Roberta told me it would be an insult not to allow people to bring food with them if they wanted to."

"She's right. There's very little any of us can do, but we can do that much and we should be allowed to." She flashed a small smile. "Somehow, it makes one feel better."

Bev was dressed in royal blue sweats and white lace-up shoes with cushioned insteps, the kind that waitresses wore. After putting the casserole dish on top of some cereal boxes, she rested her hands on her waist and stretched her back. "I'm getting old. I don't bend as well as I used to." Her gaze returned to Sunny. "Will your cousin be returning for the service?"

"Uh-huh. That's why it's scheduled so late in the day, to give him a chance to get here."

The store wasn't busy. Matthew stood at the counter, watching them and obviously listening to them, and just as obviously not inclined to be included in their conversation. When a woman entered with three young kids, Bev picked up the casserole dish and motioned Sunny outside, then led the way to the Wilkes' living quarters behind the store. Sunny was glad. She still wanted to have that heart-to-heart with Bev. Privately, and hopefully tactfully.

The Wilkes' home was small. The modest living room was adjacent to a little kitchen with a corner dinette, and along one wall of the main room, three doors opened to two bedrooms and what was probably a shared bath in the center.

The furnishings were no more elaborate than the floor plan. A portable TV sat upon a four-legged brass stand, facing a sofa in a light-blue print and a matching armchair. A sand-colored end table sat between them, supporting a lamp with a brass base. Everything appeared neat and clean.

Sunny sat on the sofa and accepted a glass of cola over ice.

Not knowing how to beat around the bush, she took a sip of the drink and threw tact out the window. "I heard that you and Franklin were romantically involved at one time."

The bluntness of the statement threw Bev for an instant. Then she executed a small shrug, admitting the romance, but giving it no present importance. "Yes. That was common knowledge."

"With that in mind, telling him a final goodbye now might be difficult."

Criminy, Sunny, you sound like that red-haired reporter.

"You think?" Apparently Bev's patience had a limit. Her voice was clipped and her dark eyes snapped. Her reaction would've been fodder for the tabloids. "Well, you're wrong—there's nothing whatsoever difficult about it." Then she pulled in a breath, drew back and looked at the blank TV screen. "Excuse me. There's no need for me to be rude."

Sunny wondered which of them was being rude. And she realized that kind of response was characteristic of Bev. Sharp words, even anger, then she'd rein herself in as if uncomfortable with her own outburst.

"But actually that is the truth," Bev went on. "I said goodbye to Franklin a long time ago. A lifetime ago. We were never suited for each other, not really."

You're right. You're not aggressive enough. He would've walked all over you.

Bev continued, "Tim Joyce has been talking to me and everyone else, trying to jog our memories. I knew he was up here—Franklin, I mean. He came in for sandwich meats. That was the last time I ever saw him."

Sandwich meats? Then he wasn't expecting to be cooking for company, or anticipating someone might come in and cook for him. Somebody surprised him? Maybe followed him from Reno?

Gee, wouldn't that simplify the whole mess? Dream on.

When Bev became silent, Sunny decided she'd pushed enough, so she drained her glass of soda and set it down. "By the way, I wanted to tell you that Matthew helped me out the other day. He's got courage and integrity. But those two boys that—"

"I know. The Bowers. The problem is that in a small community like this, Matthew doesn't have much choice of peers." Bev sighed, appearing weary with the world as well as physically tired. "I'll probably sell next year and get out of here. The hours we work don't compare well with the income the store brings in. I'm hoping to realize enough to get him into college. He's working a second job and putting money away, too."

"His father can't help?"

Sunny caught the hard glint in Bev's eyes before her gaze again broke off and darted toward the blank TV. But when she spoke, her voice was mild. "Howard? No, I expect no help from Howard. He wasn't exactly thrilled with fatherhood."

Doesn't sound like you chose your men in the past any more wisely than I did. But you did the choosing, and so did I.

Bev looked back at her guest. The older woman's eyes were a soft and pretty light brown, the lashes long and dark. With her olive complexion and heart-shaped face, she was attractive with only minimal makeup. In her youth, she'd probably turned plenty of heads.

"Sunny, I've been curious," she said. "Do you have any idea why Tom was replaced?"

Sunny shrugged. "Too close to the investigation and the people, I guess."

Either you're a good poker player, or Mavis keeps a damn good secret.

"That makes sense," Bev said, and a mask came over her face.

Sunny's senses sharpened. *You do know something.*

The phone rang. Bev answered, listened and then said, "Okay." But she appeared irritated as well as resigned when she hung up. "Excuse me, Sunny. Matthew needs me back in there. It's hard watching the aisles when you get multiple people roaming around. And shoplifting makes the difference between being in the red or staying in the black."

When Roberta arrived Thursday afternoon, she was solemn, subdued, and obviously uncomfortable at being in the house again. She accepted Ryan's offer of coffee, but then seemed incapable of sitting and waiting for it. She toured the rooms on the first floor, reacquainting herself with the house. Then she mounted the stairs and looked inside each room up there. It appeared that her mother had ghosts she needed to meet, so Sunny left her alone.

They met again at the bottom of the stairs. Each bed had fresh sheets on it so Roberta had her choice of rooms, and she chose the front bedroom on the first floor. "We'd always used this as a guest room. It only seems fitting that I sleep in it now."

Her gaze traveled to the glossy, refurbished Victrola standing in splendor in front of the windows. "And I'll enjoy sharing the room with that lovely piece. I've never seen anything so exquisite. I can understand how it captivated Jonathan."

Sunny smiled to herself, realizing that Jonathan had guessed right when wanting to offer the restored antique to Roberta. But how had he known the woman better than her own daughter did?

Roberta ran her hand over the ivory chenille bedspread. She might have found it familiar, though she said nothing. Sunny had found several bedspreads, had laundered them and they were in surprisingly good shape. She'd put a gold one on her bed in the corner bedroom and Jonathan had claimed one in powder blue.

"Where does Cat sleep?" Roberta asked, showing animation for the first time since she'd arrived. "Am I by chance depriving her of her bed?"

"She sleeps with me. But I leave my door open so she can get out if she needs to, so she might roam. You can close your door if you want to be sure she doesn't join you in the middle of the night."

"Where do you sleep? I saw your suitcase in one room, but some of your things were on the dresser in one of the front bedrooms, too."

Sunny felt the flush in her cheeks. "Oh, uh . . ."

Roberta laughed, a small sound, yet it seemed to echo throughout the house. "Oh, Sunny, that look on your face is priceless."

But the touch of lightness didn't last. Sobering, Roberta walked to the window, and as she stood there, it appeared that she was looking inward, not outward. She said, so quietly she could have been speaking to herself, "That master bedroom is a beautiful room. It should have life and love and laughter in it, and yet it has had so little of any of those things."

Then decisively she turned from the window, as if forcing herself to look to the future instead of the past. "I need that coffee. What happened to Ryan?"

Sunny was grateful Roberta hadn't suggested a walk to the beach. She didn't relish the thought of standing with her mother and looking at the place where her father had lain buried for seven years.

She'd prepared chicken salad sandwiches and potato salad for a simple, early supper. They ate quietly, then prepared to leave for the first proceeding of the weekend: the interment. Though this part was private, they invited Ryan to join them.

But he declined. "You don't need me. You need each other, but you don't need me. Not tonight." He ushered them out to the car, gave them each an affectionate peck on the cheek, then saw them off.

CHAPTER TWENTY-TWO

Sunny stood alone in the middle of the parlor trying to remember what she'd gone in there for. She couldn't keep her mind on any one task but was way too fidgety to sit and read, so she was still trying to keep busy—which was impossible when she couldn't remember what she was doing long enough to get it done.

She was hopeless. Giving up, she walked to the window and looked outside.

Jonathan should be arriving any time now. She felt as excited and elated as a teenager before a big date. So no wonder she was such a basket case. She was a bundle of emotions: expectant, joyful, both scared and happy. She didn't have a handle on anything, and didn't even care that she didn't.

The phone rang, startling her into a jerky leap. Shaking her head at herself, and glad that Ryan the psychologist hadn't witnessed her little exhibition, she answered it.

"It's me," said Jonathan's voice. Because he sounded garbled, she guessed he was on his cell phone. He quickly corrected himself. "Uh, I—I mean, it's I. It is I."

She grinned. *Nobody but you.*

Then she frowned as a sinking feeling formed in her gut. "Is there a problem? Are you calling because you can't make it?"

"I'll be there, but not on time. I know Friday traffic is supposed to be bad, but this is ridiculous. Don't wait on me. I'll meet you at the mortuary. I remember passing by it once so I won't have trouble finding it."

"Okay." She heard her relief and wondered if it was audible over the line's static. "I'll save you a seat."

"Right next to you," he whispered, his tone turning husky and now carrying well over the airwaves. She felt a tingle from her eardrum right to her groin.

"Yes," she whispered back.

"Soon," he said, by way of goodbye, and she repeated the word back to him, same promise in her voice as in his. Gently, she replaced the phone in its cradle and then looked at it. *You've got it bad, Sunny.*

Roberta's sedan was roomier than Ryan's coupe and was more presentable than his grandmother's clunker, so they chose to ride in it to the memorial service. She balked at driving, however, so Sunny volunteered.

As they'd feared, the time and place of the service had leaked out. The mortuary's parking lot, as well as the whole street, held a carnival atmosphere. Ryan took Roberta's arm and elbowed his way past the flashbulbs, and Sunny followed in their wake. Each of them knew better than to make eye contact with the news people, or even to reply to the clamored questions with a terse, "No comment."

The room filled quickly, but no one bothered them in their pew at the front. Sunny sat at the end, next to the wall aisle, leaving space beside her for Jonathan. Tom and Mavis sat behind them. Sunny suspected that some of his cohorts sat across the center aisle from them as well, for the specific purpose of fending off unwelcome visitors.

When Jonathan slipped in next to her and squeezed her hand, her breathing quickened, and she broke out in goose bumps all over. *Oh, yeah. You've got it real bad, Sunny.*

She gave him a lingering look. He was impeccable in a dark-

206

brown suit, cream shirt and oatmeal tie. Those familiar green eyes were filled with expression, longing and questions and concern, as they searched hers. His breathing had also quickened.

The buzz in the room diminished somewhat, but didn't cease, when the minister appeared and took his place at the podium. She and Jonathan turned their attention to him. The man looked out over the congregation, remaining quiet until silence fell over the room.

He was soft-spoken, brief, and respectful as he laid Franklin Corday to rest for the final time. The preceding night at 7:00 P.M. the skeleton, enclosed within a plain wooden coffin, had been lowered into the ground. Only three people had been present: his ex-wife, his daughter, and the same man who stood at the podium. Their faces had been solemn, but dry, as they were today.

Now, as Sunny thought of the crowd of people behind her, and resented most of them, an unwelcome thought broke through her subconscious and gave her a sudden chill. Barely aware of Jonathan's hand around hers, or of the minister's voice, she remained frozen for an instant.

This room was full. Was her father's murderer in it? Saying his—or her—final goodbye?

Feeling sick, she closed her eyes against her next thought, which was even more unwelcome than the first. Had his murderer been present last night as well?

Her mother as killer was incomprehensible, yet the possibility had always been there, barely suppressed, waiting to pop up. The only indisputable fact they had was that the killer hadn't profited. It had been a crime of passion, of impulse, without premeditation. Roberta had said she'd let go. But she might not have done so until she'd seen his body plummet to the bottom of the cove, followed it down, then dragged it into the vines and heaped sand over it.

When she caught Jonathan's quick glance, Sunny realized her shudder had carried itself to him. But there was no way he could know that her troubling thoughts concerned her mother, not her father.

For the reception Sunny had invested in more outdoor furniture: two cushioned lounges, a round tempered-glass table equipped with an umbrella, and four matching chairs. She'd given Ryan carte blanche, in both purchasing and placement, and had noted how quickly and totally he'd become immersed in the project. This was an outdoorsy, domesticated side of her smoothly put together housemate and best friend that Sunny had not seen before.

Only a handful of people were invited to follow them home: Tom and Mavis, Tim Joyce, Bev and Matthew, and they all milled about the house and yard. Matthew stayed outside with his face turned toward the ocean. He was so painfully ill at ease that Sunny wondered why he'd attended at all, and for his sake she hoped Bev would take him home soon.

A pair of men was stationed outside the house on the road leading in from town. She doubted they were here in an official capacity, however. It was more likely they were doing Tom a favor. She was grateful for their presence; they'd already stopped and turned away several media members. Before she got a chance to send food out to them, she saw that Jonathan had commissioned Matthew to take plates to them. The act served two purposes: telling the men they were appreciated and giving the obviously uncomfortable teenager something purposeful to do.

Because of the late hour, their guests—Sunny had difficulty with the word mourners, though she wasn't sure why—probably wouldn't be staying long. She was also grateful for that. Her mother concealed it well, but she was under a strain. Roberta needed peace and quiet and solitude. Sunny was also tired and on edge. And she was acutely, almost painfully, aware of Jonathan Corday.

He was uppermost in her thoughts, constantly in her vision, and if he didn't have his hand on hers or his arm around her, it was the other way around. She'd dressed in a dark-green skirt, straight and short, and an ivy-green sweater. She even wore stockings with her conservative pumps, and several times she'd noticed him looking at her legs. She was both flattered and flustered, feeling like a teenager again, raging hormones and all.

At one point, the kitchen was empty except for the two of them. He saw it first, pushed the porch door closed and then wrapped his arms around her.

"It's about time," he whispered as his lips lowered to hers.

When they came up for air, either seconds or minutes later—Sunny doubted either of them knew how much time had elapsed—he murmured, "I've never seen you in a skirt before."

"Maybe not, but I wear shorts all the time." Her voice was as breathless as his. "You've seen my legs before."

"Yes, but shorts and skirts are different. Maybe it's the stockings. Stockings are sexy." His hands rested on her waist while his teeth nibbled at her lip. "Please note my admirable control. My fingers are itching to check out those stockings, but I'm afraid someone might disturb us."

As if on cue, the door opened. "Oops," Ryan said.

"Get lost," Sunny said without looking at him.

"Please," Jonathan agreed.

The door closed.

Their hands behaved themselves, but their mouths were locked for another long while, then finally Jonathan raised his head. "We need a breather. This is getting, uh . . ."

"Yeah," she agreed. They broke apart and stared at each other.

He took a deep breath, looked at the outside door and exhaled noisily. "How long do we have to wait before we can graciously tell everybody to go home?"

"I don't know, but we'll still have Roberta and Ryan."

"Oh. Yeah." He gave her a cautious, almost panicky look. "That doesn't mean you want to move back into your old room, does it?"

She smiled, then laughed.

"Good," he said.

Ryan opened the door again. "Okay, that's long enough. You make excellent potato salad, Sunny. Got any more?"

"No."

"Actually, the bowl of green salad was the first one emptied. Mavis's frittata wasn't bad, either, but I could do without the macaroni and cheese. And that was the only hot dish out there."

"You'll survive," Jonathan said.

Ryan grinned. "So will you." He could be a master of innuendo when he wanted to be, and he was presently pouring it on.

Jonathan frowned, as if trying to decide if he'd read the comment correctly, and Sunny smiled. "What do you want, Ryan?" she asked. "Besides more potato salad."

"I want you both to come out to the porch and sit down with me. I brought up three chairs and positioned them in such a way that no one should take it upon himself or herself to join us."

"And why did you do that?" Sunny asked, tilting her head curiously.

He gave her a level look. "Because I want you back home where it's safe, and I don't think you'll go without a fight until you've exhausted every investigative possibility. Your suspects are all here. Come look at them, and we'll talk about them. Which is exactly what those two deputy sheriffs are doing, or at least what they should be doing."

"Except that Tom's one of the suspects," Jonathan said dryly. "I admit I've not been involved in a murder investigation before, but this one seems quite unorthodox."

Ryan's idea seemed like a good one, so they went outside and sat down. Sunny felt guilty about spying on her friends, and feared that the three of them might be conspicuous, but neither did she want to forego this chance of looking at everybody at the same time.

"We're missing a few people," she said. "Langley Bowers and his sons, except that his boys would've been mere children seven years ago. But his wife, Louise, is definitely in the running. And Roberta said that Bev's marriage wasn't a good one. Howard Wilkes might've blamed Franklin, her first love, for that."

"Okay," Ryan said. "Anyone else?"

"Yeah." She made a face and shook her head. "The murderer. How can we believe that any one of these people actually swung a bat at somebody's head hard enough to kill him?"

"Someone did, Sunny. Be quiet and look around. What are your impressions?"

She did as bidden. Her gaze traveled from person to person, and then she met Matthew's eyes as he stood alone in the yard, but he didn't quickly glance away as he usually did. Sullenness darkened his eyes as he looked back at her. His mouth was a harsh, straight line, and his posture was so stiff he appeared wooden. Then he took a half-step to turn toward the ocean, showing her his back, and Sunny wondered if it had been her imagination or if the anger she'd read in his expression had really been there.

Bev chose that moment to stand. She wore a pearl gray sweater dress that showed off her figure, not bad for over fifty. She'd been seated with Roberta and Mavis, and it appeared she was saying goodbye to them. Sunny felt her eyes narrowing as the fact struck her that each of those three women had been physically intimate with Franklin Corday. They each had known of his various involvements, yet they were seated together, out of choice, following his funeral. She shook her head, wondering at the variances of human nature.

Roberta also stood, elegant as always in a straight brown skirt that reached her calves and a print over-blouse that was tied at the waist with a cloth belt. Sunny noted how much the women resembled each other. Each was tall and slender and carried herself well. Mavis, in a simple tan sheath, matched them in height. Franklin had been of small stature but had been attracted to tall women. Was that why he'd been compelled to prove himself over and over again? Woman after woman? Had his own insecurity made him a small man emotionally?

"Quicksilver," Ryan murmured, and Sunny saw that he meant Bev. "Her moods can turn rapidly, but she doesn't try to hide them. She just goes with them."

"That might make Bev more honest than some," Jonathan observed. Then he added, as if in afterthought, "And it might not. It certainly doesn't make her less complex than anyone else."

Ryan nodded, his attention on the people in the yard, but casually so. If anyone looked this way, Sunny realized that they most likely wouldn't realize they were being scrutinized.

"And Tom," Ryan mused. "He's a good man, but sometimes I get the impression he's trying too hard. Part of his persona is a facade. I just don't know how much. And I wonder if Mavis knows that next to Roberta, she looks like a maid in waiting." He paused, then added, "She might know it and just rolls with it. There could be a downside to that . . . but I don't see it."

Sunny continued to study the three women. Similar in stature, yes, but Roberta carried a regal air that would always outshine others. No wonder she'd caught Franklin's eye.

Ryan raised one leg to rest the ankle across the other knee and glanced sideways at Sunny. "And what's wrong with your friend Matthew?"

"You saw it, too?" she asked and noted Jonathan's nod, signaling he'd also caught it.

"Something's bothering him," Ryan said. "Got any idea what?"

"He obviously doesn't want to be here," Jonathan said.

"Uh-huh," Ryan agreed. "But why? My gut tells me there's more to his mood than just reluctance."

Sunny stood. "Do me a favor? Looks like Bev's on her way out. Waylay Matthew for a minute or two, and maybe you can even answer your own question. I want to talk to Bev."

Playing the role of hostess bidding a casual goodbye to her guest, Sunny walked Bev out to the pickup. "Thanks for coming. And for the casserole."

And that was the end of small talk. There was only one way to get information, Sunny figured: ask for it.

"I want to talk to you, Bev. Please don't be offended or clam up on me."

Although Bev frowned, appearing apprehensive, after a short moment she shrugged in acquiescence. "Okay, shoot."

"I got the impression the other day that you knew more than you were telling me. Was it about Franklin, and . . . and anyone around here?"

"Oh, shit," Bev said softly. She looked at the pickup, beyond it to the eucalyptus grove, and then her gaze returned to Sunny. "Okay. I already talked to Tim Joyce. If you're asking, you might as well know." She laughed wryly. "You may know anyway and that's why you're asking."

Then with a sigh, she nodded. "Yes. I saw Franklin one more time after he came into the store that day. He was having dinner at Sal's that night with Mavis. But the meeting didn't look like it'd been planned," she added quickly. "She was almost through eating, and he came in and sat down at her table. Whether invited or uninvited, I wouldn't know."

Still appearing edgy, she glanced away at the expanse of ocean. "That in itself is nothing, of course. But that was at a time when Mavis and Tom were separated, or close to it, and that's why it caught my attention. His parents were having problems, health wise and even marital, I believe, and it was tearing him apart. He spent as much time out of town as he did at home with his wife."

Bev grew quiet, but Sunny sensed there was more. She waited. Bev didn't seem to know what she wanted to look at; her gaze darted from place to place until it once more settled on her hostess.

"It bothered me," Bev confided. "I'd hoped Mavis was smart enough not to get involved with Franklin. She had a good marriage, Tom was a good guy, and then her friendship with your mother, but . . . whoever knows? Sometimes we go with the moment. You know what I mean?"

Sunny didn't doubt that the meeting between Mavis and Franklin had been accidental, but if Bev had sensed something beneath the surface that evening, anyone else in the restaurant could've also seen it. Tom might have heard about his wife's transgression before she'd told him.

Bev's attention moved beyond Sunny. "There you are, Matthew." She seemed relieved. "Are you about ready?"

He hesitated, gaze traveling uncomfortably between the two women, as if he suspected they'd been talking about him. Then he walked around the pickup to the passenger's side. He stopped and looked at Sunny over the empty bed of the truck. "Uh, thanks, Sunny, for, uh . . ." He broke off, as if not sure what to thank her for.

She nodded and smiled, easing him out of the need for words.

He looked grateful for that, but still somewhat wooden. She watched them drive off. As the pickup gained distance, Sunny's thoughts were no longer of Bev, but of her son instead.

Where did that hurt and whipped look come from, Matthew? What's going on with you?

CHAPTER TWENTY-THREE

Jonathan and Ryan had joined the deputy sheriffs by the time Sunny returned to the backyard. The men sat in chairs in the shade of a eucalyptus tree, and Roberta and Mavis remained at the table under the umbrella.

"Oh, for Pete's sake." Sunny put her hands on her hips. "I refuse to allow this to turn into boys over there and girls over here. This is coeducational. Now one of you two groups, pick up your chairs and go mingle."

Everybody looked at her, but nobody moved.

"She may know how to make muffins, but she's also a bit on the bossy side," Tim Joyce observed.

Ryan thoughtfully rubbed his chin. "Uh, Sunny, if you're thinking that we should pick up our chairs and do the moving, isn't that being just a little bit sexist?"

"You want me to help you out of that chair, Ryan?"

He gave her a slow grin. "No, thanks." He put his hands beneath his head and crossed his ankles as he reclined in the lounger. "I'm quite comfortable right where I am."

Roberta picked up her chair, took it to the tree, and plunked it down. "Daughters," she said, clearly irritated with hers. "I was perfectly comfortable where I was."

Mavis followed suit. "Move, Tom. You're hogging the shade."

Sunny was without a chair, didn't want to sit on the ground in her skirt, and wasn't inclined to traipse back to the porch to retrieve the one she'd left there. Ryan, quite possibly reading her mind, watched her with smug amusement that she ignored. Jonathan started to pat his knee, signaling that she should sit in his lap, then abruptly aborted the motion as if becoming aware of their audience. He started to rise instead, but Sunny shook her head. She wasn't going to let anyone, including him, surrender a chair to her. No way would she give Ryan the satisfaction.

Ryan had one lounger, and Timothy Joyce had the other. At the moment, she preferred the police officer to the psychologist, so she motioned for the deputy to move his legs to make room for her. He did, and after a brief hesitation, Jonathan settled back into his lawn chair.

Sunny sat modestly and uncomfortably at the end of the lounger with her back straight, knees together, and both feet on the ground. There was so much freedom in pants, and so little in a skirt. She folded her hands in her lap and inclined her head toward the man she shared the chair with.

"So, Joyce, how's it going? Have you located anyone? Like Louise Bowers or Howard Wilkes, maybe?"

He gave her a long look. "You don't mind putting a man on the spot, do you? May I remind you that this is an ongoing investigation?"

"I certainly hope it is. A simple yes or no will suffice. And while we're on the subject, have you come across any other interesting possibilities?"

Contrary to his speech, his expression held no real reticence. He even had a slight smile.

"Ignore her if you want to," Tom told him.

"I wouldn't recommend it," Ryan said mildly.

Sunny was aware of Jonathan's gaze on her. But he seemed more interested in how she was conducting herself than in the conversation, and she realized they'd shared few social situations. Out of necessity, her pose was prim and proper, but she, the person, wasn't. *What you see is what you get, Jonathan. Reserved, I'm not.*

Her eyes nailed the long-legged cop. "I'm not asking for state secrets, Deputy Joyce, just if you've located anyone?"

"Yes."

Sunny waited for elaboration, which wasn't forthcoming. "Which one?" she prompted.

"Louise."

She waited again, then prompted again, "And Howard?"

"Haven't pinned him down yet."

Carefully, she crossed her legs and clasped her hands around the uppermost knee. "And what did Louise have to say?"

"About what?" he drawled.

Ryan burst out laughing. Sunny didn't. She gave Joyce a long, silent, unkind look.

"Come on, Tim," Mavis coaxed. "You're not jeopardizing anything by talking about it. Your investigation consists of hearsay. You might pick up something from us, too, if you keep the lines of communication open."

Joyce nodded at her, then directed his attention back to Sunny. He had a very disarming smile. "Sorry, Sunny. Something about you brings out the worst in me."

She was aware that something in Jonathan's manner changed. He was sitting just a little straighter than he had been. Sunny glanced at him, trying to keep her expression casual.

Yeah, I thought he was flirting, too.

As her gaze moved from him, she caught her mother's eye, and Roberta gave her a minuscule smile.

You caught it, too, huh.

Joyce's long legs must have made it difficult for him to be comfortable in the position he was in, half reclining with both feet on the ground on one side, because he sat up and re-arranged himself next to her and stretched his legs out. He was also long-waisted, so he towered over her whether they were sitting down or standing up.

"Louise remarried two years ago and now lives in Arizona." His tone was conversational, his manner casual, and it appeared that he was talking to the trunk of the eucalyptus tree. "Seven years ago she was living and working in San Francisco. She's not off the hook. She had motive. She had opportunity. Langley doesn't know where he was or what he was doing. He was experiencing blackouts around that time. This is vouched for by his boys, neighbors, and employer. He managed to hang on to his job by joining a substance abuse program his company had for employees."

We all have our problems.

"No alibi and plenty of motive and opportunity," Joyce continued. "He's not off the hook either. Because of the blackouts, he looks good for doing in Franklin in a rage that he can't remember. But the fact that that possibility is so convenient bothers me."

He paused, still staring at the tree in a thinking attitude. Then he went on. "Howard returned to Oregon, where he'd come from, and he's worked for a couple different logging firms up there. He's hopped around a bit more than anyone else has, but we'll run across him in time."

He turned his head to give Sunny a dazzling, sideways smile. "Anything else, Ms. Corday?"

"Yes. How about Reno?"

"Zilch. Nothing whatsoever promising about anyone or anything in Reno."

"It's local," Tom said under his breath.

Joyce looked at him and nodded once.

"I've got a question," Jonathan said. "I want to know whose prints are on that bloody bat we found."

"I'd like to know that, too," Tim Joyce said. He looked pointedly at the two women sitting opposite him. "And the best way to do that is to first figure out whose prints aren't on it. At the moment it's still a voluntary action on your part, and I'd like to keep it that way."

"I know, I know," Roberta said. She gave Tom an apologetic frown. "I promised, and I will do it. I just haven't gotten around to it."

"So will Mavis," Tom said, and she nodded. She didn't appear uneasy at the prospect.

"That will be a help," Joyce said. "Another question, of course, is who it was that the bat walloped. But we can only take one step at a time."

Tim Joyce left at dusk, and Mavis and Tom quickly followed. Sunny said goodnight from her seat in the backyard, allowing whoever was inclined to play host and hostess to do so.

Within a few minutes, Jonathan returned by himself. The kitchen light flicked on and she heard Ryan and Roberta clearing up. Ignoring the empty chairs, Jonathan motioned for her to move her legs to make room for him on the lounger she'd confiscated from Joyce. She turned onto her side, bringing her knees up, and he sat at the end. Somewhere along the way he'd lost his suit coat and tie. The two top buttons on his shirt were unfastened and his cuffs were rolled up to his forearms. Nothing persnickety about him today. He looked at ease, comfortable, and sexy.

But she didn't feel sexy. She felt her brow wrinkle. How come?

"It would never work," he said, staring toward the ocean. It was dark enough that it couldn't be seen, but it was always heard.

She thought that over, then had to ask, "What won't work?"

"You and Joyce. He's too tall for you. You look like Mutt and Jeff."

She smiled. "Yeah?"

He smiled back. "Yeah."

He reached for her feet. She'd kicked her shoes off once she'd gotten the lounge to herself, and he grasped both her ankles and pulled until she was forced to change position. As she supported herself on her elbows while she lay on her back, he captured both her feet in his lap.

"I warn you," she said. "If you start tickling, you've made an enemy."

Instead of tickling, he massaged. It felt good, but it seemed that her bones were too rigid to allow her to relax. After a moment she lay back and stared at the stars, wishing she could just give in to what could be a very sensuous massage.

You're not making sense, Sunny. You were so mellow earlier that you were ready to melt, and now that you've got him to yourself, you're so uptight you can't even enjoy his touch.

And he must have sensed it. He'd admired her legs and appreciated her stockings, but there was nothing sexual—overtly sexual—in his touch. He finished one foot and started on the other. "I don't have to ask what's wrong. I can't think of a more stress-filled topic of conversation than who killed your father."

When she didn't respond, he glanced sideways at her.

"Did you get anywhere with Matthew?" she asked.

He shook his head. "He was too uptight, almost defiant, and neither Ryan nor I wanted to push." He waited a beat, still watching her, then asked, "Is there one thing that's bothering you more than another?"

Her sigh was deep. "That question's a little late. I already got off of worst-case scenario and was on to wishful thinking. For instance, wouldn't it be convenient if someone showed up and swore they saw Langley Bowers push Franklin off the cliff? Or if Louise arrived tomorrow and said she'd killed Franklin and couldn't stand keeping it to herself any longer? Or maybe when Howard Wilkes is found, he'll confess and surrender with his hands up? But none of those things is going to happen."

"Okay," he said mildly, gaze returning to her feet in his lap as his hands continued to rub them. "Then what is going to happen?"

With her eyes on the stars she drew in a breath, blew it out slowly, then refrained from drawing in more air for several seconds. That simple activity sometimes worked wonders in settling nerves.

"I don't know what's going to happen," she said softly. "But I can't rid myself of the thought that my father's killer was sitting in the backyard with us today."

His hands stilled. He didn't look at her. "Who?"

When she sat up, the muscles in the backs of her legs stretched. She rested her hands on her knees. "Think about it, Jonathan." Though she hadn't raised her voice, she heard the agitation in her tone. "All that motive and opportunity that was sitting out here with us today. Every time I turn around I'm reminded of Mavis's assignation with Franklin. It happened the last time he was up here. It's like it was a catalyst. And Tom . . ."

Exhaling heavily, she lay back. "And Tom is an investigating officer. I don't care that he says he was relieved. He's still on it. Unorthodox doesn't even begin to describe this situation. Ludicrous is more like it. And, while we're on the subject, who checked his prints against those on the bat?"

"I think you're underestimating Tim Joyce." In contrast to hers, Jonathan's voice was mild. His hands resumed their massage. "He's not a fool. He's got his eyes and ears open. And a trained expert checks prints, not the investigating officer."

"Yeah, I guess so. But that's not the worst part anyway. The worst part . . ."

When she didn't finish, he looked her way and prompted, "What?"

Go ahead, Sunny, you've gone this far. "If it wasn't a convenient outsider, and if it wasn't an inconvenient insider, then it's my mother."

He said nothing.

"It's not even farfetched, Jonathan. I hate it, but it fits. It fits so well."

"Okay. How?"

"That was when I was being released from rehab. She was very much aware of my pain and anger, and how I couldn't stop punishing myself because my father had tried to disown me. She also had her own pain and anger to deal with. Her emotions would've been high right about then. She knew he was up here, and she might've wanted to talk to him, maybe ask him for financial help—that place I was in cost a mint—and one thing led to another, and . . ."

She stopped. "No, there's nothing else. That's all. That's enough."

With each hand he squeezed a foot. "No wonder you're so uptight I can feel it all the way into your toes." He gave her a long and serious look. "But you're skipping some important points. For one thing, I'm more concerned with who pushed you off the cliff than who pushed Franklin. And your mother didn't push you."

She looked at the stars. "You're still hung up on that. One thing has nothing to do with the other. They just don't . . . fit. I can't explain it, and it scares me, too. I still don't feel comfortable on my own because of that. But it could've been a stray hiker, or even a beach bum. We get them sometimes. Someone who's long gone but is still muddying up the picture."

"I disagree. I think that if you can find the person whose prints are on that baseball bat, you will also find the person who killed Franklin, shot at you, and pushed you off the cliff."

"Yeah? Now that's farfetched if I ever heard farfetched. Look at the time element. We have no idea how long that bat was in the attic, and Franklin was killed seven long years ago."

He said nothing as his gaze returned to the dark ocean, and she sensed his growing tension. And it somehow worked to ease hers. She wriggled her toes. "You want to know what else I'm thinking?"

She waited to tell him until he looked back at her. "I'm thinking that's a beautiful moon up there. And if we got a blanket we could find a nice secluded spot on the beach and—"

He pushed her feet off his lap, jumped up, grasped her hands and pulled her up. "Well, let's go. What are you waiting for? Someone to come out here and start up a conversation?"

The next morning Sunny found herself dodging three people as she tried to make French toast. Waiting for Ryan to move so she could open the drawer and get the eggbeater out of it, she forced a smile.

"Wouldn't you all like to go lounge on the porch with coffee?" she asked nicely.

Ryan looked at the coffeepot and Jonathan looked at the porch, but no one moved.

"Let me help," Roberta said. "If I don't have something to do, I'll go crazy."

So will I. "You can cut the cantaloupe, Mom."

"Where . . . ?"

"In the refrigerator, Mom. And the knives are in that drawer. Jonathan, maybe you and Ryan can set the table." *And then sit down nicely and wait.*

She reached for the cinnamon then double-checked to make sure she had what she thought she had. *What do you want to bet I'll do it one of these days just because he suggested it?*

Next was the vanilla flavoring. It was a new bottle and the cap was tight. When she couldn't twist it open she handed it to Jonathan. Maybe he could do something in here besides take up space. After working with it, the small bottle almost lost in his hands, he frowned and handed it to Ryan. Ryan twisted the cap, grunted, got nowhere and also frowned. Roberta took it from him, tapped the solid end of a knife against the stubborn cap three times, then twisted it open and gave the bottle back to Sunny.

Sunny grinned. "Thanks, Mom."

Once breakfast was ready and they sat down to eat, Roberta still couldn't settle. She continued to act as if she had ants in an uncomfortable place. She got through half a piece of bread, one slice of melon, and then simply could wait no longer to get out of there.

"I'm sorry, honey, I just . . ."

"Never mind. I understand." Sunny let her own breakfast go and followed her mother outside, where the suitcase was already in the car. The men joined them on the front porch.

Sunny initiated a hug. "It's over, Mom," she whispered. "It's finally behind us." *Please, please, let it be over.*

Roberta drew back to meet her daughter's eyes. "Yes, honey, it's done. But it took a long time to get to where we are, and it's going to take some time now to get beyond it." She managed a weak smile. "But I'm working on it."

She exchanged a hug with Ryan, and then shook hands with Jonathan.

"Thank you, Jonathan, for that lovely piece of furniture. I'll take possession once both of you are out of here, and I'll take loving care of it. I promise."

Sunny followed her down the stairs to the sea green sedan. After getting into the car, Roberta motioned for her daughter to lean down so she could talk to her through the open window.

"Jonathan is good for you," she whispered in her ear so no one else could hear. "You deserve to be happy, and your mother deserves to see you happy."

Then Roberta turned away to twist the key in the ignition, but not before Sunny caught the moisture in her mother's eyes.

CHAPTER TWENTY-FOUR

"No," Jonathan said later that morning as he took the packaged roast out of Sunny's hands and returned it to the freezer. "You've done enough cooking. We're going out for dinner tonight."

Ryan nodded in agreement. "Matthew was telling us about this place where he moonlights." Frowning, he glanced aside. "That was hard on the ego, I must admit, batting a solid zero with the kid. Jonathan was the one who got him talking, but even then only about Sal's."

Evidently he had a fast-healing ego, however, because his gaze quickly returned to Sunny. "It's an Italian restaurant where he claims they make excellent lasagna, not to mention their minestrone." With his expression going through yet another fast transformation, he added on a critical note, "You never make soup."

"Well . . . dinner out." Thrown by the unexpected development, Sunny looked around the kitchen, wondering what to do now that she didn't have to cook. "How about that." Then she looked back at her companions and decided to take full advantage of the moment. "I'll tell you what, how about I go on vacation for the whole day and let you guys make lunch, too?"

Ryan appeared surprised. Jonathan looked at the refrigerator, then the cabinets with a game but dubious expression. He lived on his own, but she didn't know how he existed. TV dinners and takeout was her guess, which meant that lunch was most likely going to be Ryan's baloney and mustard sandwiches. She debated about telling Ryan there should be at least as much baloney on the bread as mustard, but didn't trust him not to slap extra mustard on her sandwich if she did, so she kept quiet.

She opened the porch door. "Ryan, may I have a Sprite with my lunch?" she asked nicely, then glanced at Jonathan. "Would you mind getting my book for me? I think I left it in the parlor."

Relaxing under the umbrella at the picnic table, waiting for her soda and book and lunch, she smiled complacently at the ocean. *Gee, life is good.*

She chose a blouse and skirt to wear out to dinner. The fact that Jonathan had liked her in feminine garb had much to do with her choice of outfit, she admitted to herself, but she skipped stockings. The skirt was a flared red print and she topped it with a white cotton blouse that had a squared neckline decorated with tiny strawberries. Jonathan watched her tuck it in at the waist then slip on a pair of white strappy sandals.

"Casual," he said. "And pretty."

So it's not just stockings that turn you on.

When she walked downstairs, Ryan took a double take. "Two skirts in two days?"

The restaurant got Ryan's approval. He concentrated on his dinner, wasting no time on small talk. "Excellent," he said, sitting back and pushing away his empty plate. "So good I didn't save room for dessert. Highly unusual."

He studied the last piece of French bread. Apparently deciding he could manage just that little bit more, he reached for it, then looked up questioningly.

Jonathan shook his head, indicating he didn't want it, and Sunny said, "Go for it."

Then she said, "Ryan, dear, may I ask you a question?"

"Shoot."

"What are you still doing here?"

The butter knife paused in midair.

"I seldom catch you speechless." She gave each man a wry glance. "And I noticed that Jonathan caught his breath for a second there." She settled back. "Okay, guys, may I ask what your plans are, regarding me, for the next week?"

"Go ahead, Jonathan," Ryan said. "I've got my mouth full." He stuffed half the piece of bread into it.

Jonathan met her eyes. His stuffiness was back, and along with it was a steely look she'd not seen before. Apparently he could play hardball when he had to. "Both Ryan and I have to depart on Monday." His speech was precise. "If you won't go home with Ryan, Marcus will be here by noon to relieve us."

She put her elbow on the table, her chin on her fist, and stared at him. His expression took on a touch of wariness, but never lost its resolve. Then she sat up straight with a getting-down-to-business attitude.

"Okay, now let me tell you what my plans are. The three of us could've talked this over in the first place, but that means the two of you would've had to forego your behind-my-back scheming of which you are so fond." She folded her hands in her lap. "I've got to go home, get back to work, and make some money so I can afford to find my own place and feed my cat. I'll follow Ryan home on Monday."

Ryan had taken a sip of water and now choked on it. He got his breath back, used his napkin, and said, "What?"

"You're obtuse about as often as you are speechless. I'll spell it out for you. The house is done. Franklin has been adequately provided for. It's time for me to go home."

The men looked at each other. Their expressions were similar to the ones they'd worn when the doctor had informed them that Sunny hadn't broken anything when she'd taken the plunge off the cliff.

She pursed her lips. "You know, you two work together quite

well. But just think, if you put all that time and thought toward solving a problem that actually exists—"

"Shut up, Sunny."

"Please," Jonathan agreed.

"Sure, guys." *Gee, life is good.*

Matthew appeared, gathered their dishes and utensils with minimum effort and noise, left and then quickly reappeared with a pot of coffee. Sunny shook her head, but her companions nodded theirs.

"How many different cheeses were in that lasagna?" she asked.

"I'm not sure," he answered. "But there's a lot."

Yesterday's sullen mood was behind him, she was glad to note. His gray-blue eyes were easy and friendly. In these lights, his hair appeared more blond than sandy-brown, and he had long-fingered hands that looked strong and capable. When he reached for a cup with his left hand, Sunny noticed an imperfection in his little finger. It was bent outward at the knuckle, giving it a bowlegged appearance compared to the straight ring finger next to it.

He finished pouring the second cup. "Cindy will be back in a minute with dessert menus."

The suggestion of more food raised frowns and groans from the men. Sunny said nothing. She was staring at Matthew's hands.

Matthew looked amused by the audible reaction. "Sounds like I better head her off before she gets here."

When he left, Sunny put her left hand palm down on the table. The same long fingers and narrow wrist. His hand had been bigger and adorned with fine hairs, the nails blunt, but a perfect male match to hers, even to the slightly bent, bowlegged appearance of the pinkie.

"Sunny?"

She became aware that was the second time Jonathan had

said her name. She looked up.

"Is there something wrong?" he asked. "You look like . . ."

"I saw a ghost? That's what I feel like."

Twisting around in her chair, she watched Matthew carry the coffeepot from table to table. He was lithe, friendly, and had ample charm to draw from. She'd not seen this side of him before, but he'd always been in the store or overshadowed in some way by others. On his own, his charisma shone through.

She wondered what Howard Wilkes looked like. Was he tall, short? Dark, light? Introvert, extrovert? Where could she find a picture of Howard without having to ask Bev for it?

"Sunny," Ryan said pointedly, "should we worry about you?"

Turning back, she folded her hands in her lap and looked at each man in turn. "Look at Matthew. Try not to be obvious about it, but give him a really good look." They were seated at a corner table in the back, with only one table near them and it was empty. She wasn't concerned about being overheard.

She gave them a moment before asking, "Could he be Franklin's son?"

Their disbelief was evident in their silence. Their eyes narrowed, but settled on her instead of on Matthew. She pushed her chair back and stood. "Wait here. Watch me. Watch us."

She tracked Matthew. He disappeared into the swinging doors of the kitchen as she approached, and she paused, hoping she didn't look as out of place as she felt standing by herself in the middle of the dining room. Fortunately, he quickly reappeared.

"Oh, hi, Sunny." He looked surprised. His gaze moved beyond her to her table. Realizing she stood in front of him, not presenting the view to her companions that she wanted to present, she stepped to her side and he turned with her. Now the occupants at her table had a clear view of their profiles.

"Can I get you something?" he asked, appearing puzzled.

As usual, you thought this one out well, Sunny. What can he get for you?

"We changed our minds about dessert. Could you bring us some menus after all?"

"Sure. But you didn't have to come after me. I would've—"

She waved away his words. "I was feeling so stiff I had to get out of the chair for a minute." When she returned to the table and sat down, no one said anything. "Well?" she prompted.

Ryan shook his head. "You're grasping at straws, Sunny."

She looked at Jonathan. He said nothing, his gaze still on the spot where she'd stood with Matthew.

Ryan continued to shake his head. "Okay, you both have light complexions and are slightly built. But there are other people in this room that are blond and blue-eyed and slim, and you're not related to any of them."

When her gaze returned to Jonathan, his eyes warned her. Turning, she accepted the menu from Matthew, and then he gave one to each man.

"Cindy will take your orders," he told them. "She'll be right here."

He walked away, and Sunny looked back at Jonathan. "Maybe," he said. "Maybe."

Cindy appeared before they'd even looked at the menus.

Okay, Sunny. You've got to order something. You asked for the stupid things.

"Oh," she said, stalling for time and reading fast. Her companions were no help. They weren't even pretending to read the selections.

"Oh," she said again, pleased. "Spumoni. It's been forever since I had spumoni."

"Good choice. Ours is excellent." Cindy looked questioningly at the men, but they shook their heads.

Matthew appeared on her heels, refilled coffee cups, and then

Cindy and the dish of spumoni were there. The hostess seated a couple at the next table, removing the opportunity for private conversation. Though Sunny hadn't really wanted dessert, she was glad now she'd ordered it. The ice cream was as good as Cindy had claimed.

"That does look good," Jonathan said and gave her a questioning look.

"Sure," she said, and he scooped up a small taste with his coffee spoon.

"Hmm," Ryan said, looking interested. He spooned out half the mound of ice cream and put it on his saucer.

Jonathan's spoon was on its way back again. She shoved the dish toward him, sat back in her chair and watched her dinner companions, who were too full for dessert, finish hers. Jonathan at least had the grace to look sheepish.

Apparently the spumoni had merely titillated Ryan. When they walked in the back way of the old Victorian, he headed straight for the freezer and the banana nut ice cream. He emptied the container into three bowls, and then they sat outside with their treats and watched the descending sun.

But the men appeared more interested in Sunny than the sun. At length, Ryan asked, "Well, do you still think you might have discovered a brother you never knew you had?"

She looked into her bowl, not meeting anyone's eyes. Then she held her left hand up, palm facing her, and looked at it. "Notice how my little finger is malformed, just slightly. I never thought much about it. It was just the way my finger grew, but Matthew had the same look to his pinkie, left hand." She lowered her hand, still not meeting anyone's eyes. "I know it's skimpy. But, well, I always had a feeling . . ."

Making a sound of disgust, she shook her head. "I know how lame that sounds. But I like Matthew, and, yes, I feel a kinship with him. He's a good kid. But . . ." She gave up. "Oh, dammit anyway, I don't know."

"It would be simple enough to ask Roberta if Franklin had a misshaped finger," Jonathan said. "And she'd know what Howard Wilkes looks like. So should Tom and Mavis. Matthew may resemble Howard more than the Cordays, and in that case you could discard this theory. But, until then, it's not a bad theory."

"Yeah?" Ryan asked. He looked both skeptical and thoughtful. "Feel free to expound."

"It would answer a couple of questions. Franklin kept coming up here, but it might not have been the view that attracted him. His first love might have been his strongest love." He paused to give Sunny an apologetic look, as if he'd insulted her mother. "Perhaps he was never quite able to break away from Bev. And vice versa."

"Okay," Ryan said, rubbing his chin. "Keep going."

"No," Sunny said. "Let me." The answer to a long-standing question had occurred to her, and it made her both angry and sad.

"Matthew is about ten years younger than I am. When Bev became pregnant, she would've told Franklin if the child was his. If he refused to accept the baby as his, that would've started the ball rolling toward his act of disowning me. If he'd ever had the slightest glimmer of mistrust—and why wouldn't he? He could only judge others by himself—that could have been the final straw."

Neither man said anything.

"What a cold-hearted, hateful bastard." Her fingernails were digging into her palms. "He didn't deserve to live. Two children, and look what he did to both of them."

"You don't know that for certain, Sunny," Ryan cautioned.

"Of course I don't. But you're going to be as surprised as I am if I'm wrong. It fits too well."

"We need to talk to Tim Joyce," Jonathan said. "The sooner, the better. It has suddenly become vital that he finds and talks to Howard Wilkes."

"But this poses more questions than it answers," Ryan said. "If Matthew was Franklin's son, why didn't Bev also file a paternity suit? Especially after it was proved that Franklin wasn't sterile?"

"She was still married to Howard," Sunny answered. "Matthew has his name. No one ever questioned that."

Absently, she put her bowl on the ground instead of stretching for the table. Cat leaped for it and Jonathan rescued it and put it atop the table. Then he patted his lap and the animal jumped up and made three complete circles before settling down for a nap.

"And it answers as many questions as it raises," Sunny continued. "Bev said Howard hadn't been thrilled with fatherhood. She sounded both resigned and bitter. If he'd suspected it wasn't his child, he wouldn't have been jumping with joy."

"But she kept it to herself," Ryan mused, "for all these years. That doesn't make sense. Unless she wasn't sure herself who had fathered the child."

In the long silence that followed, Sunny stared into space. Then she said, "I'm reminded of what my mother said, about this being a hellish mess. And what a mess each of them had made of their lives. It's so sad that it's frightening."

"Yep," Ryan agreed. "It's downright scary. Man and woman are unique on this earth. They are capable of immeasurable love, relentless hate, and amazing stupidity."

CHAPTER TWENTY-FIVE

"Hi, Sunny," Roberta said at the other end of the phone line. "I'm glad you called. You've been on my mind since I left up there." She'd evidently recovered from the strain she'd felt at the memorial service because the bounce was back in her voice. "When are you coming home? Soon, I hope."

"I was planning on following Ryan home tomorrow." Sunny laughed, relieved she didn't have to force it. "It's hard not to salivate when I think about exchanging that clunker for my own car."

But as more small talk followed, Sunny heard her voice growing tight. She'd stayed up half the night with Jonathan and Ryan, discussing their suspicions. They were well aware of the hurt their theories could inflict, and Sunny hadn't yet figured out a way to ask her mother what she wanted to know without Roberta guessing why she was asking.

Come on, Sunny, the only way to do it is to do it. "By the way, Mom, that update from Tim Joyce started me wondering about Louise and Howard. Who they were, what they looked like, their personalities . . ."

After a short silence, her mother asked, "What are you after, Sunny?"

Damn. How can she zero in like that? "I'm curious, Mom. We all are. These are major players we've heard about, but never met."

"Well, okay, I guess I can understand that. But I can't help much. Louise, I know very little about. She entered the picture long after I'd left it, and all I can remember is that she was on the quiet side. I'd met Howard, of course, but wasn't impressed with him. He was self-centered, self-important. He wore on my nerves."

"What did he look like?"

She could almost hear her mother's shrug. "He was dark-blond, blue eyes, I think. He was physically attractive, I guess. He wasn't a big man, either, but strong, very athletic. He played some minor league baseball, and at one point was even considered for the majors. But he never made it that far."

Sunny froze in mid breath. Her gaze became unfocused.

"Oh, for . . . I just heard what I said." Roberta's words rushed together. "Baseball bats! Sunny, call Tim Joyce. He may already know about Howard's baseball history, but maybe not. Tom certainly knew it. But it could've slipped his mind, too."

"Yeah, I'll call Joyce right now. Bye, Mom."

But after replacing the telephone receiver in its cradle she stared at it, marveling at what people knew yet didn't know they knew it. Tom had remembered Franklin's military stint, but somehow Howard's baseball past had escaped him, as well as Mavis, apparently, and even Bev.

"Well?" The men spoke in unison, one voice inquiring and the other impatient.

"Howard was a baseball player. That was his bat." Grabbing her phone index that rested next to the phone, she rifled through the cards. "No proof it was his, of course, at least not yet. But like you said, Jonathan, we've got way too many coincidences to continue calling them coincidences."

She found the number of the Deputy Sheriff's office and punched it in. Tom's recorded voice told her to call nine-one-one in case of an emergency and then recited the number of the Cullen County Sheriff in case one wanted to call there instead.

And they'd refer me right back to Chester Beach. Come on, come on, come on . . .

Biting her lip as her gaze darted impatiently around the room, she waited for Tom's voice to run down, then for the beep, and then she said, "This is Sunny. Call me ASAP." She started to hang up, caught herself, brought the receiver back up to her mouth and recited her number into it.

Dummy.

Ryan gave her an incredulous look. "You had to leave a message?"

"Yeah. I don't like it either, but it's Sunday. And this is Chester, not San Francisco."

"But this is the communications age. Haven't they heard? Everybody's got a cell phone, a beeper, a pager, but you had to leave a message for the deputy sheriff?"

"You want Hendricks?"

"Who's he?"

"You don't want Hendricks," Jonathan said. "He'll tell you to take two aspirins, go to bed, and call someone else tomorrow."

Sunny again reached for the phone. "Sunday's a busy day for Mavis, but Tom might be home."

This time, Mavis's recorded voice invited her to leave a message.

"We found the owner of the bloody bat," Sunny said then hung up and massaged the bridge of her nose. "I could try calling Joyce, but I don't have his home number. And I'm a little tired of disembodied voices anyway."

Then her fingers stilled, and she scrunched her face up. "Idiot," she muttered, "idiot." Out of deference to Jonathan, she bit back stronger words. Her gaze traveled sheepishly from one man to the other. "I got sidetracked with the bat and forgot to ask Mom if Franklin had a crooked pinkie." *And what would she have read into that question, I wonder?* "But Howard was blue-eyed, dark-blond, and close to Matthew's size. So they could be father and son after all."

The three people stared at one another, and then each set of eyes looked elsewhere. The sense of anticlimax lay over the room like a heavy blanket.

Leaving the men to hash it out, Sunny headed for the kitchen and rummaged through the refrigerator. It was early for lunch, but she had to have something to do. She filled a plate with tomato sandwiches, emptied a bag of chips into a bowl, lined a plate with macaroons and then called her companions.

Ryan sat at the table, appearing preoccupied, picked up a sandwich and then came to life. "A vegetable sandwich?"

"Tomato and onion," she explained unnecessarily, since he'd already removed the top piece of bread and was frowning at what he'd found under it. "Give it a try. It's not bad."

"A vegetable sandwich?"

"Oh, for Pete's sake. Eat a cookie, Ryan."

"Vegetable sandwiches," he muttered, replaced the top slice of bread and bit off a small piece of sandwich. "Hmm." He held it out, gave it a longer look, then took a bigger bite. "Okay. Pass the plate. I'm going to need another one."

The phone remained silent. But the men suddenly realized that since it was Sunday, there would be a football game on TV, and that took care of them. Sunny went upstairs and dragged out her suitcase, opened it up on the bed and then stared at it.

Don't even think about changing your mind. You've got car payments to meet. Her gaze traveled between the closet and the dresser. *Not to mention those two guys downstairs. Ryan will start yelling at you, or even worse, go all patient and preachy, and Jonathan will look at you like you said a bad swear word.*

Her eyes caught her reflected image in the dresser mirror. *So when did you start making decisions based on what someone else wants you to do instead of what you want to do?*

She turned her back on the suitcase and the mirror and went downstairs to sort laundry. Whether she stayed here or went home, sheets weren't going to wash themselves. As she worked in the utility room, she overheard the men in the backyard hosing down their vehicles, a job they'd shared every day. So she figured the game was over, it was halftime, or the picture tube had blown up.

"Much better looking truck without that big dent in it," Ryan said.

"Yeah, they did a good job."

"But I hope you realize it's twice the size and work of my coupe."

Jonathan sounded unfazed. "I hope you realize that you've got two vehicles to my one."

"The Reviler isn't my responsibility. Sunny's driving it."

"Do you want to make a deal with her? You can cook dinner, and she and I can wash the Reviler."

"You can forget about the Reviler," she muttered. "It's going out for a ride." After putting the basket in the backseat of the car, which was parked in the front yard, she hollered at the men from around the corner of the house. "Laundromat. Give me an hour."

Jonathan looked up with a frown. "Uh, Sunny, wait a minute. I'll go with you."

But she ducked back around the side of the house as if she hadn't heard. *I swear. You guys are gonna give me a complex.*

The Laundromat was deserted. She filled three machines and was inserting coins in the last one when she felt a presence looming behind her. She whirled.

Tim Joyce jumped back a step. "Hey! I'm one of the good guys."

Her heart started beating again. "Criminy. You're as quiet as Cat."

She turned back around, plunged in the coins and got the machine started. He dumped the contents of one of the bags he carried into the machine next to hers. Her eye caught a white shirt among the dark uniforms, jeans and sweats. That shirt wasn't going to stay very white for very long if that was his usual sorting style. Was it thrown in there for expediency's sake, or did he really not know any better? He filled the next machine with blue-and-white-striped sheets.

"Have you checked your phone messages?" she asked.

He gave her a sidelong look. "At home or the office?"

"Office."

He eyed the wall telephone. "Shall I check now, or will person to person suffice?"

"Howard Wilkes used to play baseball."

He studied her, eyes narrowing, and then his gaze shifted to the list of Laundromat rules tacked on the wall as if vital information was stored there. "Well, now, how about that." With thoughtful lines creasing his forehead, he pulled a metal chair out from under the table that was used for folding clothes and sat down.

Sunny was glad. Her neck felt strained from looking up at him. "How tall are you?"

She was still standing and he looked up; he didn't have to look up far. "Six-three. You?"

"Almost five-two."

He grinned. "In cases like this, spike heels make sense."

She sat in the other chair. "Tell me how far you've gotten in tracing Howard?"

"Guess it can't hurt. It's not classified." He clasped his hands behind his neck and slumped in the chair. His legs stuck out from under the other side of the table. "He and Bev didn't make a clean break of it. They were on again, off again for several years, and finally they filed for divorce when Matthew

241

was about a year old. Nice guy. Left her flat with a kid and never paid a dime in child support. He'd worked for a logging firm over near Grizzly Camp, but then he moved on to Oregon and got on with a company there. Trouble is, that place folded, and so did the next one he went to. We ran into a blank, and it's been a lot of years, but we got people on it. It's just a matter of time."

"So, as far as you know, he hasn't been around here in . . . what? Fifteen years or so?"

"So Bev tells us." He was staring at the machines. He seemed to think best when focusing on inanimate objects. "And nobody else remembers seeing him around, either. But I'll be talking to her again. Today, in fact. I'm not much of a believer in coincidences, and this one is a biggie."

Folding his arms, he leaned back, directed his gaze straight ahead and crossed one huge sneaker-clad foot over the other. It appeared he was falling asleep with his eyes open. She settled in with her paperback. When she became aware that the deputy's attention had shifted back to her, she looked over at him and instantly recognized the look of male to female interest. It was universal, needing no translation in any language.

"I get the impression you and Jonathan are an item. That so?" His eyes, not exactly brown, closer to hazel, were partially concealed behind lazy, half-closed lids.

Sunny simply nodded. Though she wasn't interested in Joyce's attention, she was flattered by it. The deputy sheriff was a prime example of the male species. Cupid had really engaged his funny bone with this one—the uninhibited Tim Joyce was more Sunny's type than Jonathan, yet the staid Jonathan was the one who turned her on.

"Too bad," Joyce murmured. "Personally, I have nothing against spike heels, short women and spunk. In fact, I like spunk. If it doesn't work out with you and Jonathan, I hope

242

you'll look me up. I guarantee that if I hear about it, I'll look you up." He gave her a slow grin. "Agreed?"

She couldn't stop her lips from curving in response. "Nothing shy about you, is there?"

He held the lazy but gorgeous grin. In self-defense, she turned back to her book. *That smile you've got could melt hearts by itself, Deputy Joyce.* Inwardly, she smiled. *John Grisham comes in second but you're a close third.*

Ryan was sitting on the front porch steps with Cat on his lap when Sunny returned home. He rose when she walked around to unlock the trunk, and Cat settled in the corner of the step to give herself a bath.

"Well, you sure took off in a hurry," Ryan said.

"Where's Jonathan?"

"He took off, too. Didn't tell me where, just said there was something he wanted to do." He picked up the basket of clean laundry, and then they both stood there until he gave her a pointed look. "Are you going to go open the door? I've kind of got my hands full."

She mounted the steps, held the door open for him, and he led the way inside. Cat dodged between them, padded into the parlor and hopped up into her favorite chair.

"Mavis called," Ryan said. "And she was a tad on the frantic side. As I would be, too, after that message of yours. I calmed her down, told her everything we knew but nothing we'd surmised. Tom won't be home until late tonight." He stopped, turned to look at her. "I don't like waiting on this. Maybe you should go ahead and call this guy Hendricks, whoever he is."

"Not necessary. I already talked to Joyce. He was doing his laundry, too."

"Good." He nodded decisively. "Then it's out of our hands and in his." He looked up the stairs. "Where do you want this basket? Not up there, I hope."

She pointed to the front bedroom. "In there is fine. It needs sorting."

After putting the basket atop the ivory bedspread, he gave her a studying look. Curiously, she looked back.

"What's with you?" he asked. "You look like . . ." He snapped his fingers as if the proverbial light bulb had switched on in his mind. "A cat with a bowl full of cream. Joyce made a pass, didn't he?"

Sunny's mouth fell open. *How can you do that?*

He chuckled. "How about that? You hide out for four years then attract two men at the same time."

Floored, she scrunched her eyes closed.

"Hey, this has got to be good for the ego. And you needed the boost. Sunny, sweetheart, I couldn't be happier for you."

She opened her eyes. "Will you stop?"

"So who's it going to be? The doctor or the deputy sheriff?"

She drew in a controlled breath. "Ryan, there are times, like now, when you overstep yourself."

His face sobered. One reason she'd always trusted Ryan was that he heard more than mere words. As flippant as he could be at times, he was always listening. He stepped forward to cup her shoulders. "I couldn't love you more even if you were my sister. You know that."

She nodded, conveying that the brother and sister feeling was mutual.

"Then listen carefully. Jonathan wants to talk to you. When you left he wanted to go with you, but not because he didn't want you off on your own, which is how you probably took it. He's not a spontaneous person. He has to plan what he wants to say and then look for the opportunity to say it. My presence here has gagged him, and I regret that. When he returns, invite him to go for a walk on the beach. Or give me a signal and I'll go for a walk."

She frowned. "When and where did you pick up on this? I haven't—"

"Trust me, Sunny. The man's got something on his mind. Something important."

CHAPTER TWENTY-SIX

Whatever Jonathan was doing, it was taking him a while, which meant that Sunny had nothing to do but wonder where he was and what he was up to. She'd given up on packing, had finished her book at the laundromat, and she didn't feel like going for a walk. She watched football with Ryan for as long as she could stand it, and then she got busy in the kitchen making a potato salad.

Once done with that task she rejoined Ryan, who was sitting on the sofa with his feet adorning the coffee table. She chose the corner chair, propped her elbow on the arm and her chin on her fist while she watched grown men fight over a football. And take time out to regroup, then another time out, and then another one.

Returning to the kitchen, she cut up all the fruit she could find into another salad.

"Got some chips you could bring back with you, Sunny?"

The fruit was healthier but if he wanted chips, he could have chips. He accepted the wrinkled bag with his attention glued to the set. He angled his head to see around her and then it snapped back the other way when she stepped out of his way.

"Awright!" The crowd roared at the same instant his fist hit the arm of the sofa.

Pitiful.

Sunny thumbed the newspaper. When she got up to get a pencil so she could work the crossword puzzle, she evidently passed in front of the TV set one too many times.

"Sunny, dammit, you're like a yo-yo! Will you settle somewhere?"

"Oh, for . . ." She tried to make her frown more severe than his. "You want me to settle? That's your problem? We've got a skeleton with a dented skull, a bloody baseball bat, a missing victim with at least one murderer, maybe two, questions and puzzles all over the place and you're watching a stupid football game?"

"Yes. I'm watching a stupid football game and would appreciate your settling down while I do it. It's really not that hard. Shut up, be still, and you're halfway there."

Sunny glared at the ceiling, blew her breath out in a long exhale, then settled in the chair with her pencil and puzzle. At halftime, Ryan surfed channels until he found another game that then also went into halftime. He put the TV on mute and wandered toward the kitchen. She watched the silent commercials; they were more interesting than the game was.

On his way back, Ryan came to a dead stop in the middle of the doorway, a can of beer held inches from his mouth as he stared into space as if hypnotized. Sunny looked up. "What's the matter?"

"It's a grave," he whispered.

His shock was contagious. Sunny rose. "What's a grave? What are you talking about?"

He set the can on top of the TV so fast that beer sloshed out of it. "A shovel. I need a shovel." He headed down the hall.

"Ryan!" She sprinted after him, caught up in the utility room, slammed the outside door he'd just opened and placed herself in front of it. "What . . . are . . . you . . . doing?"

It took visible effort for him to stand still. His eyes snapped at her.

"It's a grave, Sunny, in that clearing in the trees. The flowerbed is almost a perfect rectangle and nothing else is growing anywhere else. Unless I miss my guess, that's a grave and I'm going to prove it. Now get out of my way."

He elbowed her aside and went out the door. She followed him to the tool shed. "Will you hold on a minute? If you're right, you need Tim Joyce. You can't just go over there and—"

"Yes, I can. I might be wrong and I hope I am, but I can't, absolutely cannot, sit here and wait for some uniformed cop who's out of uniform to take it into his head to check his messages."

The tool shed wasn't equipped with electricity, and impatiently Ryan mumbled while waiting for his vision to adjust to the dim interior. Then he grabbed the one and only shovel that leaned against the wall, checked the edge and frowned, then slammed the door shut.

"At least wait for Jonathan," she suggested. "And while we're waiting, I'll look for Tim Joyce's number. This isn't like you, to go off half-cocked."

He gave her an are-you-serious look, and then went into long-winded mode. He didn't often exhibit stress, but when he did he expressed it through verbiage. "This isn't like me? Just how many skeletons have we discovered? Unless I've drastically lost count, it's been one and this would make two. How could either of us know how either of us would react in a situation like this?"

She'd positioned herself in front of him, so he walked around her. She wished she had a rope. She watched him, looked at the house, back again at his fast-moving figure, swore loudly and then she ran after him.

"All right, Sherlock, suppose you find your skeleton," she said when she caught up. "Whose is it? Have you figured that out yet?"

"Howard Wilkes."

She stopped, but he didn't. She ran again to catch up. "Howard?"

"Think, Sunny, think. It adds up. It makes sense. It's the only answer that answers everything."

"Bev?" she whispered and stopped again. "Bev killed Howard?" Then she had to break into another sprint. "Ryan, please, I can't keep up. Slow down."

With visible effort he waited for her, then matched his stride to hers. "She had equal access to whatever bats were around the house. He might've guessed the baby wasn't his and confronted her. Maybe she swung at him in self-defense, probably did. However it happened, she panicked and called Franklin for help. He had to have been in on it at some point because he hid the bat."

"Insurance," she murmured. A stunned daze threatened to overtake her, and she fought it back.

"Exactly. He helped her bury the body, and then he stole the murder weapon."

"So she was trapped. She couldn't force his hand. As long as he had that bat he had complete control over her."

"But she snapped. In time, something made her snap and she killed Franklin, too. But she was still trapped. She didn't know where the bat was that she'd killed Howard with."

"I was right," she said tonelessly. "Mavis and Franklin's affair was the catalyst. Bev had seen them together, guessed the rest, confronted him and then lost it."

The trees loomed. Sunny found herself wishing she'd stayed behind. She didn't want to discover another grave.

A rifle shot cracked, and Ryan went down.

Sunny dropped with him. "What—"

"The trees, Sunny. The trees. Get in there."

"But . . ."

"Move!"

She half crawled and half rolled until she was in the blessedly dark and safer shade. He was at her side.

"Ryan, are you . . ." She choked on the words, mesmerized by the spreading stain in his shirt. "Blood," she whispered. "You're bleeding."

"I got shot, Sunny. Of course I'm bleeding."

Still on their knees, they looked back across the field toward the house and the pickup parked in front of it. Neither of them had heard the vehicle approaching, but Bev now stood at the driver's door, rifle in hand.

She's here because Joyce talked to her. She's running out of time, and she knows it. She already saw the shovel so she knows we've guessed.

And the shovel now rested behind them where Ryan had dropped it when he'd been hit. They couldn't even use it as a weapon.

His wound had dulled Sunny's wits but seemed to have sharpened his. His gaze darted everywhere. Then he pointed toward the beach. "You go that way. I'll lead her this way. Go."

"I can't leave—"

"You have to. You can't get back to the house, and she can cut you off from the road. You've got to get to the beach and then to town that way. That's our only chance."

They scampered back several more feet before feeling safe enough to stand upright. Ryan was bleeding from his left side. He wore a long-sleeved shirt that he tore down the front, not taking time with buttons, and with her help he pulled it off. She winced at the raw, ugly hole gaping in his side. The blood was seeping steadily, but, thank goodness, wasn't gushing.

"Help me with this, Sunny, then get out of here." He wadded the shirt and put it in place, and she tied the sleeves at the right side of his back. Her fingers trembled.

"Okay. Now go," he ordered.

"But . . ."

"But nothing!" He grabbed her arm and squeezed so hard she winced. His eyes resembled hard gray marbles. "Listen to me." He bit off the words. "I think the bullet went clean through, but I'm bleeding and will leave a trail. I can't move as fast as you can on your own. If you're worried about me, then you need to get help back here as soon as you can. Now get the hell out of here."

She couldn't think coherently. If he weren't holding on to her, she would've held on to him. "Ryan, I can't—"

"It's you she wants, dammit! I'll be safer without you than with you. Now go!"

Shoving her away, he moved inland toward the eucalyptus trees and the road. His walk was just short of a stagger. She looked back across the field. Bev was almost halfway across it. With an audible sob, Sunny turned and ran toward the ocean.

He's on his feet. He was thinking coherently. He'll be all right.

She tripped over a trailing root and sprawled headlong, knocking the wind out of herself. Gasping, she got onto all fours, then to her feet and took it slower. Panic wasn't far away. She needed to slow down in more ways than one.

The shirt padding may absorb the blood and keep him from leaving a trail.

But Bev is going to expect us to go to the road, not the beach. She'll follow him anyway.

Uh-huh. That's why he sent you this way, dummy.

A shot rang out. Sunny froze.

No. No!

"Sunny?" Bev's voice.

"This way," Ryan hollered, and Sunny sagged in relief at the sound of his voice.

"Sunny!" Bev sounded angry. "I don't want your friend, but I'll go through him to get to you if I have to."

"Why, Bev?" Ryan asked. His voice was mild, as if he had nothing more on his mind than idle chitchat. "She didn't do anything. It was Franklin. Roberta, too, I guess. But Sunny had nothing to do with anything."

Their voices were a little distance apart. Bev could easily zero in on him, but Sunny had to trust that he knew what he was doing. Sunny had entered a dense cypress thicket and was trying to work her way out. The limbs didn't bend so she had to maneuver around and under and over.

"I'm out of time, but I don't care anymore." Bev's chilling lack of emotion lent credence to her words. "Matthew should get this place, but I can't do that for him. But I can make certain she doesn't get it. You didn't know you had a brother, did you, Sunny?"

"Actually, we had figured that out, Bev." Ryan sounded closer to her. Was he stalking her now?

Get the rifle, and we'll be home free.

"Matthew knows, too, doesn't he?" Sunny called out. She was giving away her position, but distracting Bev now seemed more to their advantage. "But he doesn't hate me like you do. In fact, I think he's been trying to protect me from you."

Silence. Was Bev too smart to be distracted?

The ocean was getting louder and would mask traveling sounds Sunny made but would also cover Bev's approach. One more tree stood between Sunny and the edge of the ravine.

Goad her. You've got to find out where she is. "There have been phone calls at strategic times. He must've missed you the day you pushed me off the cliff and guessed you were out here. The men came after me and sent you running because he'd called and asked for me."

More silence.

"You gave him an alibi, as I remember, but it must not have

occurred to anyone that no one asked him to give you the same alibi."

Still nothing from Bev.

Smart, Sunny. You're trying to play her, but it seems she's playing you instead.

But she went on anyway; what else could she do? "You may hate the idea, but Matthew doesn't seem to mind having a sister. Did he guess, or did you tell him his father wasn't the man you were married to? If you did, that's a tough thing to do to a kid. Had your hate warped you so much that you lost consideration of him?"

Ryan, I haven't heard anything from you for a while. What are you up to?

As if in answer she heard a sudden sound of surprise from Bev, a high-pitched squeal, and then another shot cracked. In the relative silence between crashing waves, Sunny caught muted sounds of a struggle and then a loud grunt of pain.

She froze, listening with every nerve.

Ryan was wounded and weak but had taken her by surprise. He'd have the upper hand and should be able to keep it. Sunny waited, standing on the bluff. For balance, she placed a hand on the cypress at the edge of the sheer drop.

Then she heard Bev's voice, sounding winded, yet basking in victory. "He's down, Sunny. It's just you and me now."

Sunny felt such a heavy weight inside, she could barely breathe. "Ryan?"

No answer.

"Ryan? Talk to me."

The beach, Sunny, the beach. Get down there. It's his only chance. If he's still alive, it's his only chance.

But it was a long way down. She stood still, staring at the sand, working on building her strength and hanging on to her wits by sheer will. She had to get down there, but how?

Jump. You survived one fall. You can survive another one.

Another rifle shot had her snapping her head around, and she almost lost her footing.

It wasn't even close. She's fishing, Sunny, because she doesn't know exactly where you are. And she's got that rifle to hang on to, so she'll be slower getting here than you were.

She looked back at the sand. Jump and roll, it was the only way. She closed her eyes, praying for the courage to do what she had to and then again she froze.

The ladder. Nature's ladder, stupid. Remember?

Where was it? Where is it?

She knelt at the edge, craning her neck to look down.

There!

Wrapping her arms around the trunk of the tree, she duck-walked around it, careful of the slippery ice plant at its base. Then inch by careful inch, she lowered one leg until her foot found the uppermost part of the root that snaked its way halfway down to the sand. She regretted the cutoffs she wore that allowed the cliff to scrape her legs.

Once her foot settled on the root, her position became less precarious. So far, so good. Next she needed to reach down and get her hand around the root that her foot rested on, and that was going to be a neat trick. With each hand grasping a fistful of the flimsy ice plant, she managed to get her other foot onto a lower part of the trunk's root, and she extended her right arm until she got fingers around the protruding part that her highest foot rested upon. Her other hand groped for purchase in the uneven side of the cliff as she lowered herself a couple more inches.

"Sunny?" Bev's voice was close, too close. She'd made good time. But her tone was tentative, still fishing. She hadn't seen her prey go over the side.

Sunny held her breath, then let it out slowly and forced even breaths. If she made any kind of noise, she was a sitting duck. One foot found the edge of a protruding rock, and her hand got a good grip on the root that was pressing into her stomach, and she lowered herself several more inches. Then her foot slipped off the rock and the knife-sharp edge of it gouged a line up the inside of her calf.

Locking her lips together, she fought off a yelp. She directed her gaze down and watched a thick stream of blood pour down her leg. The gash was long and deep. She raised her head, closed her eyes and forced another deep, even breath. There was one more handhold. Then she was going to have to trust free fall. Once she'd grasped the lowest part of the root in both hands, her feet still dangled five feet above the sand. She let go.

She hit and rolled, scrambled to her feet and then dove for the cliff on the other side. A bullet whined past, struck a beer can and sent it flying, then Sunny was in the relative safety of the far cliff. Gritty sand stuck in her wounded calf but she didn't pause. She had another problem besides Bev and her rifle. The tide was rising.

Her pursuer couldn't follow her down the cliff while holding the rifle. She'd have to backtrack to the end of the crevasse, cut across the field to the road and then to the beach path, and try to head her prey off at the cove. Sunny could get there first, but if the tide cut her off she was out of luck and options. The water swirled around her ankles and dragged at her feet.

The next wave caught her at the knees. When the salt water filled the gash in her leg she couldn't contain her scream. She lost precious seconds waiting for the water and the burning to subside. Then she got her breath back and ran. She made it into the cove, beating Bev. With her gaze on the beach path, Sunny waited for the wave dashing against the opposite cliff to ebb. Still no Bev. Sloshing through, she reached the far side and then hugged the cliff as the water caught her again, now almost reaching her waist.

It wanted her, dragged at her. Pressing her body into the cliff wall she held on to the slick, uneven surface, digging her fingers into the claylike muddy wall, consumed by the burning in her leg. When she thought she could stand it no longer the water level dropped but continued to pull at her legs. She trudged ahead, made it around the curve, and the next wave reached no higher than her ankles.

No more obstacles existed between her and Chester and help. She ran as fast as the terrain allowed, feet leaving deep gouges behind her in the wet sand, barely aware of the tears streaming down her face.

CHAPTER TWENTY-SEVEN

Sunny's mind was racing as fast as her feet as she sprinted along the water's edge. The ice cream place would have a phone. Nine-one-one, ambulance and the authorities, find Jonathan—

Fear struck again, and again froze her in place.

Nothing prevented Bev from driving into Chester, beating her prey there, and then doubling back on the beach to cut Sunny off. If Bev threw a sweatshirt over the rifle, no one would give either her or it a second look.

Sunny sagged, but she couldn't give up. She crossed over to the base of the cliff and trudged ahead. It was slower going in the dry, loose sand, but safer in case she spied Bev in the distance.

But it was Bev's son, not Bev, who met her. And Jonathan was at his side.

Sunny flew over the remaining distance and plowed into him. She held on as if he were a lifeline. Then she jerked back.

"Ryan. He needs an ambulance. He—"

"I know." Although his eyes intently searched hers, his voice was calm. "We know. The ambulance is on its way to the hospital. Ryan's okay. He was on his feet, weak but coherent."

"Oh." She stared at him, hearing him but unable to grasp the facts. "But . . ."

Jonathan stepped back to look at her leg. "What did you do? You need attention, too."

"But Bev. What about Bev?"

When Sunny looked at Matthew, she wanted to cry at the desolation in his expression. And her eyes must have held her anguish when she glanced back at Jonathan because he pulled her to him almost roughly, and one hand cupped her head against his chest. His heart was pounding furiously, belying his calm tone.

"It's okay," he said. "She's with Joyce. And Matthew's all right. He knows, and he understands."

How can Matthew be all right? How?

"First things first," Jonathan went on and drew back. He took time to pull in a long breath before finishing. "Let's get you to the truck and then to the hospital. I can explain on the way. Matthew will go with us."

But the young man hung back. "No, uh, you take care of Sunny. She needs you. She needs, uh . . . I'm okay, and I need to . . . I should . . ."

Sunny pulled away from Jonathan and went to Matthew. She put her arms around him, buried her head on his shoulder and cried. She let go completely, not holding anything back. At first he remained rigid. Then he grew limp, except for his arms that tightened around her, and finally he lost the fragile hold he held on himself. She felt matching, shuddering spasms throughout his body.

"Sunny, I'm sorry, I'm sorry, I—"

"Shut up, Matthew." She drew back and swiped her forearm across her eyes. "Come on. We need to get to the hospital. I have to check on Ryan, and Jonathan's going to bug me about my leg until somebody looks at it. I need you, Matthew. Please come with us." Questioningly, she looked at Jonathan. "The store must be locked up?"

He nodded, and she said, "Then let's go."

When they reached the SUV, Jonathan made her sit on the passenger seat while he got out the first aid kit. A small crowd had assembled around them, probably because the bloody leg was an attention grabber. Sunny ignored the rubberneckers.

"No," she warned as Jonathan snapped open the bag. She shook her head, too drained to realize the absurdity of refusing treatment. "Don't even think about it. That stinging stuff—"

"Save it for the ER physician." He rolled the gloves on so fast he would've won a competition if he'd been in one. With a professional gaze on her leg he unraveled a long swatch of gauze. Apparently if he had something familiar to do, like medical stuff, he lost his emotional involvement. "All I want to do is wrap it up before you do any more damage to it. They'll numb it before they clean it out and stitch it up."

"Stitch it? With a needle?"

He cut the material, giving her a look out of the corner of his eye. He wrapped the bandage around her calf. "You have a thing about needles?"

"Stitches? You really think I need stitches?"

"Yes." Deftly he tore the end of gauze back into itself, separated the pieces and then tied them together. He'd been kneeling on one knee. He pulled back, resting his forearms across his upright knee, and gave her a level look. "Do we have a problem here?"

Matthew stood next to him. Her gaze rose to the teenager. He looked scared, anxious, overwhelmed, full of doubt and insecurity, and in great need of guidance.

"No," she said. "No problem. I'm fine."

Jonathan had been aware of her glance, and just as clearly had read her thoughts. He waited until her eyes returned to his. Then he smiled, leaned forward to peck her lightly on the lips, and then he stood. "Good," he said.

"Look at me, Sunny, not the needle." Jonathan's voice was mild, and it had a smile in it that made her want to hit him. But with her fists clenched and teeth gritted, she did as he suggested.

The needle full of anesthetic poked her once more and she yelped again and tried to pull her leg away again. But the doctor was the same sex and size as Sunny, had a good grip on her patient, and wasn't about to let her get away. "Now come on. That wasn't as bad as the first one, and this next one isn't going to be as bad as that one."

As tense as a rock, Sunny blew her breath out, laid her head back down on the hard pillow and stared at the ceiling as she waited for the next stinging prick.

"There," the doctor said. "See what I told you? Did you have a problem with that one?"

"Huh?" She frowned and lifted her head.

Jonathan grinned. "Nope. No problem with that one."

"What have you been doing, anyway?" the doctor asked. "Wallowing around in a sandbox?"

"Yes. And the tide caught me. The water was . . ."

"I'll bet it was." The doctor seemed to understand there wasn't an adequate word to describe salt water washing an open wound.

Sunny stared hard into Jonathan's eyes. "You're sure Matthew's okay?"

"He's okay." He held her gaze then said quietly, "He needs his space, too. He's nursing a cola in the waiting room."

The doctor stepped sideways to the head of the bed and gazed benignly down upon Sunny. "Promise not to run away if I leave you alone for a minute? Just long enough to let that medicine do what it's supposed to do."

Sunny gave her what was probably a weak smile. "Promise."

The doctor left, and Sunny squeezed Jonathan's fingers. "Thanks for holding my hand." Now free from the threat of the needle, she felt friendly again.

"You're welcome."

"You didn't give me much information in the truck. Is there anything else I should know?"

"How about I just go over the whole thing? Without having to be conscious of Matthew's ears this time." His eyes, voice, body language, everything about him was again calm and matter-of-fact. Which worked well for Sunny because she was short on peace of mind and it seemed that Jonathan had enough to share.

"I didn't see Bev at first," he said. "I'd parked in back, and she must not have seen me either. I heard shots and then saw her tearing across the field. She looked deranged, and that's not hindsight. She really was. Once she reached the pickup, I got behind her and grabbed the rifle, and she didn't even resist. She just stared at me and mumbled something about being out of time. Then she told me my friend was in the trees and needed an ambulance. I thought she meant you, but then I saw Ryan staggering across the field and I really got worried. Between the two of us, Ryan and me, we got the story out of Bev while we were waiting for the ambulance. She was . . . cooperative. Even friendly. She told us about Howard, Franklin, how much she hated you. She held nothing back. I . . ."

He looked at the examining room's closed door. When he next spoke, his voice was flat. "I felt sorry for her. I still do, and yet I'm mad as hell at her. And I can't comprehend the fact that she didn't even once mention Matthew."

"So full of guilt and hate that she let it rule her." Sunny felt sad, weary, and sick inside. "She was so close to the edge. I don't know how we missed it. I think Matthew saw it, but he was helpless. It was probably my moving back here, the official declaration of Franklin's death, the will, the whole works. It just did her in."

"Yes. There is very little accountability there. She's no longer close to the edge. She's over it. That was not an act today."

Ryan's eyes were closed.

Sunny had been told he was conscious, out of danger, and that he'd asked for her. But the sight of him, pale and still in a hospital bed, undid her. She was the unsteady one; he was the rock. She stood silently in the doorway for a long time.

Then she walked to the chair next to his bed and sat down. She'd made no sound that she'd heard, but she must've disturbed the air because his eyes opened and focused on her.

"Hi, doll." He sounded out of it, probably still drugged. "I'm glad you chose the doctor instead of the cop." It seemed he was trying for that characteristic flip in his voice, but it eluded him. "He got there first."

She swallowed, nodded. "He told me."

"What are you so choked up about? We did it, Sunny. We made it."

Then he looked at the ceiling, and added, "No thanks to me." His gaze returned to her and he went on. "I had her, Sunny. I had her and the rifle, but she outsmarted me. She went limp and I thought she was giving up, but instead she made a fist out of both hands and walloped me really good right in the middle of my bloody shirt. I blacked out."

"I forgive you. You were the one who finally figured the whole thing out."

"Tom was close to getting it. It was his remark about it being local that kept rattling around in my subconscious. The other victim, the missing one, had to be local, too."

She leaned forward to put her hand on his. "I tried calling Marcus, on Jonathan's cell, but I got his voice mail. I didn't want to leave a message like this one."

"Just as well. I'll call. He'll want to talk to me anyway." He frowned, and then looked at the phone on the stand beside his bed. "My cell is probably still on the coffee table next to that empty bag of chips. But he'll accept charges."

Sunny didn't know where her cell was. Probably in her purse, which was . . . she didn't have the slightest idea where that was either.

Ryan shifted his head to look down at her bandaged leg. "And what happened to you? Dammit, Sunny, it's not safe to let you out of my sight."

"I had an argument with a rock on my way down the cliff."

"One immovable object meets another?" He managed a smile, but it was strained. "I was right about the bullet, and lucky as hell. It went all the way through. They're going to let me out of here tomorrow, and you're going to have to put up with me for a while longer. I'm not ready to even think about sitting in a car for the couple of hours it'll take to get home."

"Oh. Well." She exaggerated her frown. "But I promised everyone I'd go home tomorrow. Can you manage out there at that old house by yourself?"

"You're funny, doll. Very funny. Now get out of here and let me get some sleep. I feel all dopey."

Unable to resist, she broke into a grin.

His words must have taken an instant longer to reach his ears than hers. Because belatedly he laughed, flinched at the pain the action caused, and then he pointed his forefinger at her in warning. "Shut up, Sunny. You say it and I'll make you sorry. I promise."

CHAPTER TWENTY-EIGHT

As they stood atop the bluff overlooking the ocean, Sunny held on to Matthew's arm for support while she lowered herself onto one knee. Then she settled on the ground with that leg crossed under her and the wounded one positioned with the knee bent. They'd remained at the top of the cliff instead of descending to the beach because she'd promised the doctor she'd stay out of the sandbox until her leg healed.

She'd been living in sweats for three days. She'd been told to wear what she wanted to, as long as she kept the leg clean, but Jonathan was back in mother-hen mode. He didn't want her injury exposed to the tiniest chance of infection, which meant air, sun, light, sheets . . .

At first she'd resisted, but by the third or fourth or fifth argument she'd concluded the only way to save her sanity was to humor him. Ryan had said nothing, simply watched and listened to them with a bland manner that Sunny had found irritating. Anyway, shorts were out, the legs of her jeans were too tight around the bandage, so . . .

She was getting awfully tired of sweatpants. She even had to sleep in the stupid things.

Once she was settled, Matthew sat next to her and wrapped his arms around his knees. His face was strained as he kept his gaze on the ocean. It had been like pulling teeth to get him to take this walk with her.

Matthew and Jonathan had prepared a bedroom for Matthew

at the old Victorian, getting everything the teenager needed from his residence behind the store in one trip. He'd been given the choice of upstairs or downstairs, and he'd chosen a room near the kitchen. He'd been doing some of the cooking, keeping the meals simple, but he managed it so effortlessly that Sunny suspected he was a better cook than she was. She wondered if the feel for cooking was a legacy from their father.

"We need to talk," she said.

He nodded without looking at her. His Adam's apple was prominent.

"If it's agreeable with you," she said, "I want to petition the court for legal guardianship."

He was silent. With the feeling she was fighting her way uphill while standing in place, she went on. "I have to look for another place, in San Francisco, and I'll find one big enough for both of us that's in a good school district. But that means you'd be starting all over again in a new school. What do you think about that?"

His throat worked as he swallowed. "I don't have any ties here. Not really. Maybe I'd be better off getting away from everything and starting all over."

She took in a long breath, hoping her relief that he'd finally spoken wasn't too evident and that her lack of confidence wasn't overly obvious. She'd talked this over with everybody but Matthew, yet his concurrence was the most important. "Good. I'll need time to set everything up. Mavis and Tom want you to stay with them until I get it rolling, and that will give you some transition time. Will that work for you?"

His head bobbed as he kept his gaze on the horizon. "They're good people."

"We'll need help, all kinds of legal help, in dealing with the store and its inventory. That's a biggie, but we can do it. And Roberta will help, if that's all right with you. She's got a good business mind."

Again he nodded, but said nothing.

"Whatever gain is realized from the sale of the store and that's left after your mother's legal expenses should go toward your education. That's what she wanted, too. She'd told me so."

Still he remained silent. His gaze hadn't left the ocean, but she wondered if he really saw it.

"College is right around the corner," she continued. "But it shouldn't be a problem, not financially. Corday Cove belongs to you as much as it does to me. Jonathan and I got in a couple minutes of discussion about this, and I think it's going to be a three-way split, but the least you'll have is half of mine. The only stipulation is that it goes toward your education first, then into a trust fund until you're twenty-five."

He looked at the ground, then his eyes squinched shut. "Sunny, you don't have to—"

"I know I don't. I'm doing it because I want to and it's right."

Sunny had been of two minds regarding the age stipulation. If she'd had any real money before she was twenty, she would've blown every cent of it, yet she suspected Matthew was smarter than that. Jonathan had leaned toward the age requirement, however, so she'd gone along with it.

Matthew's face turned away, to where she now saw more of the back of his head than his profile. Silence stretched. Then she said quietly, "We need to get to know each other. We need to find out what works and what doesn't. And we need to be honest. If we can do that, everything else will fall into place. And the truth is that I want to make the familial bond between us legal. If that's what you want also, that's where we'll start."

Matthew, help me out. Please. In a lot of ways you're more mature than I am. I don't just need your cooperation. I need your help.

"Well?" she prompted. "Shall we get this ball rolling? Shall we go for it?"

"Yes," he said simply.

"Thanks, Sunny," Mavis said as she accepted the can of beer. It was Sunday, a busy day in the real estate game, but she'd refused to work.

"If I don't deserve a day off today, I'll never deserve one," she'd said when climbing down from her husband's four-wheeler. With one foot on the ground and the other one still on the truck's runner, she'd given her hostess a pained look with some heavy aggravation in it. " 'We found the owner of the bloody bat.' The mother of all messages."

Because it appeared a peace offering might be in order, Sunny had gone after the can of beer.

Settling in the lawn chair, wearing khaki shorts that exposed slightly veined but still shapely legs, Mavis popped the top and took a long slug. "Umm. High society can have their champagne. I've got a weakness for beer. It'd be better with a cigarette, of course, but it's still good."

Sunny stretched her legs out and crossed her ankles. Unable to endure the lackluster gray sweats a day longer, she'd bought a bright-red pair, and in response to the warm day she wore a skimpy white tank top over the pants. "By the way, thanks for taking Matthew to see Bev. He seems more at ease now."

"Good. When he told her he was staying with you, she gave him a hard look and then directed it at me. But she didn't argue."

They sat in the shade of the eucalyptus, watching the men work. The yard resembled a community car wash. The Reviler had been finished and returned to the front, and Tom had been invited to drive his truck around to the back. Matthew was hosing it down for him. Ryan stood on the sidelines, nursing his wound and enjoying his role of supervisor.

"You missed a spot there, Tom."

"You're missing more than that, Ryan."

Sunny giggled. "One can shy of a six-pack, maybe?"

Executing an excellent parody of a slow burn, Ryan turned to look at Sunny. She held her soda pop can up.

Mavis chuckled. "You seem to be holding up okay."

Sunny echoed the laugh. "I guess. I feel punchy, to tell the truth. And rummy. Like my head's not on straight yet. Roberta is working on the legal end of things, I'm glad. She's got the mind for that. I never did, even at the best of times."

"When are you heading for home?"

"In another couple of days Ryan should be up to it. That's why I want Matthew to go home with you today. Give him some time with you and Tom before I clear out. For his sake and yours." She hesitated. "And mine. I just want to, well, make sure he's okay? I don't know how to explain it."

Mavis smiled her understanding.

Then Sunny changed the subject. "I don't know how he wrangled it, but Jonathan got this coming week off, too. It's going to seem strange leaving him here on his own, instead of the other way around."

Mavis gave her a surprised sideways glance. "Jonathan only has one more week? I thought . . ." Then the surprise that she must have seen on Sunny's face seemed to induce Mavis into silence.

"You thought what?" Sunny prompted.

"Well, he told me he didn't want to put the house on the market after all." Mavis spoke slowly, as if feeling her way. "He's been asking around about contractors, and . . ." She rolled her eyes and looked at the car washers. "Oh, hell. Me and my big mouth. When am I going to learn to keep it shut?"

You and your big mouth, and him and his closed one.

Sunny sat back and stared straight ahead.

So, okay, Jonathan. What's with the contractors, and how come I'm in the dark here?

Sunny kept her cool for the rest of the day, not barging up to Jonathan like she wanted to and demanding answers. Not because of him, herself, or social niceties, but because of Matthew. She kept her misgivings to herself through dinner, maintaining an easy manner that even fooled Ryan. After seeing Tom and Mavis and Matthew off, Sunny sat out on the back porch by herself.

This isn't good, Sunny. When you keep things to yourself, you explode.

Eventually Jonathan joined her. "I was wondering what happened to you." Instead of sitting down, he crossed to the screen and watched the fast-disappearing sun. "It's getting chilly out here. Are you ready to come inside?"

"I'm fine."

He glanced at her. "Sounds like there's more chill to you than there is in the air. What's wrong?"

"Is there something about not selling the house that you want to talk to me about?"

"Oh." He frowned. "I should've realized that—"

"Yes, you should have."

"—Mavis might mention it. I hadn't thought to tell her—"

"To keep it to herself?"

He gave her a level look. "Yes. Until I got a chance to talk to you."

Elaborately she looked around the porch. "It's just you and me right now. Go for it, Jonathan."

After a long silence, he asked quietly, "Am I on trial, Sunny?"

With her gaze fixed steadily on him, she enunciated precisely, "Let's not . . . get off . . . the subject. What, exactly, are your plans regarding the house?"

He waited another long moment, matching her stare, and

then he crossed the porch and opened the door leading into the kitchen. "We'll talk about this tomorrow. Maybe you'll be more receptive and less contentious in the morning."

"Contentious, hell!" She jumped up and slammed the door closed. "We'll damn well talk about it now."

"Don't swear. I don't like it when you—"

"And I don't like not being consulted about a major decision like this."

"I planned on consulting you. We're equal partners, and I can't do anything without you. I wanted facts and figures first, for myself as well as for you, and it's been a little on the hectic side lately. Even you must see that."

"Even me? What's that supposed to mean?"

He gave her a long stare. "Something tells me I'm not going to be able to say anything right tonight. All you're capable of right now is an argument, and this is too important to discuss in the mood you're in."

He opened the door again, and she closed it again.

"It's too important to put it off," she snapped. "Too important not to have already discussed it. And it's not my mood at fault here. It's you and your lack of candor."

He frowned. "Lack of candor? What are you trying to say?"

"Oh? Now you're insulted? If I remember correctly, we talked once about my being used to taking care of myself. It looks like you're used to that as well. Being equal partners with you evidently means that you do all the thinking and make all the decisions. Then when it suits you, you let me in on it."

He held his silence for a long while, then said, "You've got quite a temper in you. I've seen glimpses of it before, but never the full force of it."

"And you think you're seeing it now? Not even close." She forced herself to unclench her fists. "Do what you want with the damned house. Mail me the papers. I'll either sign them or I won't."

She opened the door and this time he closed it. "Oh, no, you don't. You started this, Sunny, and now we're going to finish it."

"Oh, really? You mean you've got a temper, too?" Just when she was wondering how much longer she could hold out before smacking the wall with her fist, the kitchen light switched on. Their gazes, Jonathan's now as hard and angry as she felt hers must be, remained locked on each other.

"Sunny?" Ryan called curiously.

"I'm out here, Ryan, on the porch." She looked pointedly at Jonathan's hand, which still gripped the doorknob. "The door's stuck. I can't get it open."

With his face taking on the appearance of a tight mask, Jonathan removed his hand. He also looked like he wanted to hit something.

When she flung the door open, she almost hit Ryan with it. He backed up, looked at her and then beyond her at Jonathan's back, then again at her. His face fell. "Oh, Sunny. No."

She passed him without a word.

CHAPTER TWENTY-NINE

Did you have to come on quite that strong, Sunny?

She'd slept fitfully in her old bed in the back bedroom, her nagging inner voice giving her no mercy during the long night. She blinked into the dark room, wondering what time it was, ready to give up and get up regardless of the time.

Sure, he should've talked to you, but you've made mistakes, too. Will you give him a chance to make amends?

No.

Why not?

Because it's over.

The blankets and sheet were tangled, the pillow lumpy. It was impossible to get comfortable. She wrestled her way onto her side, wondering again if it really had to be over. Then she swallowed, throat so tight that it felt sore, and slowly she nodded to herself.

She had enough going on without having to deal with a romance and its complications. She was now responsible for a teenager. Talk about an instant, ready-made family. Life had become pretty heavy of late. Which was an understatement and a half.

The ceiling didn't appear as dark as it had the last time she'd noted it, and light was slowly becoming discernible behind the frilly Priscilla curtains. She threw the covers back, dressed, and then quietly made her way downstairs, hoping she wouldn't have company for a while.

Sunny, wait. Maybe it doesn't have to be over.

Pressing her lips tightly together, she wondered precisely where and when this diehard sentimental side of hers had been born. But Jonathan had the same opportunity that she did right now to either patch it up or end it. Give him some time, and he might be grateful for the clean break. He was less volatile than she was, so he should see their incompatibility even more clearly than she did.

As she drew water for the coffeepot, she turned the kitchen tap on to a mere dribble, trying for as little noise as possible. Yes, the relationship had been good, very good, while it lasted, but they both needed to move on. The house was the only thing they had in common, and even it had come between them. It was time to go home.

When she reached for a coffee cup, movement at the hall doorway startled her. She jerked, bumping her hip against the corner edge of the counter hard enough that it'd probably leave a bruise. Then calmly she reached for a second cup.

"Criminy, Ryan. You scared the hell out of me."

"What I'd like to do is scare some sense into you."

"Don't start. Please." She filled both cups, crossed the room and handed him one. He was barefoot and unshaven, hair uncombed, and he wore slacks and a pullover. His expression was closed.

"Do you want to talk about it?" he asked, accepting the cup but not sipping from it.

"No."

"Okay. *Will* you talk about it?"

"No." She turned away. "Are you ready to go home?"

"No."

She looked at the wall instead of at him. "I want to get out of here, Ryan. I have to get out of here." She sounded both pleading and belligerent and didn't like either emotion.

"Then go," he said flatly. "I'll drive myself when I'm ready."

She turned back. "But you said—"

"I know what I said. And I'm telling you now I'd prefer to drive myself. Take the clunker, and you'll have to leave it on the street. Your car is in your parking slot, and the keys are on the dresser in your room."

She hesitated. "Just like that?"

"Just like that." His eyes reminded her of cold steel. "You want to run scared, then run."

She felt her eyes also growing hard as she returned his gaze. Then wordlessly she passed him and walked down the hall.

When she entered the empty San Francisco apartment two hours later, it seemed to Sunny that she'd stepped back in time. She looked around the familiar place, feeling too lonely for even the kitten to help.

Cat had been a nervous passenger and had left an accident on the Reviler's floorboard. Sunny didn't think she'd ever get the smell out of her nostrils. Cat now looked warily about the room, seemingly no happier in the apartment than she'd been in the car. Her mistress hoped she wasn't going to have any more accidents to contend with. She quickly set up a litter box, and Cat promptly showed her she knew how to use it.

Sunny had skipped breakfast and was hungry. She found a solitary egg in the fridge, but dropped it when she reached for a frying pan, and it broke on the floor. Cat investigated and decided that she liked it.

"Well, that takes care of you. But what about me?"

She found American cheese slices and stale crackers and washed them all down with a cold soda. The apartment got more silent and empty with each passing moment. She cleaned up the eggshells, stripped her bed and remade it, and managed two trips to the laundry room without losing Cat out the door.

Every time Jonathan came to mind, she pushed him right back out again. It was also difficult not thinking about Ryan. She hadn't liked leaving on the note she had. He'd seemed to be washing his hands of her.

Well, gee, that's tough. I'm a grown woman, and I make my own decisions. He doesn't have to agree with me. He doesn't even have to understand.

Do you understand, Sunny?

She whirled and smacked the wall with her open hand.

Cat was investigating bedspread corners that dangled near the floor. Panicked by the violent motion, she raced out of the room. Sunny nursed her sore hand, tears burning behind her eyelids. Then she heard Ryan at the door. He must've changed his mind and followed her after all.

Relief at having company made her mood lift, but she didn't want him to catch her with wet eyes. She rubbed her face with the palms of both hands, pulled in a deep breath and went to meet him, but then a knock sounded and she realized that had been the first sound as well. It wasn't Ryan.

She stood on tiptoe to check the peephole, and when she spied the familiar face on the other side of the door, slowly she fell back onto her heels.

"Oh." She stood there as if in a stupor.

"Sunny?" No more knocking, just his voice.

She swallowed. Her wits had deserted her.

Now what do I do?

Let him in, stupid. He knows you're here. He would've seen the clunker on the street.

After opening the door, she realized that not all her poise had abandoned her, just a big chunk of it.

"Well," she said. "Hi." That casual note wasn't fooling anyone, not even herself. She motioned for Jonathan to come in and then closed the door. "How does San Francisco compare with Bakersfield?"

"Not well. I know my way around there."

Cat appeared and wrapped herself around his ankle. When Jonathan stooped to greet her, Sunny looked away. Tears burned.

With his hand stroking the cat, he looked up at Sunny from his position on the floor. "We need to talk."

She nodded, which was the only response she was capable of.

He stood and looked at the modern living room arrangement in stark black and gold, and the dining room area beyond it with its mirrored table and tall-backed ebony chairs. His eyes met hers. "This is Ryan's place. Not yours."

"Uh, yeah."

"It looks like him, not you."

She looked around her. She'd never thought about it before, but the room and everything in it reflected Ryan, not her. Jonathan knew her well. The wits she'd collected were threatening to escape. Then she got a sudden thought and grinned. "I set up the cat box in my room."

He grinned back. "Good idea."

Cat sat on the floor between them, looking up and back and forth as if trying to figure out the new surroundings and the familiar people and how everything fit together.

Let me know when you figure it out, Cat.

"Can I get you some coffee?" she offered.

"No, thanks. But I wouldn't mind sharing a Sprite with you. I acquired a taste for it."

"Sure." She motioned toward the plump black sofa with its black-and-gold-striped throw pillows. "Sit down and I'll get it."

But he followed her into the kitchen. She was uncomfortably aware of him standing behind her.

"You left early," he said, no accusation in his voice. "I heard your car, but you were gone by the time I got to the window."

"Uh-huh." She got glasses and filled them with ice from the

refrigerator's door dispenser.

"You were right," he said. "I should've talked to you first about what I was thinking. We could've collected facts and figures together and decided then if it was a worthwhile idea or not."

Carefully she emptied a can into the two glasses so the fizz wouldn't overflow. "What idea is this?"

"I don't want to sell."

She put the empty can on the speckled granite counter and stared at it. "So I gathered. Then what do you want to do?"

"I want to gut the whole place, from top to bottom. I want to expand the kitchen, add a dining room, modernize the windows, and we need a new heating system. I want to enlarge the bathrooms, both of them. Top floor and bottom floor each must have a shower. And I want a master bedroom with a private bath—a third bathroom—on either the first floor or the second, wherever you want it. I want to retain the back porch, much as it is already, and utilize more of the yard. We need landscaping, professional gardening help. The location and size of the house are made to order. We could turn it into a lucrative bed and breakfast inn." He paused. "Think about it, Sunny. It's perfect."

"Bed and breakfast?" she echoed, gaze remaining on the counter and her voice sounding small.

"That's where you come in. I don't know how to cook breakfast."

"Bed . . . and breakfast? An inn? A business venture?"

"And a home. There is presently no mortgage against the place, so we could borrow what we need to get started. I want to do what I can with it as well. I'd enjoy working on a major refurbishing job like this. And I can also hang out my shingle in Chester or Castleton. Maybe Mavis wouldn't mind some competition from you, just until we get started, and then we'll figure out our work schedule and where we're needed the most.

And I'm not forgetting about Matthew. He'll be an equal partner. There's enough money in the place to get him through school, and he can share in both the physical labor and the accomplishment. We can play that by ear. See what works for him, for all three of us. Think about it, Sunny. There's no end to the possibilities."

She hadn't moved. He put his hands on her shoulders but didn't attempt to turn her around. His hands felt tentative, hesitant, telling her that he wasn't sure of her.

"But I can't do it without you," he said, voice so soft it was like a caress. "I don't want to do it without you. If you want to sell, we'll sell. But I remember a comment you made, in the beginning when you were talking about Ryan, that if you ever found a better friend you'd have to marry him. In our short time up there, we became friends as well as lovers."

He paused. "Didn't we?"

Sunny was trembling. His hands were still on her shoulders, and she wondered if he felt the emotion shuddering through her.

"This is a major decision," he went on. "And we've been through an emotional wringer the last few days. It's not surprising we clashed last night. But there's more to it than that. You've been hurt in the past, very much, and I think you're scared. That was why you came on so strong last night. If we hadn't run into conflict over the house, it would've been over something else."

That's Ryan talking.

"And that's not Ryan talking," he said, and she spun around.

He blinked, took a half step back. "What? What is it?"

"Nothing." When she started to turn back for their drinks, he cupped her shoulders to hold her in place.

"Never mind that," he said. "I want to know if I've got a chance. If we've got a chance. Do we, Sunny?"

Slowly, feeling both scared and hopeful, she lowered her gaze to the linoleum and its glossy black and white squares. Heaviness weighed in her gut, yet her heart felt buoyed, and the contradiction scared her. More than anything, she wanted to trust Jonathan. But to do that, she also had to trust herself, and that was a very hard thing to do.

"We've got everything going for us," he coaxed. "Everyone is rooting for us. Roberta likes me, so does Ryan, even Cat, and Matthew has no problem with me either. But your vote counts the most, Sunny. What about you? Do you like me?"

She squeezed her eyes closed. Never before had anyone asked her that simple question. Throughout her life both the romantic and emotional meaning of the word love had been elusive, and he was asking her now if she *liked* him?

Sunny finally knew what each word meant, and more important, what each emotion felt like.

And she was beginning to think it might be possible to be free. Free to learn how to live and to love. To have faith in herself. And faith in a significant other person. But she was scared. Oh, she was scared. So scared and choked that she wondered if her throat would work if she tried to speak. But she was going to do it. She had to do it; at long last, she sensed fissures breaking through the armored shell of the emotional prison she'd lived in for such a long time.

"Like you?" she echoed, her voice sounding small.

She kept her eyes trained on his shirt buttons.

"Yes, I like you, Jonathan," she whispered, and she swallowed hard. "And I love you. Heart, body and soul."

She was conscious of the tension draining out of him. Gently he put his knuckles beneath her chin and tilted her head up until she met his eyes.

"Good," he said.

ABOUT THE AUTHOR

Bobbie O'Keefe enjoys reading so much that she eventually tried writing her own stories and fleshing out her own characters. She loves just letting her imagination go where it wants to—and often she's surprised where it lights.

Her first novel, *Second Thoughts,* is a romantic comedy that garnered favorable reviews, including reviews in *Publishers Weekly* and *Romantic Times Magazine. RT'*s staff of reviewers chose *Second Thoughts* as one of the best they'd reviewed in 2009.

Bobbie has also written *Lone Tree,* another 2011 release from Five Star. A contemporary ranch romance evolving and revolving around a family saga that spans three generations, *Lone Tree* will make you laugh and maybe even cry.